ARMAGEDDON'S SON

Part 1 of
HYBRID: The Ethereal War

GREG BALLAN

Hadrosaur Productions, Mesilla Park, NM

Armageddon's Son
Hadrosaur Productions
First Edition, first printing, continuous printing on demand

First date of publication: March 2019
Copyright © 2019 Greg Ballan
Cover Art Copyright © 2019 Laura Givens

ISBN-10: 1-885093-87-X
ISBN-13: 978-1-885093-87-5

To my amazing, talented children:

Thomas. You taught me how to chase a dream and helped make that dream a reality. You believed in me when I didn't believe in myself and gave me the confidence to keep pushing forward. No father could be blessed with a better son. I have had the joy of watching you grow into a wonderful, caring young man.

Rachel. Every day you inspire me with your tenacity and God given ability. Never stop reaching for the stars, there is a place for you among them. The world is a stage, and you, my daughter, are in the center spotlight.

Chrisite. You are the rainbows in a dreary, gray world. Your inner light shines like a beacon providing illumination and warmth for those around you. Never lose that quality. I am truly blessed to be your father.

Acknowledgments

Where to begin? This book is more than a story from my often-disturbed imagination. The idea, the story seed is mine, nurtured into reality on the pages of my beat up laptop, stored safely inside bytes on a hard drive. But writing the tale is only the beginning of a journey. Along this journey I've hounded friends and family to read my endless rewrites. I've trapped my patient son, bribing him with caramel iced coffee to discuss plot points and character development. I've met an incredible editor who worked to make the tale shine like a like a ruby and sharper than the edge of my prized katana. There wasn't just wordsmithing, there was a fresh perspective on scenes that were too over the top or needed a bit more punch. The journey contained a talented cover artist adding her special magic creating the eye-catching packaging, the bow and wrapping holding the carefully edited tale. Then there's the publisher; the entity coordinating all the aforementioned activities to bring the story to the public and mark one journey's end and the beginning of another.

I owe all of these people a debt of gratitude. Without their efforts this would just be an idea unshared and a tale untold. David Lee Summers, my editor and publisher, you gave my work a chance and I will be forever grateful. But you've given me an even greater gift; a new friendship to treasure.

ARMAGEDDON'S SON

Prologue

Vatican City, Rome. St. Martha's Chapel

Burning pain scalded bone-white flesh as the hooded specter crept through the seldom used catacombs below the chapel. He'd been to St. Peter's Basilica several hundred years ago, as a man, and remembered celebrating Mass at the large open courtyard. Time had changed the church—more security, more politics and more deviation from the basic tenets. Like with everything else over time, the church had been infiltrated and even partially corrupted by the fetid stench of politics. Change was a product of Man. Eternity was of God. The rules set down by Peter, Paul, and the Apostles were being supplanted by a more secular teaching. Change drove it from the faith and into the darkness. There was no more purity in the church. The time for cleansing had come.

He heard footsteps and leapt an inhuman fifteen feet straight up. Sharp bone claws dug into the soft mortar while nimble feet took firm hold of suspended pipe.

"There should be no souls here!" Silent curses left purple lips as four men in rough brown robes walked into the large adjoining chamber.

The specter crawled along the ceiling, finding footholds, ever wary of the crumbling rubble overhead. Two-inch black nails sunk into the soft ceiling and support timbers. Each movement drew it closer to the opening and intensified the scalding agony inside his body. He dropped from the ceiling landing silently, then glided wraith-like toward the dull glow of the chamber. The specter hissed as he spied the large crucifix suspended from several heavy chains. The being looked up at the Son of God's image and cursed violently. The four men turned and screamed. Angry hands grabbed the eight-inch thick steel doors slamming them closed. The chamber echoed as the heavy doors crashed against the cast-iron frame and jamb. There

1

would be no escape from judgment for these souls.

The men stood frozen in fear staring at the black-hooded specter walking toward them. He stumbled as pain pierced his dead heart. "You are not worthy!" Four claws dug into nearby wooden benches gouging out shards of hundred-year-old oak. "You must be cleansed!"

One of the four approached. "Friend, there can be no violence in this consecrated place. How did you get here?" Terror lingered on every spoken syllable.

The man's fear was a cancer contaminating his whole being. Even through the protection of its robe, the sickening palsy of compassion swept through heightened senses. The specter felt the ambient warmth of life and the flow of sustenance surging with each rapid heartbeat. The sweet smell of blood drove him to react. Clawed hands grabbed and held the mortal man's shoulder, clamping down like an inhuman vice. The sound of cracking bone and the gasp of shock and pain fed the specter's dark desire. Hungry fangs punctured pale pink flesh. The creature savored the salty, scarlet warmth of human nectar.

He slurped two large gulps then, with a vicious, clawed slap, severed the throat and jugular veins of his victim. Blood sprayed from the wounds staining his black garment and momentarily covering his eyes. He slowly wiped the blood from his face, licking his claws with a long, forked tongue savoring the stray droplets which dulled the burning and pushed him forward. The next man shouted a prayer for protection before the enraged entity plunged his right hand through the terrified man's rib cage tearing out his heart. The man's last sight before eternal judgment would be his own heart, grasped by the being, still beating and spraying blood.

"Give my regards to the Father!" With a nonchalant toss, the entity heaved the heartless corpse twenty feet across the chamber, decorating the wooden benches and stone tile with more scarlet fluid.

The burning agony increased, almost intolerable. Something smashed against the top of his head. The sound of his own skull bones cracking and jawbone breaking echoed inside his enraged mind. He staggered back falling against the cold flagstones. His own poisoned blood mingled with those now dead. The man facing him held a large cross, covered in dark purple blood, mounted on a pole. An angry bubbling hiss filled the air as the fluid boiled and burned off the holy object.

"Run Brother Peter! Get help! I'll hold it off as long as I can. The cardinals must know what happened here!"

Jaw reset and skull bones refused, the entity stood up and howled angrily at the puny thing that dared defend itself. There was no fear in the man, only a sense of moral duty. In some warped way he admired that, a quality he too possessed several hundred years in the past. The specter rushed forward to attack only to be rebuked by the searing pain. The protective garment had been torn and he felt and smelled the stench of burning flesh. He picked up a large oak bench and hurled the twelve-foot object like a missile. The weak man was pinned, desperately struggling to free himself. He really shouldn't take the time, but he wanted to make this victim pay for what it had done. The doors rattled and creaked as the fourth man struggled to open them.

The being took one single claw and cut the entire length of the pinned man's torso, then another slice across the midsection opening up the man's belly. The cries of pain and agony echoed pleasingly off the stone and masonry.

It took the man fifteen minutes to finally expire. Intestines and internal organs littered the floor drenched in a sea of warm blood. The being looked up and realized his fourth victim had escaped. The doors were still sealed but there must be another doorway unknown to those that sent him. He had to move swiftly now. The frenzy of the torture was gone and the burning pain returned. His flesh once again began to sizzle and burn. He walked toward the tabernacle, painfully ascending the three stairs. He tore off the linens spilling a small golden goblet of sacramental wine. The pain increased as his hand reached under the most holy table. Scalded, desperate claws found the hidden button and depressed it. The large chains that suspended the large crucifix were drawn back into the far wall raising the cross. A heavy stone panel slid open exposing a formidable safe.

The being grabbed the handle of the safe and tugged

applying more and more inhuman effort. The sound of shearing, tortured metal echoed through the chamber. The specter reached inside a pocket freeing a heavy black cloth. He took another moment to carefully pull the ebony monk's hood on the enchanted garment further over his head. He opened the safe and was bathed in a white light. The pure white light enveloped the being and he shrieked in agony while his flesh cooked despite the unholy shielding. Burning hands reached inside the glowing safe wrapping the object in the charcoal-black fabric. He stepped away, staggering like a drunkard struggling to recover from the crippling pain while his body healed. The being still felt pain and realized his hands were still scalding and smoking. Another wave of pure agony rippled through his arms. In sheer panic he tossed the prize onto the crimson carpeting. The being toppled over shivering, his body smoked and broiled enduring the effects of holding an object only one being in the entire universe could ever control. Even shielded by dark power, the object still made its true nature felt.

The specter lay unmoving for five minutes then struggled to his feet.

"Damn them! They said the sack cloth would contain it!" He looked around desperately. Time was running out. He spotted the white linen tossed away earlier. He covered the black cloth within the linen and spied a dirty burlap sack in the corner filled with trash. He emptied the garbage and stuffed the twice-wrapped object into the sack. He held the sack in his arms and waited. The object still scaled his skin, but he could bear it now. Satisfied with the improvised containment vessel, the battered entity painfully limped toward the doors. He looked back at the massive image of Christ and laughed holding up the stolen prize.

"You see, Prince of Light? Your time has passed. Your creatures are corrupted and will become our own servants. The age of Mankind will cease and the Lords of Light can now only watch in dismay as their eternal plan comes unwound." With the last bits of its remaining strength he opened the doors and moved through the stone labyrinth, each step further from the chamber seemed to rejuvenate palsied flesh. He could hear shouts as men finally entered the chamber from the hidden passageway and discovered the theft. The creature's masters would reward him well if he could escape Vatican City with his prize.

Chapter 1. For Friendship's Sake

Milford, MA

Shanda stared at the small plastic indicator. Erik struggled to find the right words. There were only so many ways to give the same encouraging speech he'd been giving for almost three years now. Shanda's composure cracked and her tears fell freely. In despair she hurled the pregnancy test across the kitchen. The plastic indicator bounced off a cabinet and landed on the floor, the "Negative" indicator face up as if fate attempted to mock her further.

Erik picked up the device, wrapped it in a paper towel, and tossed it into a nearby wastebasket.

"We'll keep trying Hon. It'll happen for us."

She looked up. "When, Erik? When?"

Erik walked over and wrapped his arms around her. "Soon, baby. I gotta believe it'll be soon. Until then we'll just keep trying and living our lives and loving the son we already have."

Shanda sniffed, wiped her nose and nodded. "I know. But, a part of me has always wanted a baby girl, a daughter to dress up in pretty pink bows and tiny leopard print jackets and baby boots." She leaned up and kissed him then moved toward the large picture window staring out at the woodlands behind their home.

Erik smiled. His wife broadcast her thoughts loud and clear. She desperately wanted a large family and feared getting too old to bear children. They were in their mid-thirties and it was an understatement to say Shanda felt her biological clock ticking. To her, it was more like a raging alarm clock constantly ringing in her ears. Erik had no real objections against his wife's desire for a large family, but he wondered if the world was ready for multiple hybrid offspring. He wasn't totally human and neither was their son. Any other children they had would share his Human/Esper lineage.

Erik wondered how the government would react to three

6

or four additional Esper hybrids running around Massachusetts. He knew several intelligence agencies still surveilled them, but they did keep a respectful distance. Since the aftermath of the Observer Incident the clandestine intelligence agency known only as 'the firm' kept him at arm's length, calling upon his special talents just twice in the last three years. Erik understood he was being punished for violating the firm's confidentiality agreement. He'd leaked sensitive documents to a news reporter, Eunice Kim. The reporter wrote a devastating expose on the Hopedale Mountain incident and Pendelcorp's involvement in corrupt defense contracting. His old handler, Martin Denton, pulled some strings allowing the ex-cooler to still work cases in the firm's small private clients' agency. Martin had recruited him into the agency and had a fondness for the promising agent, but even the Senor Bureau Chief was unable to protect Erik's position. Erik got what he wanted—his nemesis, Richard Pendelton behind bars. The cost was his career as a CIA operative.

Erik ran a hand through his long hair absently shaking his head. He looked back over at Shanda as she gazed out the kitchen window. He could still feel her pain; the waves of hurt were palpable to his Esper senses. Sadly he could do nothing to ease this particular burden.

"Why don't we see if Alissa feels like babysitting tonight? We haven't had a Friday night out in months. With the hours you're putting in at the store, my case list, and getting the gym running we've barely had a moment to ourselves. Let's just go out for an evening—the two of us. We can have an early dinner at The Blue Dog and then catch a double feature at the Mendon Drive In. You always said how much you loved the Mendon's ambiance. How about it?"

Shanda kept staring out the window. "Can we sit at Dave's Tiki Bar?"

Erik laughed. "Indeed we can. It's a date then?"

She turned and smiled. "It's a date." She grinned wickedly. "We have 45 minutes until I have to get EJ from pre-school. Shall we make the most of this time, Mr. Knight?"

Erik laughed, "Hell yeah, lead the way!"

The phone rang interrupting their moment. "It could be

the store. Meet you in the bedroom?"

Erik nodded, walking down the hall. He stopped short when he heard Shanda utter a name he hadn't heard in several months: 'Martin Denton.'

"...Yes Martin, I'm fine. EJ is growing like a weed ... Erik's right here, hang on a sec and I'll put him on for you." She covered the receiver. "Why would Martin be calling you now?"

Erik shrugged as he reached for the phone. "Let's find out." He put the phone to his ear. "Good afternoon, Counselor. It's been a long time."

Erik nodded and grunted a few times. His brow furrowed. "Multiple homicides! Where?"

The detective's demeanor immediately shifted. His warm blue eyes turned frosty while his face adopted an analytical squint forming a partial wrinkle in his forehead.

Erik held his hand over the phone and glanced up at Shanda. "What time are you leaving for the store?"

"I'm working the five to closing tonight. This sounds serious, Erik. I can take EJ with me. Lisa will be on with me and EJ loves to play with her. It seems like you and Martin need to get reacquainted."

Erik nodded and put the phone back up to his face. "I'll meet you at Dawkens' Gym off route 16. I assume you can find the place?"

His shoulders slumped as he took a deep breath. Martin had asked the hard question.

"Madame's is gone, Martin. So is Jeff. He passed away last year." Erik closed his eyes momentarily. "Thanks, he was a good man. I'll see you there at six o'clock, we can talk in my office. A lot has changed, Counselor."

Erik hung up the phone, reliving the loss again in his mind, broadcasting the emptiness through his psychic connection.

Shanda placed a comforting arm around his shoulder. "Are you okay?"

Erik nodded. "Yeah, I'll be okay. It's just that I have this feeling in my gut that things are about to get crazy. I've had this hunch for the last few days, like something big happened only I don't know what. Martin calling me and being cryptic like he just was only confirms my worst fears."

* * *

Shanda nervously twirled the purple streak in her long hair. If Erik sensed trouble then some kind of storm was brewing. Her husband's hybrid senses were acute to all types of physical and metaphysical disruptions. Even after five years of marriage she wasn't really sure of the full extent of his powers; and she knew her husband had been reluctant to explore the exponential increase in his capabilities after his battle with the Observers. The feats he'd performed during that conflict were beyond anything she'd ever imagined possible. Her husband was the equivalent of a god capable of commanding the elements by sheer will and possessing physical strength that exceeded any comic book superhero. The fact that Erik was able to keep his myriad powers in such check amazed her. A lesser man would have used such talents to achieve wealth, power, and influence, perhaps even total world domination. Erik simply wanted to be a regular man with regular problems and everyday issues.

She took her husband's hand and led him to the bedroom. "We're running out of time, babe, and I assume you'll be busy most of the evening catching up with Martin. I assume our date night will be postponed for a bit so let's make the most of the time we have."

Erik chuckled and pulled her to him. He kissed her deeply, kicking the door closed with his foot.

* * *

Erik parked his truck at the far end of the parking lot. The gym was busy this evening and there were sparse open spaces. "We may finally start turning a profit if this keeps up."

He nodded toward the front desk girl and spent a few minutes conversing with the health club's regular members. He spent another few minutes rearranging dumbbells and working small issues with the floor staff. Neal Dawkens' style of management was much more aloof and his marketing was archaic at best. Neal hired Erik to give the gym a facelift and manage the MMA program but more importantly to make the facility a profitable enterprise. The newer 'Box Gyms' were pushing Dawkens' Gym closer and closer to insolvency with every passing month. Erik shook a few more hands and dispensed with some specialized advice to patrons before he entered the facility's martial arts section.

The sounds of punches striking canvas and the *kiaia* shouts from a kids' martial arts class made him feel at home. The instructor teaching the class paused and bowed to him. Erik stopped and returned the gesture of respect before entering the narrow hallway leading to his office. He briefly remembered the first time he'd seen this space. Neal Dawkens had been sitting at the head of a large desk surrounded by trophies and photographs informing him of the Lisa Reynolds abduction. Now he sat behind the desk and photographs of Shanda, EJ, Brianna and a few close friends decorated those walls. He didn't feel the need to hang his certifications but rather had photographs of students achieving new ranks or trophies. In his mind the success of his students was a better reflection of the facility he was trying to create and the impression he wanted to leave with potential students.

"I thought you were taking the day off. You're allowed at least one day to relax, Erik."

Erik leaned himself into his chair, picking up some enrollment papers and studying them. He smiled at the lean woman peeking onto his office. "I need to get some paperwork taken care of for the bank and I'm having a guest stop by—" he glanced at the clock "—in about fifteen minutes or so. You remember Martin Denton?"

Alissa tilted her head in confusion. "I didn't think after the Eunice Kim news story and your pseudo firing the two of you would be on speaking terms."

Erik laughed. "The media made more out of it than they actually had. I gave Eunice just enough to bury Richard Pendelton—no more, no less. Martin and the feds are pissed because they had plans for Richard and they wanted the whole mess covered up and buried. I upset their apple cart a bit, but not enough to cause any real damage. I'd never do that and Martin and his superiors know it." Erik rolled his eyes. "Well at least I hope they do. The fact that we haven't been audited by the IRS means we're pretty much off the government's watch list." Erik steepled his hands. "I am being punished though, that much is certain."

"Let's hope your punishment isn't severe or prolonged. You did the right thing for the right reasons. On a happier note, six of the ten kids you talked with last week have signed up for lessons. Two prepaid for six months. The checks are in your top desk drawer. I didn't think it would be possible, Erik, but you're turning this place around bit by bit." Alissa walked in and sat in the chair facing his desk. "Did Mr. Denton give you any idea of why he wants to see you? Do you think he's going to pull you back into the CIA?"

The ex-CIA cooler shook his head no. "I think I burned that bridge. But he does have a multiple homicide case he wants to discuss, so I assume I'll be doing something along the line of heavier investigative work. It's been several months since the firm has thrown any lucrative work my way and I have bills to pay as well. Shanda's store is struggling in this economy. What I pull down here gets us by, barely. The small cases from the firm allow us to breathe a little easier and let us put some more funds away for Erik Junior. Plus I told Margaret I'd foot part of Brianna's tuition." Erik sighed. "Money is tight without the larger cases I had before Eunice's story dropped."

The young woman shook her head. "Margaret is swimming in Richard's wealth. I heard her telling you not to worry about that in this very office. Your actions against Richard and Pendelcorp made your ex-wife a very wealthy woman." She leaned forward looking at him intently. "Don't obsess over this Erik. You're building something special here. I feel it. In a few more months this place will be a huge success."

Erik leaned forward his face a scowl. "Thanks, Alissa. Sometimes I think I let my desire to bury that bastard overrule my better judgment. Shanda would never say anything to me, but I get the feeling she wishes I towed the company line. We'd certainly be better off financially."

"Come on Erik, you know that's not true. That's your own self-doubt talking. You did what you felt needed to be done—the right thing, in my opinion. I know your wife well enough to know if she thought you were wrong she'd certainly let you know. Shanda isn't one to shy away like a wall flower and keep some kind of resentment buried. If she thought what you did was wrong, she would have been the first one to tell you."

The ex-CIA operative and detective now turned gym manager leaned his head on his hands as his elbows rested on the top of his desk. He contemplated Alissa's remark. "You're right of course. I'll admit I didn't expect the firm to respond like this … I figured I'd get a hand slap and things would go back to normal. Don't get me wrong, I like being home every night and I like the peace. This is a far cry from battling alien monsters or Observer combat platforms." Erik looked up at his friend, studying her.

"What?" She looked away blushing.

"Sorry. Let's change the subject from my self-pity party for a minute. Have you sensed any kind of disturbance lately, any subtle shift or hint of some cataclysm looming on the horizon?"

She stared at the floor growing uncomfortable. Her body language became closed and defensive. Lean arms folded across her chest.

"I'll take that as a 'Yes'." Erik leaned back in his chair. "A few days ago I got a sense that something changed. Something big happened but I can't lock it down. I was hoping the feeling would fade but it's getting stronger. My gut tells me Martin's visit is going to pull me into the heart of it."

Alissa unfolded her arms. "I sense darkness, Erik—a kind of darkness that makes the Seelak warrior feel like a warm puppy."

Erik's mind flashed back to the dark hate-driven creature that haunted the Hopedale Town Forest several years ago, the creature that forced him to embrace his Esper genetics and transform into an Esper/Human hybrid soldier. "May I ask why you didn't mention this to me when you got these impressions?"

Alissa tilted her head. "I could ask that same question of you, Mr. Knight."

Erik winced. "Touché."

The phone rang interrupting their morose discussion. "Dawkens' Fitness, this is Erik Knight speaking, how can I meet your fitness needs today?" Erik recited his standard greeting.

He looked over at Alissa. "Thanks Mike. Tell Mr. Denton I'll have Alissa walk him back to my office." Erik looked at his assistant. "Would you please escort our esteemed guest?"

Alissa stood up. "Can do, but let's finish this conversation later. If something that dark is on the horizon let's circle our wagons and prepare a defense—or at least an exit strategy."

Erik nodded. "Let's hope it doesn't come to that and we're both misreading the disturbance in 'The Force'." Erik tossed out the *Star Wars* analogy since it was the closest thing he could come to describe the anomaly they'd both detected in the psychic fabric surrounding them. Something inside him—his Esper sense—warned him of danger. Alissa's doom-filled revelation did little to ease the sense of foreboding.

Erik heard Martin engaging Alissa in small talk as she led him down the narrow hallway to his office.

"Right through that door, Mr. Denton, Erik's waiting for you."

"Thank you, my dear," Denton replied lightly. "You're still as beautiful as a spring day."

Alissa laughed as she headed back up the hallway.

Martin Denton quietly stepped into the office. Erik could read the uncertainty radiating off the old man's body. He sensed deep sorrow from his old friend and colleague. Erik stood, walked around the desk and extended his hand toward the old man. Denton's grip was soft and weak, not the sure grasp he'd known from his friend from years earlier.

"Have a seat, Counselor. I'd offer you a cup of coffee or some hot food but as you can plainly see, my circumstances have changed greatly over the last three years. I can get you a bottle of water or a bottle of juice." Erik continued to study his former boss. He'd aged the last few years as if some great pressure weighed the man down, leeching away his vitality.

Denton's foot tapped an unsteady rhythm on the tiled floor. Tired hands shook to the point he placed them under his thighs.

Erik never had the opportunity to speak to Martin. Three anonymous feds in black suits and sunglasses had dismissed him from the agency. He was told not to have any contact with Denton or the law firm and that the firm would contact him as needed on small client cases. They'd only spoken once since his dismissal as an agent and it was only briefly regarding a case file he still possessed.

Alissa knocked on the door and entered. The young woman had two cups of Honey Dew coffee and some assorted muffins. "I had one of our staff make a coffee run earlier."

Erik looked toward his assistant and smiled. She magically knew how to break the tension and ease both men through the awkward moments of this first reunion.

Denton took a coffee cup and smiled graciously. "Thank you, my dear, this is perfect."

Erik took the other cup and Alissa placed the tray on his desk. "Will that be all Mr. Knight?" She used the same tone when he ran his agency back at Madame's.

Erik smiled. "This is perfect, as always. I'd be lost without you."

Alissa nodded, closing the door behind her.

"It's nice that some things haven't changed." Denton sipped his coffee. "I was devastated when you told me Madame's was gone and Jeff passed away. Wasn't there anyone willing to step forward and keep the business going?"

"Jeff's brother wanted nothing to do with the business after he passed. The offer he got to sell was extremely generous. I understand why he sold out. Running a restaurant is grueling work. You either love it or you don't. Jeff loved it; his brother, not so much. I had to scramble and my agency suffered while I found a new base of operation." Erik gestured around his office. "It's not exactly what I had before, but it's home, so to speak."

"I liked that place, and your little back office was very comfortable. Sadly we can't always control what happens around us." Denton pointed his finger towards the gym area. "But, this is a nice place and you seem to be making a go of it."

Erik nodded. "It was tough leaving Madame's after so many years but this is starting to come together."

Martin's facial expression softened. The old man put his coffee down and leaned forward. "I'm sorry about what happened, Erik. I really am. I understand why you gave Eunice that material. Unfortunately the internal politics of that action reverberated all the way up to the executive office. Many more people on both sides of the aisle had their hands in that corrupt cookie jar than we'd anticipated. The CIA had plans to use Richard Pendelton and Pendelcorp. Your little bombshell shook up too many people and it was decided that you needed to be put on ice. Normally someone who commits such an act would fall off the face of the Earth." Denton took another sip of his coffee. "After the feats you performed fighting the Observers nobody in their right mind was going to come after you and risk obliteration."

Erik shook his head, "I didn't have much of a choice, Counselor. This shadow government abducted my wife and wanted to use my son as a lab rat in a cloning project. Not to mention that maniacal idiot, Ross, was picking a fight with an alien race bringing our species to the very brink of oblivion. Maybe the executive office should have given those facts some consideration before judging me and my actions. The President even convinced me to help root out much of the shadow government pulling Ross' strings. As I'm exposing these players, the administration went in and simply replaced the crooks with their own crooks. There were no trials. As far as I know, the shadow government still exists; only now it's being run by the executive branch of our government!"

Denton sighed. "Agreed, the corruption runs deep, Erik. I can't deny that. But there are more players involved, things going on that I don't understand. I dug for answers after you were let go but was stonewalled and reprimanded for my efforts. It seems I've been reduced to the political equivalent of a 'Water Boy.' I was politely told to mind my own business and if I continued to look into certain things my body would be found on a park bench in Boston Commons. So for the past two years that's exactly what I've been doing, minding my own business marking off the days until I can retire."

Erik cringed, there was more going on than either of them had deduced. The corruption they'd worked so hard to expose and bring to justice was barely a scratch on the surface.

Denton continued. "I didn't want to see you fired, Erik. I promise you I did everything I could to prevent that from happening. Originally the firm was instructed not to give you any case work and put a quarantine on you and your family.

The powers that be are still afraid of you and don't want you getting involved in intelligence work of any kind. Believe it or not, they don't think you can be trusted. I told them a level three quarantine would impact you financially and potentially ruin you. I told them you'd come after them and bury anyone involved. They settled for a level five instead; just giving you the bare minimum in case work and making sure no one approached you with any outside clients. I also know they used the push/pull tactic on Neal Dawkens to convince him to give you this job."

Erik leaned forward. "Push/pull?"

"Yeah, they pushed the idea to him and pulled him along with a sizable sum of money in the form of a buyout. I hate to tell you this, Erik, but the firm owns Dawkens' Gym. You've been an employee of the firm all along only you didn't know it."

Erik fell against his seatback stunned by Denton's revelation. "Sonovabitch!!" Erik slammed his fist against the desk, the heavy wood surface creaked under the powerful impact spilling some of his coffee. He removed the papers and checks then toweled up the spill. He looked up at his old friend. "So this whole thing is a farce?"

"No, not really. Dawkens ran the place into the ground. The firm figured with your background you'd get immersed in rebuilding the business and would cease being a threat to anyone save some overweight person looking to shed a few pounds. They figured it'd take you five years to turn things around but you've proven them all wrong. You've done amazing things here, Erik. The business plan you wrote for the bank was impressive, they didn't need us to cosign your loan, but we did anyway just to make sure you got the fifty thousand seed capital you needed with none of those pesky strings or floating interest rates banks love to attach to business loans."

Erik rubbed his hand through his hair, clearly angered over Martin's admission. "None of it was real. This whole thing was a setup from day one."

"No Erik, you didn't have to take this job at all. You had the chance to opt out. The firm was genuinely glad you took the opportunity to step in once they bought this place ... Imagine if you passed and they'd have to find some poor schmuck to unload a failing enterprise. Your sweat equity's paid off and this place seems to be climbing out of the sewer Mr. Dawkens dug for it."

"Oh boy, I saved the firm from a bad investment." Erik looked at Denton with suspicion. "Why are you telling me all of this now, Martin? You're sticking your neck out."

"I put my 'Sixty Day' papers in yesterday, Erik. I'm done. Something happened a few days ago that gave me a reality check and I'm hoping you can help me work a murder case—multiple homicides, as I said on the phone earlier. I'm really not so concerned with all this secrecy and layers upon layers of intrigue anymore."

Erik tossed the coffee-soaked towels in the trash, then wiped his hands. He offered his friend a muffin before helping himself to one. "It's not exactly fresh baked from the kitchen of Madame's, but they're not too bad." He looked toward his old friend. "Okay Martin, let's get to the point, what the hell is going on? Give me the whole story."

Martin took a bite of his muffin, sipped his coffee and began his tale.

"I got the call three days ago from Rome, a triple homicide in Vatican City. Three clergy were slaughtered in a chamber under St. Martha's Chapel."

Erik stood up shaking his head vehemently, "Not interested, Martin. I'll take a pass on this one."

Denton's jaw dropped. "What? You didn't even hear me out."

"I know. I heard enough, though. I'm not interested in doing any work for the Catholic Church." Erik's tone was icy and final.

"But...."

"There are no buts, Counselor."

"Then how about a reason. Can you at least give me that, Agent Knight?" Denton snapped, his own tone icy and confrontational.

Erik's hands balled into fists and his eyes began to burn a fiery ice blue like two young stars burning bright with anger and rage. "When I was seven, I was placed in a foster home with two very Catholic parents. They were nice enough people. My foster brother and I went to church every Sunday, Sunday school afterwards and the whole religious nine yards. My foster mother decided that her son would be a wonderful altar boy and approached Father Lucas hoping Timmy would be accepted. Well she was overjoyed when, despite Timmy being so young, Father Lucas would make him a junior altar boy but he'd need some special training and classes at the rectory."

Denton groaned, the grip on his coffee cup increasing.

"I remember waking up one night around two in the morning after four of Father Lucas' classes. Timmy was up late packing. I asked where he was going and he told me he was running away so he didn't have to be an altar boy any more. I didn't understand what was going on but he told me that Father Lucas was touching him, and forcing my brother to do things. I remember the look of agony and horror on my brother's face and the tears as he told me what went on during those tutoring sessions. My brother told me the priest said his soul would burn in Hell if he ever said anything to anyone. I'd only been with Timmy for about ten months but he accepted me as his little brother and I thanked God for giving me a big brother. Timmy didn't care about Hell anymore. He just couldn't take going back there and we both knew our parents would never believe him.

"I threw some clothes in a bag and went with him. We climbed out of the bedroom window and headed off, neither one of us having any idea what to do next." Erik paused, tears rolled down his cheeks. Denton sat stone still, a look of shock on the old man's face.

Erik shook his head sadly and continued. "We were picked up by a police car in the next county two days later. We were caught stealing some Ring Dings and Twinkies. We were cold and hungry at that point and it didn't seem like taking the food was a bad idea. The clerk called the cops and it was only a matter of time before we wound up back home. We had to go to confession because we stole and got our backsides tanned for running away. Father Lucas took our confessions, of course. Timmy was forced to go back to being an altar boy and the private tutoring at the rectory continued. I remember clearly.

Three weeks to the day after we ran away, my brother came home from his 'tutoring'. He was different. His face looked like he'd seen a ghost or something. Over dinner he just sat stone still staring off into space. Our father asked what happened and Timmy just started crying saying he couldn't tell. But I did, I told. I shouted it at the top of my lungs. I remember the backhand I got like it was yesterday, I can still taste the blood in my mouth from my split lip. We both got the belt that night for telling such blasphemous tales." Erik laughed sickly. "Blasphemous he said ... not what was done to his son but what I said was blasphemous. At that point I hated that man, I hated my foster father and I hated Father Lucas." Erik started to whimper. "The next morning, I awoke to find my brother had slit his wrists with his pocket knife and bled out while I was sleeping. He left me a note saying he couldn't go on and he couldn't take Father Lucas' boy part touching him anymore.

"I screamed out and my foster parents came running in. I showed my foster father the note which he crumpled up and threw away. They called an ambulance and the police came. I was asked a few questions but was warned by them not to mention Timmy's letter. I kept the letter, Martin. It's still in a safety deposit box. Do you know what the real irony was? Father Lucas holding vigil and saying mass at my brother's funeral and offering comfort to my parents and the community. I'll never forget him telling my foster mother that when I was old enough I should become an altar boy too." Erik snorted an ironic laugh. "And that stupid ignorant woman had the nerve to thank him and hug him after he killed her son—my brother. That stubborn religious idiot of a man shook the priest's hand and accepted his blessing after they put my brother in the ground. They didn't believe their own son. Even his dying words were dismissed as ravings. I sat up that evening crying and praying to God for some kind of salvation, some kind of explanation for what happened to Timmy. God was apparently busy in some other corner of the universe because my prayers went unanswered. Around four in the morning I snuck into their bedroom and emptied the old man's wallet and her purse. I took a few things and I hit the road."

"Erik, I'm sorry. I had no idea."

Erik took a deep breath. "I should apologize to you. I shouldn't have gone off like that. What happened certainly wasn't your fault. But hopefully you can understand my reluctance to do anything for the quote 'Holy' Catholic Church."

"What happened? Did you ever see any of them again? You were a seven-year-old runaway. Surely you didn't get too far."

"I made it from Massachusetts to Upstate New York with two hundred forty-five dollars and sixteen cents." I followed the Mass Pike and the New York Thruway avoiding as many people as I could and buying food at highway rest stops while sleeping in the woods or inside dumpsters when it rained. I was on the road for about five weeks before a New York cop spotted me from a BOLO. At that point I was flat broke, cold and hungry, not to mention I smelled like an open sewer. The police were nice enough and I got turned over to social services and back into the lovely foster care system. I was in and out of different homes until I joined the Marines. I got the early waiver and was at boot camp at the tender age of seventeen and in Special Forces by the time I was twenty. When I had my first leave I paid a visit back to Timmy's parents. It took them awhile to remember me but I was very convincing. I even showed them the letter they threw away. I asked them if Father Lucas was still ministering in town and they said he wasn't. It didn't take too much looking to find out where the pervert priest was located." Erik's face turned to stone. "I paid Father Lucas a call. I wasn't a helpless little boy anymore. I made him regret that he ever laid a hand on my brother and I made sure he'd never do the same thing to another innocent boy."

Denton squirmed. "Good God! Tell me you didn't kill the man!"

Erik looked over at his old friend. "No, but he begged for death a few times before I was finished with him. He left the priesthood once he was discharged from the hospital. He's living in Arizona at a retirement community. The dry air is good for people suffering from multiple broken bones."

"So you've kept tabs on him?"

Erik nodded slightly. "One of my Special Forces friends also specializes in my kind of work, he calls me once in awhile and pays Father Lucas a visit from time to time to assure that he's leading a virtuous life."

Erik sipped his coffee. "Then the whole scandal erupted in 2001. I had no idea how vast the clergy abuse was. I'd just assumed my experience was a freak occurrence. I was wrong."

Martin chimed in gently. "The press did a great deal of wild reporting, Erik, and in fact the number of cases compared to the overall priesthood was very small."

Erik shook his head vehemently. "There's supposed to be an extra level of trust there, Martin, more so than a school teacher or some other institution. These were supposed to be men of God, men beyond reproach. They held a position of esteem and trust within the community and, just like Father Lucas, they warped and perverted that trust. And to make matters even worse, the Archdiocese covered up the truth, moved these problems from parish to parish writing glowing letters of recommendation for these monsters so they'd be free to prey on more innocents. Is that Godly? Is that the act of a holy organization? Hell, I read articles where the Archdiocese was actually blaming victims!"

"I agree, Erik but you're broad brush painting an entire organization and condemning everyone for the actions of a few. That's not justice. That's a witch hunt."

Erik shook his head. "Do you remember how Cardinal Law crept out of Boston to hide in Vatican City to avoid being forced to testify under oath? He knew what was going on and deliberately buried it. Do you remember how the Mass AG Kevin Riley balked on forcing the warrant for the 'good' cardinal? The powers in Rome used their influence to pull the protective blanket of the Vatican around him to keep what he knew buried. It was a perfectly orchestrated cover up right down to paying off some victims and ferrying the guilty away from justice." Erik sighed. "Look, I know the whole church isn't dirty. I know the vast majority of priests are good, decent men doing incredible work. I know the church does amazing charitable work around the world. I get it. I just can't let it go, Martin. The hurt runs deep and some shit just doesn't fade even after all these years."

An air of silence hung between the two men as Erik reburied the painful memories.

"You've had a difficult life, Erik. You've suffered more than any man should have to in one lifetime. As far as what happened I can't blame you for how you feel. No child should ever be exposed to such horrors." Denton began to shake. "I'm going to ask you, plead with you if I have to, for friendship's sake to please put aside your hatred for just a little while."

Erik sensed his friend's wave of pain and misery. "What is it Martin? What aren't you telling me, Counselor?"

The old man looked up, his face tortured, enduring some unknown agony. "My son, Erik. One of those clergymen murdered was my only son. No one in Vatican City has any leads or the slightest clue what happened. All I could glean from our intelligence gathering was that an artifact of some significance was stolen and my son and two other men were slaughtered. I did some checking on my own and I know one man survived the attack and the church hierarchy is sitting on him. He's the only witness to what occurred there. Our firm has some relations with the Bishop's Council and the Papal staff at Vatican City and they've consented to allow a team from the firm to investigate the crime scene for clues. I need your Esper senses, Erik. I need to know what happened to my son. Will you please put aside your hatred for a short time and help me find my son's killer?" Denton stared down at the floor. "A father shouldn't outlive his son."

"No, Martin, that shouldn't happen." Erik stood up and extended his hand toward his wounded friend. "Congratulations Counselor, you just managed to make me feel like shit. I'll do whatever I can to help you. I'll need to juggle my schedule with Shanda. Is it safe to assume that the firm has a staff of fitness gurus to fill in for me here while we're gone?"

Martin's posture stiffened and he managed a smile. "I told the firm I'd be hiring you and that you wouldn't be cheap. They want the mystery solved as much as I do. I get the sense that whatever was taken has some historical significance. The brass on the top floor is in a tizzy and Washington has been inundating our offices since news of the theft and deaths were discovered. Vatican City police and the Papal staff want this kept at a high clearance with no publicity and Washington is echoing those sentiments."

"Then there's some unspoken truth yet to be told. This reeks of hidden agendas and politics. It seems our religious friends in Rome have more secrets that need keeping." Erik smirked. "Okay Martin, let's go overturn the Vatican's apple-cart."

Denton smiled for the first time since he'd been at Erik's office. The old man reached inside his coat pocket and tossed an envelope on his desk. "Here's what I forced out of the accounting department for your fee. Consider it back pay for all the cases we steered away from you the last two years."

Erik picked up the envelope and opened it. His eyes widened, "That's a lot of zero's, Counselor, just for me looking into a homicide."

"Agreed, but the firm acknowledges that they overreacted to your little rebellion. I made a point of reminding them about who saved the planet from interstellar war while at the same time mending our diplomatic fences with France. Some of the higher ups needed a reminder of just how valuable an asset they were shelving for spite's sake. Also in your absence the terrorist cells in the Arab nations have skyrocketed. Al-Qaeda is no longer 'On the run' as our dear leader once said and several splinter cells and new factions have emerged in Iraq, Syria, Afghanistan, and Libya. You were our biggest weapon against them, and from what I heard, they were dancing in the streets when news of your termination spread."

Erik chuckled. "I got a few good riddance e-mails from some Al-Qaeda regulars I'd tangled with in the past. Sarina Fahaad's brother actually sent me flowers. Black roses, of course."

"The Fahaad family still blames you for Sarina's death, despite the fact you two were working together to protect the LaSalles." Denton shot his friend an evil grin. "I also reminded our friends higher up how the overseas problems have drastically escalated during your absence." The old man pointed toward the fat check. "Consider this their version of an apology and an invitation back to the 'family'."

Erik pocketed the check nodding, "I accept the apology. But I'm not sure I'm ready to travel around the world chasing terrorists and international bad guys again. It's nice being home with Shanda and EJ. The firm doesn't plan on inciting a riot in the next star system, do they?"

Denton laughed and nodded. "As far as I know we have no plans regarding interstellar warfare. One battle was sufficient. I understand your reluctance, but we've missed your insight and we've been suffering on the higher end private client cases. Our field detectives are good but none of them have your intuition or ability to dig into the weeds. The firm wants you back at the helm of Private Clients if you're willing. For that matter, they might possibly drop you in to cool a few hot spots in northern Iraq." Denton sighed. "But that's a discussion for another time. I can have a corporate jet ready to take off in two days. Will that give you enough time to get things squared away here and at home?"

Erik nodded. "Yeah, just let me know whose going to show up here so I can let the staff know what to expect. I've got good people here and I don't want a bunch of strangers walking in and trying to take over. Just send me two competent bodies willing to work with our clientele and maybe a bean counter to check my math. My bookkeeping skills are far from perfect."

Erik looked up at his friend. "Speaking of aliens, I wasn't privy to how things finally played out with 'Diplomat' and the negotiations for relations."

Denton shook his head. "The proposal was rejected. Our representatives were extremely disappointed. Humanity was deemed too unfit and ill prepared for intergalactic relations. We were also informed that Sergeant Phelps would not be returning to Earth. He chose to stay with Gray and his family."

Erik smiled. The young sergeant was a gentle soul living an unimaginable life of adventure no other human being would ever believe possible. Phelps was the first man in history to move beyond the solar system. A part of Erik was alien and he often wondered about the cosmic mysteries that lay beyond man's reach. His alien lineage came from a species long extinct. The Espers and Seelak fought their final war on Earth, over ten thousand years ago. The Observers claimed to know much of the Esper history and Diplomat, the Observer leader, had expressed an interest in discussing that history with the hybrid soldier at a future point in time. Erik felt a pang of regret at losing that opportunity.

"I wish I could say I'm surprised but I'm not. Diplomat didn't think much of our species and the case he made against us was pretty damning. The meeting at Area 51 for the peace negotiations was terse for awhile." Erik chuckled briefly. "Has the military finished rebuilding? We kind of decimated it during our difference of opinion."

Denton sighed. "The underground facilities were pretty much intact and you spared most of the tarmac and runways. It's on its way back to operational status but the alien craft we were studying and the Tesla prototypes were obliterated. I know they're reworking the Tesla models and the Phoenix fighter program but as far as testing any intergalactic hardware..." Denton slid his index finger across his throat. "That's all dead and buried."

"If they had another craft, would you know about it?" Erik shot his friend a doubtful glance.

Denton paused, as though weighing his answer, then shook his head. "Truth be told, probably not. This is becoming a younger man's business, Erik. High tech computer wizardry is rapidly replacing sleuth and investigative skill. It appears I've become a dinosaur after so many years. I was looking forward to retiring on my own terms, reconnecting with my son and seeing some of the world as a tourist and not a spy." A brief sob escaped. "Maybe even visiting William in Rome. It doesn't matter now; my son is gone and my career is over." Denton's head fell forward, another grief-wracked sob escaped him. Erik walked over placing a comforting arm on his friend's shoulder.

"I'm so sorry, Martin. I wish there was something I could do or say to ease this burden."

Denton's weathered, shaking hand reached up covering Erik's. "Helping me find his killer is the best thing you can do for me. Thank you."

Erik nodded. "You're more than welcome."

Erik spent the next two hours catching up and getting re-acquainted with his old friend listening to stories of Denton's son growing up. The gym was closing as Erik escorted Martin to his car.

"I'll have someone contact you tomorrow with the details.

I'll have a limo come by your place in two days to take you to the airport." Denton shook Erik's hand again and there seemed to be a bit more energy in his friend's grip. "Tell Shanda hello and I'm looking forward to a dinner invitation once we wrap up this unpleasantness."

Erik nodded. "Will do Martin, see you in a few days."

* * *

Erik was alone in the dojo punching and kicking a massive heavy bag. The force of his blows cracked like thunder and the bag swung like a child's piñata under the powerful strikes. The hybrid threw a triple combination then stepped in, launching a powerful roundhouse kick. The heavy bag creased under the impact, then rocketed upward. Only the protesting chain links kept it from flying into the air. Erik's mind raced through several images of his childhood and his blows increased in intensity. His hands were no longer visible. He launched strikes and counterstrikes faster than the human eye could follow. The sound of creaking chain and tortured canvas echoed throughout the empty dojo.

The ex-CIA agent saw images of his friend, Steve Forrest, and recalled the tragic passing of the brave Hopedale police officer. His mind took him back to Madame's and he saw his friend Jeff's body being taken away in an ambulance as the wait staff looked on in shock and horror. Erik put more force into his blows exhaling in rhythm with each series of punches and kicks. His mind kept recalling the painful memories like an endless waking nightmare.

"Enough!" he screamed aloud. A blue haze of bio-organic energy enveloped Erik's body. His skin had a faint silver hue. His eyes burned like two blue orbs of lightning. His final blow tore through the heavy canvas and snapped the heavy chain links. The two-hundred pound bag sailed across the open floor as sand and dense polymer stuffing fell from the gaping hole. The destroyed bag landed forty feet away, slamming into the far wall tipping over several chairs as it fell. The noise reverberated through the empty studio, echoing off the walls, knocking down several pictures. The hybrid stared blankly at the destroyed bag and the damage his last punch caused. "Wonderful." He approached the destroyed equipment lifting it by the severed chain with one arm. He casually tossed the bag in a corner and went back righting the chairs and hanging the fallen pictures.

"That heavy bag will cost a few dollars to replace."

Erik smiled as he turned toward the voice. "Don't you ever go home?"

Alissa stepped out of the dark walking toward the destroyed fitness equipment. She stuck her hand through the gaping hole caused by his fist. "What brought on this late night aggression?"

"Just exorcising a few of my own demons so I can approach what's coming with a clear mind." Erik grabbed a towel, then studied his body. "Forty-five damn minutes and not even a drop of perspiration. Goddamn Esper genetics, I can't even work up a sweat."

"You've known that since your change. Why should today be any different?"

"I know Alissa, still, the training is therapeutic and does help me work through my..." Erik made quotation marks with his fingers "...issues." Erik tossed the towel in a laundry bin and sat on a chair. Alissa picked up some errant bag filling, brushed the sand contrail with her foot and sat next to him.

"I'm sorry about Mr. Denton's son, that's just terrible."

"It is," Erik nodded staring off into the dark studio. "Martin never talked much about his family. I know he lost his wife some years ago but I confess we never really talked about our personal lives all that much. I'm ashamed to admit that for all the years I've known him I really don't know the man all that well." Erik sighed. "Another of my personal failings, I guess."

"You're in a melancholy mood this evening, what else is going on?"

Erik turned toward her. "This." He gestured all around the empty gym. "This is all a ruse. The firm bought this gym from Neal Dawkens. Not only that, they cosigned the business loan I took out from the bank to finance the renovations and the new equipment. We're not helping out a friend. The feds are babysitting us. I wonder how many of our members are employed by the firm?"

Alissa giggled.

Erik stared at his friend, his eyebrow raised.

"That's terrific news, Erik!"

"Enlighten me, please."

"You've been stressing over that loan and making the payments and you've been worrying about letting Mr. Dawkens down." Alissa patiently explained. "Mr. Dawkens is no longer a problem for you to be concerned about and if the business loan gets behind, the bank will simply chase down the firm for the money and leave you alone. Banks always go after the one with the deep pockets." Alissa placed a hand on his shoulder. "Think about it Erik, they just took all the pressure off you to make this place succeed. Let them have all their employees join up here if they want. Hell, we'll enroll all of them if we can. Why should you care? We're making money either way, and the firm's cash is just as green and spends just as easily as anyone else's."

Erik considered her words for a few moments and burst out laughing. "Very well put."

"You'd have arrived at the same conclusion, eventually, but not after breaking more equipment and brooding for hours on end." Alissa's face turned solemn. "Also you don't need this weighing you down. I have a feeling you're walking into something very big and you don't need to be distracted by this place. We'll handle things here and I'm sure Margaret will pop in on Shanda and EJ as will I."

"Thanks, Alissa."

"You're welcome. I gather 'welcome back to the world of espionage and intrigue' is a bit premature so I'll just say get off your ass and go find who killed Mr. Denton's son."

Erik tilted his head and nodded, "I'll get right on it."

* * *

Erik pulled into his driveway much later than he intended. Shanda was already home from work and was no doubt worried about him. Erik made as little noise as possible walking down the hallway to their bedroom. He quietly peeked into

EJ's room. His son was fast asleep. Erik crept over and gently stroked his son's hair.

"Sleep well little man. I'll see you tomorrow."

He crept back out and tiptoed into the master bedroom, slipping under the covers.

"Like I wasn't waiting up for you." Shanda's whisper broke the silence.

"Sorry, there was more to the meeting than I'd anticipated. We need to talk."

Shanda reached over and turned on a lamp. "This sounds serious."

Erik sat up and described the meeting's details. Shanda was stunned and saddened over the loss of Martin Denton's only son but not surprised that the firm was still directly involved in their lives. She sat up, adjusting the pillows.

"I agree with Alissa, the firm's done us a big favor, and that fat check certainly goes a long way toward making amends for the last two and a half years."

Erik flexed his powerful arms. "Don't take this the wrong way, babe. I'm glad for the money, for our family's sake, but I don't like the firm's tentacles wrapped around our lives. I admit we were struggling but we were getting by just fine without the firm of Denton, Ross and Priscoli hanging over our heads. We're not living a flashy life but we're doing okay, aren't we?"

Shanda spun toward him. "Hon, I love our life and I love what we have here. I don't need riches or bells and whistles to be happy. We've got a nice home, great neighbors, and an amazing son. I'm proud of all you've done and I'm proud of the stand you took with Eunice Kim against Richard and the firm. They need your skill set and you need to help our friend, Martin. God works in mysterious ways, Erik. We just have to have faith that this is all part of the big plan. But truth be told, a big fat check with lots of zeros makes life just a bit sweeter."

Erik laughed and tussled her hair. "You're such an optimist."

"That's why you married me, Mister Glass-half-empty."

"Funny you mentioning God, I thought with all that I am, all that we've seen, you'd have a different perspective about God."

"My view of God is my own and probably wouldn't get me

any preacher's spot in any conventional church. I do, however, believe in a binding force that created and guides the universe. I don't believe we're just a random occurrence. Now do you want to discuss religion or make love to your wife before you fly off to Italy?"

Erik leaned over her and turned off the light. "Do you even have to ask?"

Chapter 2. Getting Back on the Horse

Erik woke up, uneasy. EJ was crying in his bed. His screams were not just that of an upset child, but of a child terrified. Erik leapt from the bed and ran to his son's bedroom. He grabbed the doorknob but it refused to turn. Erik pushed on the door but it wouldn't give. He increased his force and still the door refused to open. Shanda came up behind him panicked. Erik applied another burst of strength and the doorjamb split. He pushed the door open, ignoring the fragments of wood, and both parents ran to their screaming child. Erik scooped up his son and held him close.

"It's okay buddy. I got ya. Mom and dad are here."

EJ held on to his father, clinging desperately to his shoulders while Shanda gently patted his back reassuring him that he'd had a bad dream. Once the child settled, Erik gently placed him in Shanda's arms and approached the ruined door and frame. He tried to turn the doorknob but it was frozen solid. He looked over at his wife, baffled.

"I left the door ajar like we always do after I checked on him. I'm guessing there was a good cross breeze last night causing a draft strong enough to close the door." Erik pointed toward the half-open window. "The inner mechanism seems to be jammed. I'll replace this before I leave."

Shanda nodded absently as she held EJ close. "That scared the crap out of me."

"Me as well." He studied the frozen doorknob. He tried again to turn the knob and it still refused to budge. Erik grasped the doorknob in a grip of steel and forced it counterclockwise under his enhanced Esper strength. The knob groaned and creaked as tortured, overstressed metal parts yielded to the immense applied pressure. The doorknob sheared clean off and several bent pieces of metal fell to the floor. He studied the remnants carefully. Some of the metal was corroded but that corrosion wouldn't account for the mechanism freezing up completely. "To hell with it. I'll pick up a whole new pre-hung door this morning. I'll take EJ with me. He loves tooling around the hardware store."

* * *

Vatican City, Rome

"Do we have any more information on the theft? Is there anything at all that you've uncovered in the last two days?"

A Vatican police officer was visibly uncomfortable. He'd been on the receiving end of a verbal bombardment from the papal hierarchy for nearly an hour and could only say he had no answers so many times before his grip on civility began to slip.

"You refuse me access to the one witness who survived this attack, refuse to allow my coroner access to the bodies for autopsy and won't let a team of forensic techs touch the crime scene and you have the gall to pressure me for my lack of any credible results, Bishop O'Malley. Even a pampered Vatican hack must see the insanity in your line of questioning."

The bishop reacted as if slapped. "I don't like your tone, officer."

"And I don't like being stonewalled, Bishop. When you decide to get off your high horse and allow us to do our jobs, maybe we can get you some answers. Until then, don't bother me with this anymore. Maybe your team of Americans can get you the answers you desire while keeping whatever obvious political secret you so desperately want to keep, buried. Let me remind you though, the Americans didn't take a solemn oath to serve God and the holy orders like my men and I have."

The bishop did a poor job keeping a poker face. No one was supposed to know of the Americans coming over to investigate. "Where did you hear this?"

"Like the Papacy, we have our own channels of information and our own methods of gathering intelligence. I gather by your reaction the information we obtained is accurate."

O'Malley steepled his fingers, "Yes. We've reached out to a branch of the Central Intelligence Agency. Two men will be arriving tomorrow to investigate the murders and the theft. Our purpose is twofold. One of the men is of interest to the hierarchy and requires vetting. The other is the father of one of the deceased. It's not our intention to be deliberately vague, but this act has all of us aghast. This theft will start the final war between Dark and Light in a matter of months instead of the decades we expected. The butchery committed by the Dark factions in our city cannot go unpunished, but the implications to the war already being fought are catastrophic."

The seasoned Vatican cop rubbed his brow. "I don't know about holy wars between Dark and Light, Bishop. I deal with the more mundane human crimes in the holy city, and believe me, there's enough dirt and corruption to keep my forces gainfully employed. Having said that, I'm still responsible for the security here and I'd appreciate being kept in the loop. If it's going to rain cats and dogs and the plagues of Egypt are about to befall us I'd like to know beforehand."

The old bishop nodded. "I will do what I can to keep you appraised."

The defiant officer excused himself. He turned to face the robed panel before he left the chamber. "Be careful playing with fire, gentlemen. Your actions have often caused more damage to our church than good. Playing God is best left to God himself."

Bishop O'Malley raised an eyebrow. "We'll keep that in mind."

O'Malley waited for the cop to depart and he turned toward his peers. "I want a complete dossier on Erik Knight. I want information on family, friends, everything our sources can get their hands on. We need to know exactly who and what he is beyond our current information. I've heard the stories about him. Now I want some facts to either validate or refute the fairy tales. We need answers, gentleman. The Holy Father needs explanations and answers. Somebody gave away the location of the Ruby Crucifix—supposedly the best kept secret on the planet." The bishop sighed. "Let's pray this detective is as formidable as his legend."

* * *

Milford, MA

Erik examined his handiwork and nailed in the last piece of finishing trim. "Can you hand me another nail, partner?"

Tiny hands fished a long thin nail from a glass jar. "This one good, daddy?"

Erik looked down and smiled as his son. "That's perfect, bud." Erik drove the final nail in place and stepped back to admire his work. With a casual tap he pushed the door closed, the latch caught and the door closed solidly. He reached, turned the knob and the door opened effortlessly.

"Give it a try, EJ."

The young boy pushed the door closed and then reached up and turned the bright brass doorknob, the door opened easily. He looked over at is father and smiled. "It works!"

Erik laughed. "Of course it works, buddy. We fixed it together."

EJ peeked carefully in his room looking apprehensive. Erik felt a wave on unease radiating off his son. "What's spooking ya, buddy?"

The young boy looked up at his father. "I was looking for the ghost."

Erik flinched. "The ghost? When did you start seeing a ghost?"

"This morning. It was watching me and I got scared. It flew out the window when you broke the door."

Erik knelt down and held his son. "Well I think the ghost got scared and won't be back. You don't have to be afraid anymore. But if you see something else while I'm gone, you tell your mom. Okay?"

"Okay, daddy."

"Right now, head into the bathroom, do your business, and we'll head out to JJ's for some ice cream."

EJ smiled and ran to the bathroom. Erik stepped into his son's bedroom. He focused his eyes on the room, scanning. His eyes shifted through all visible spectrums looking for any traces of energy, or residual disturbances in the room. Erik's eyes burned radiant blue, shifting through energy spectra, some known only to the Esper species. Again nothing. No residual energy or evidence of any presence.

"Ancient warriors, alien constructs, and human hybrids. Why not ghosts? Just not here, not in my home." Erik tried the door again and it worked flawlessly. He shook his head and went to fetch his car keys. He didn't have to be at the gym for another two hours and he'd make the most of his time with his son. This was the first time since the birth of his child Erik would be away for more than a day. The detective had to admit he was a bit nervous and uncomfortable. He hadn't worked a big case or done any large-scale sleuthing for two years. He'd heard other detectives talk at symposiums about losing the edge over time. He hoped this didn't apply to his skills and ability.

EJ came out of the bathroom, racing down the hall, snapping him out of his thoughts.

"Ice cream, ice cream," the young boy screamed happily.

Erik scooped up his son carrying him out to his truck dismissing the unusual discussion they had, dismissing it as part of his son's bad dream.

* * *

Washington DC, Columbia Heights

He stayed in the shadows avoiding the brightly lit streets clutching a dark case in one hand. Artificial light wasn't a danger but the bright luminosity would cause his head to throb and ache for hours. He didn't want to be seen by anyone carrying an object of such immense value and importance. Human muggers and thieves weren't much of a concern but there were other entities lurking about, hiding in the shadows, looking for an opportunity to strike. He was also aware that the owners of his stolen property were scouring the planet hunting for any trace of the holy relic. The specter hoped the dark shroud concealing the relic would shield it from the forces of Light and the renegade forces of Dark that called Washington DC home.

He clung to the side of a small five-story building overlooking the "Starlight Bistro," an upper echelon establishment for men of power as well as other beings that dealt in money, power and influence. He leapt the fifteen-foot chasm separating the two buildings, scaled down the back side of the Bistro, and crept toward the entrance. He approached a tall, muscular human guarding the front doorway, who coordinated the coming and going of limousines. The man spoke into a headset, relaying some sort of instructions to another disembodied voice heard over the earpiece.

"Hey, you! Where do you think you're goin'? Not in here dressed like that!" The large man blocked his way.

"I apologize for my less-than-formal attire, but I have an urgent package for Senator Paul McMahon. He is expecting me. Can you tell him Lazarus has arrived with the object he requested?"

The doorman spoke into his earpiece again, this time addressing someone inside the ritzy establishment. Thirty seconds later the doorman nodded. "The senator is expecting you, Mr. Lazarus." The large man pointed to a young woman inside. "Find our guest a dinner jacket and a tie, then escort him to Senator McMahon's private table in the executive room."

He smiled an evil, shark-like smirk that made the human involuntarily shudder. "Actually, it's Father Lazarus, thank you, my son. God will reward your kindness."

The man laughed. "I'll take any blessing I can get, 'Padre'." He watched the man as he was escorted away. "Damn creepy lookin' holy man."

'Father' Lazarus was escorted by a curvy waitress to a large, isolated VIP lounge. A heavy, balding, middle-aged man was enjoying the attention of two barely dressed women. Next to him were two other well dressed men dining on expensive delicacies and sipping thousand-dollar-a-bottle champagne. Lazarus sat across from the large man smiling wickedly.

"Do you have my package?"

"Yes, Senator, it was no small feat mind you but I managed to locate your coveted trinket."

McMahon smiled, his eyes hungrily searching his guest.

Lazarus placed a hard leather case on the table, careless of the hors d'oeuvres and expensive entrees. "In here. Concealed within the shroud of darkness, just as you instructed." He was about to open the case.

"No!" the senator croaked near panic. "Keep it hidden. Every supernatural being in the twelve realms will feel its presence once it's exposed. I want this transaction as low key and under the radar as possible. The fewer people that know of this the better."

Lazarus cackled the laugh of the insane. "You can't hide this, Senator. Your opposition already knows their loss. Secrets of this kind cannot be kept for long. I have no doubt that the forces of darkness are also aware of this unauthorized acquisition."

The senator's face paled. He brushed the girl's hand away from his lap. "What did you do?"

"I did nothing but what you and your associates asked, Senator. I risked obliteration and committed the ultimate sin against God in the process." Lazarus cackled again showing the senator his scarred hands, "And I still have the burns to prove it."

The senator studied the scarred flesh and turned toward a waitress. "A glass of your finest blood for my friend here. He's earned it."

The senator reached inside his suit coat and produced a small, white linen bag. "Each coin is solid silver as you requested—thirty freshly minted American Eagle coins." McMahon slid the bag across the table. Lazarus undid the tie and gazed upon his prize.

"A perfect irony, Senator McMahon. It's been a pleasure doing business with you."

McMahon tilted his head. "I don't follow you, but you work cheap and get the job done. My associates will be pleased."

The waitress returned with a delicate wine glass filled with red fluid. She carefully placed it in front of Lazarus and backed away nervously. He picked up the glass, gently caressing the brim with a scarred fingertip. "What sweet nectar." His eyeballs turned black as coal and incisor teeth grew into sharp long fangs protruding from a pale, thin upper lip. Lazarus hissed happily and downed the blood in two gulps.

He licked his lips and sighed happily. "A good vintage and still body-temperature warm. You should try some instead of that fermented juice your kind obsesses over."

"To each his own, Mr. Lazarus." McMahon raised his champagne glass and toasted their success.

As the vampire raised his empty glass in celebration, a sickening crunch accompanied a fist bursting through his ribcage, spraying dark fluid on the table, soaking the senator and his two companions.

The fist held Lazarus's still beating heart captive. Lazarus, however, was decomposing into a pile of ash.

"What the Christ!" McMahon exploded looking up at the being that'd rudely interrupted their celebration. The women screamed, leaping from his lap, fleeing in abject panic.

Lazarus' heart stopped beating and disintegrated. Ash fell from his assailant's fingers falling like snowflakes upon the blood-stained tablecloth.

"You idiots! I should kill you right here for what you've done!"

The senator turned his head as three bouncers approached his table. He nodded and waved his hand in a dismissive gesture. The three men turned and left.

"Good evening, Nicadaemus, to what do I owe the honor of a personal visit?" McMahon pointed toward the blood splatters. "Was that really necessary? Lazarus was a good 'flunkie' and an excellent thief." He gestured toward the case with a casual glance.

"What possessed you to steal the Ruby Crucifix of Christ, and why would you send a vampire of all species to get it? Do you realize what you've done? What you've instigated?"

"My employer wanted the Ruby Crucifix and I tracked the item and obtained it for him. I fail to see the problem."

"Because you're a mere human, you have no idea the forces in play and the balance you've just upset. You can tell me how you found the relic before I snap your neck." The being reached hungrily toward the senator's throat, fingers curled like lethal talons.

McMahon produced a large revolver from his jacket. His

associates mirrored the action. "Get back, now! Your puffed-up self-importance annoys the piss out of me. Your people are locked in another time playing by old rules guided by prophecy from some wrinkled, forgotten parchment. This is a new era, Nicadaemus, and you're an old Model T in a land of Ferraris and Porsches."

"You think mortal bullets will kill me?"

McMahon shot his foe an evil grin. "One thing humans do that your kind doesn't. We study, we learn, and we adapt. God gave us that ability, something he seemed to have left out with you and yours. The bullets are talithum-coated hollow points blessed and dipped in holy water. The talithum will pierce your flesh and burn your insides while the holy water and blessed metal will cook you like a mini bonfire."

Nicadaemus took a step back from the table, his eyes re-assessing the threat. "Kill me and your life will be short and your death an eternal agony beyond imagining, human." The inhuman gestured toward a chair assuming a passive posture. "Forgive my overzealous reaction. May I sit and explain the chain of events your acquisition has just disturbed?"

The senator nodded. "Please, enlighten me."

The inhuman sat. His eyes spotted the white cloth sack and he casually opened it. His face formed a half smile. "Lazarus, you are indeed an ever constant source of irony." The being emptied the silver coins on the table. "Thirty pieces of silver. He escalated a holy war for thirty pieces of silver."

McMahon looked puzzled. The inhuman explained. "Here is perhaps a failing of your kind, Senator, your lack of appreciation for history, Biblical or otherwise. Your species seems doomed to repeat the same mistakes over and over." The inhuman brushed more of the ash off the chair and sat. "Jesus was betrayed by Judas for thirty pieces of silver." The inhuman picked up a coin studying it. "Were you aware that Lazarus killed three clerics at Vatican City, slaughtered them in the process of acquiring that trinket?"

The senator's faced went pale and he poured himself a glass of hard liquor, downing the shot in a desperate attempt to calm his nerves. "Imbecile. I told him stealth was of the utmost importance."

Nicadaemus continued. "One of the men he slaughtered was the son of a high-powered CIA operative, one Martin Denton. Denton will be on a plane to Rome bringing someone with him, a recently deactivated CIA cooler—a being we don't want involved in our affairs."

"What can one CIA operative do? I know Denton. He's a dedicated suit for his firm, but he's not a player in the larger scheme. He has no idea of the bigger picture. He's strictly a low level player involved in human affairs."

The inhuman nodded, reaching for the bottle of hard liquor. He started to poor himself a glass. He looked toward McMahon. "Do you mind?"

"Help yourself."

Nicadaemus downed the shot in one gulp, slamming the glass on the table when he finished. "Denton contacted the hybrid two days ago, and they're on their way to Vatican City. That Esper/human genetic cocktail has the ability to sniff out Lazarus and anyone involved with him. Though Lazarus is a dead end now. I assume you're aware of Special Agent Erik Knight and his abilities."

McMahon nodded, growing even paler. "I read the classified report on the Observer Incident. Denton wasn't mentioned, we had no idea there was a connection. Lazarus wasn't supposed to kill anyone."

"Lazarus had his own agenda. Had you studied your history you'd have realized that. He used you to get his own revenge for past slights by the Catholic Church. You gave him the reason to return to Rome and he decided to go on a killing spree. He killed Martin Denton's son and now Denton is bringing in a big gun. The hybrid has a role to play, but we're just not sure what. We're watching him, discreetly for now. We don't want Erik Knight getting involved in this war, especially now that you've gone and escalated it beyond either sides' liking. Mankind was on a slow, happy road to Hell, oblivious and ignorant of its damnation. In a few decades, maybe even half a century, we could have made a move of this magnitude, but you went and jumped the shark. You stole the most coveted relic of the Lords of Light and committed murder in the Holy City. They will be coming for you, Senator."

McMahon shook as he downed another shot of hard liquor. "Lazarus is a low level blood sucker, what kind of beef could he have with the Vatican?"

Nicadaemus smiled. "Since your kind is so fond of learning, Senator, I'll let you investigate that for yourself. I hope you and your faction enjoy your trinket. You've just unleashed a holy war of epic proportion, maybe even escalated Armageddon itself." The inhuman laughed a chilling evil cackle. "Well done, human, well done. I don't know who'll come for you first, Michael or Lucifer. You've single-handedly escalated an eons-old simmering conflict up to a full boil. I suggest you find the deepest hole and crawl into it as soon as possible."

The inhuman stood, slowly, still watching the two weapons trained on him. "I'll leave you and your advanced sense of learning to contemplate what we've just discussed. Good evening, Senator, and good luck."

McMahon looked at his colleagues. The three men contemplated the inhuman's revelation.

"Gentleman, we may have just jumped into water way over our collective heads. Mr. Bishop, get on the phone and get me all the background on Lazarus. Keep your search off the grid. We don't want the inquiry traced back to us in any way. Alex, I only have some limited knowledge of Special Agent Knight. I need a dossier on this man like yesterday." McMahon stood, grabbed the case and the silver coins.

"Where are you going, Paul?" Bishop asked, holstering his gun.

"I'm gonna find me that deep rat hole and stash this thing, then I'm gonna call our boss and enlighten him as to how this whole escapade just went fucking nuclear on us. We need to know how to proceed. I'm not bailing on you guys. We go back too far and you've saved my ass on more than one occasion. We just need to get this hot potato out of our possession and eliminate any traces leading back to us which means I have to visit a certain coin dealer at the downtown mint and have the manager there remind his employees how much I pay for confidentiality."

* * *

Milford, MA, Knight Household

Shanda and EJ were coloring in the kitchen while Erik stared at his basement gun safe. He pondered carrying a weapon on his upcoming trip. Denton was already en route. The two days of packing and preparation flew by. He didn't feel the need to be armed in the Holy City, but his detective and military training as well as his agency training had drilled into him always better to have his weapon and not need it than to need it and not have it. The ex-CIA cooler hadn't opened the safe or fired a weapon in two years. Erik knew he'd require at least a few hundred rounds to feel comfortable enough to brandish any of the weapons in his arsenal.

"A whole bunch of guns and I don't feel comfortable carrying a single one of them." An incessant drone came from inside the safe, his skin tingled as a part of his being responded to the call.

"The Sentient Staff," he mused. "Why not? Easily concealed, lethal, and portable." Erik smiled as he dialed the safe's combination. The buzzing sound grew louder as the weapon anticipated being reunited with its wielder. Erik opened the safe's heavy door and reached for the satchel that held the Esper weapon. He gently freed the chrome, metallic cylinder and held it in his left hand. His body tingled as bio organic energy cracked through his body. The hybrid took a step back giving himself room. His thoughts focused, AHNS-SOH-LAK!

The staff purred happily and began to expand in size and shape. On one end, two fearsome blades formed from the liquid metallic substance. The other end of the staff formed a savage J-shaped hook. The weapon Erik held was over six feet long and crackled as blue-white arcs of power danced along the mirrored surface. Erik's mind saw flashes of his alter ego: the massive seven-plus-foot alien soldier, bred to be the ultimate powerhouse and war machine. Something happened in the Esper genetic engineering. His powers and abilities kept growing over time, surpassing those he was modeled after. Erik remembered the kind of power he brought to bear against the Observers several years ago and how the very elements of the planet were his to control and command. The kind of power the hybrid had under his command was unimaginable.

"Yeah." The detective smiled. "That'll work just fine." He focused his thoughts on his alien weapon. *Do you remember when we traveled by plane several years ago? How we worked to conceal you from the prying eyes?* The weapon purred and responded. It seemed to melt and stream toward his waist. The staff flowed around his heavy leather belt and covered the large metal belt buckle. Erik looked down and smiled. "Absolutely perfect, well done!"

The weapon seemed pleased at his praise and the positive response to his compliment echoed through his mind. Erik closed his safe and spun the combination lock. He turned and went back upstairs to make the most of the remaining time with his wife and son.

"Well look at the two of you, coloring up a storm. Are there any crayons left for me to use?"

Shanda and EJ looked up and laughed. "Shall we let daddy join in on the fun?"

EJ nodded happily selecting three crayons and some paper with outlined pictures. He offered them to his father and smiled a wicked grin that mimicked Erik's own smirk. "Daddy you have to stay inside the lines this time."

"Yes, daddy, sloppy coloring is not tolerated in this house," Shanda echoed.

Erik knelt down on the floor laughing. "Critics, I live with a house full of critics. No one ever told Picasso or Rembrandt to stay inside the lines."

"Picasso and Rembrandt?" Shanda laughed. "That's who you're comparing your scribbling to now?"

Erik's poor coloring skills had become the focus of much light-hearted teasing. Try as he might, his skills at coloring were awful whereas Shanda could shade with crayons and make a simple two dimensional outline come to life with depth and clarity.

"You guys just don't appreciate real art."

Shanda burst out laughing. "Is that what you call it?"

The Knight family happily spent the next hour coloring and laughing. Erik kept his eye on the clock, each minute passing seemed to bring a sense of despair. He'd become accustomed to being home with his family, living a normal life with normal worries and challenges. The life of a CIA cooler and special investigator seemed foreign now. Erik wondered if he'd made a mistake accepting this job. He didn't need the firm or their money. The detective wondered if he'd let his sense of friendship overrule his obligation to his family.

Stop it hun, you're broadcasting your bad vibes inside my head. Shanda's thoughts pulsed inside his mind. His wife was telepathic—a latent gift she'd used in order to break through Erik's pent up wall during the Hopedale Mountain incident. Both husband and wife shared Esper genetics, but Shanda lacked the metamorphic capability and extreme powers he possessed. Shanda's gifts were more empathic in nature.

"Sorry, I'm not comfortable leaving the two of you alone."

"Don't worry about us. Martin needs your help right now and you need to get back in the saddle. You're a detective, and a damn good one. It's what you were meant to do. You're happiest when you're helping people in genuine need which is why you feel comfortable at that gym. But that's not who you are. Don't get me wrong. I'm extremely happy with our life and the way things are, but I can tell you're not totally fulfilled. Help Martin, do what makes you happy and that will make me happy. EJ and I will be here when you get home and you can tell us all about Rome." She grinned, "And bring home presents!"

Erik tilted his head. "What will they have at the Vatican gift shop?"

"Here's a chance to use that Picasso-like creativity you claim to have. Surprise me."

"I'll see what I can do." Erik heard a car door close. He stood up looking out the living room window. "My ride is here, and it looks like Martin decided to pay a social call."

"I haven't seen Martin since our housewarming party." Shanda stood and went to the doorway greeting the elder CIA operative as Erik gathered his duffel bag.

"Martin!" Shanda wrapped her arms around the elder agent. "I am so sorry for your loss."

Denton returned the embrace and smiled warmly. "Thank you, Shanda." The elder agent stepped back studying the young woman. "Good lord, you haven't aged a day."

Denton spotted EJ peeking out from behind a chair. "Well hello there young man." He looked over at Shanda. "He has your eyes."

"You can come say hello. Mr. Denton is an old friend."

EJ walked forward and extended his tiny hand. He looked up and smiled, "Hi, I'm EJ."

Denton smiled and gently shook the boy's hand. "Hello EJ, I'm Martin. I'm a friend of your father's."

"You and Daddy are going on a plane ride."

Denton raised an eyebrow. "Yes, yes we are. We'll only be gone for a few days and I'll have him home as soon as possible."

"Daddy and I put a new door in my room. Wanna see it?"

Shanda rolled her eyes but Denton laughed. "You helped? I'm impressed, that's no small feat." He pointed into the house. "Lead the way."

Erik excused himself and went down to his basement office. He came up a moment later carrying his bag and heard the commotion in EJ's bedroom. He walked down the hall and could hear his son talking nonstop to Martin. The boy was showing him his Lego collection, his toy cars, and model airplanes. Erik looked in and Martin was actually sitting on the floor with EJ building with Lego's while Shanda looked on smiling.

"You keep spoiling him, Counselor, and he'll never let you leave."

Denton looked up and laughed. "I spent many a time building with these blocks, Erik. It's nice to see in the age of electronics and video games some of the old favorites haven't gone out of style."

The detective caught a slight sense of longing in his friend's voice. He imagined Martin, as a father, doing all the things he enjoyed doing with his son. Erik wondered how he would feel if EJ was taken from him suddenly. The pain his friend was enduring was something he hoped he would never feel.

"Times change, Martin. Kids are into video games, digital downloads, and computers. That's a far cry from anything we had growing up."

Denton slowly stood up and patted EJ on the head. "Time

for me to go. I hope you'll allow me to come back and play again?"

EJ smiled happily. Erik walked over and picked up his son. "You be good for mom while I'm gone. Okay?"

The young boy promised and kissed his father goodbye.

Erik shifted his son to one side and lifted up his duffel bag with his other hand and walked down the hallway. He gently placed EJ on the floor and turned toward Shanda. "Time to hit the road."

"I know." She kissed Erik deeply one last time. "Have a safe flight guys and good luck."

Both men nodded and headed toward the door. Erik tuned back and mouthed 'I love you' as he headed out. Shanda re-peated the gesture as the front door closed. She held back the sudden feeling of emptiness and focused on the ever-present psychic link they shared. Shanda looked down at EJ. The child kept staring at the door. "Do you miss daddy already?"

"Yeah," the child muttered. "Wanna go with daddy."

"I know baby, me too, but daddy and Mr. Denton are do-ing big boy stuff. Why don't we go to the park for awhile then we can order pizza for dinner, would you like that?"

EJ smiled and nodded.

* * *

Washington DC, Office of the Speaker of the House of Representatives

Senator Paul McMahon paced nervously outside Speaker Andrew Collins' office. He'd passed the requested artifact on to the speaker as ordered and now had the required follow-up data on Special Agent Erik Knight and the deceased vampire named Lazarus. Nicadaemus' doom-filled proclamation was accurate. The inhuman warned that they'd kicked over a hor-net's nest.

"The speaker will see you now, Senator."

McMahon nodded to the shapely receptionist and made his way into the plush office. Andrew Collins was thumbing through the latest house bill with two aides. Collins looked up and the senator nodded, indicating he had information.

"I'm afraid I'm going to have to cut this short, gentlemen. Bottom line, we didn't get any help from them during the election and I nearly lost my majority. If they expect me to play ball now it's going to take more than the wooing of a few lobbyists. Call Mr. Flint at DuPont and tell him if he doesn't sweeten the pot this initiative will wind up in some backdoor committee until the end of time."

McMahon waited impatiently as Collins wrapped up his business. Finally the two aides gathered their papers and headed back to the House chambers to deliver his ultimatum. The large office door closed and Collins took his seat behind his antique mahogany desk.

"Paul you have the look of a man whose dog just got run over."

The senator placed two binders on Collins' desk. He sat on the heavily cushioned chair opposite the speaker. "The dossier on Erik Knight and some research on 'Father Lazarus'."

Collins picked up a file. "Father? You can't be serious. A low level bloodsucker for hire was once a human priest?"

McMahon nodded. "We didn't get a complete file, but we were able to trace down enough to know Lazarus was a priest in Italy a few hundred years ago. He was extremely fanatical and Old Testament. He didn't play church politics and was quite incorruptible."

Collins poured himself a drink from the crystal decanter on his desk and then poured one for his associate. McMahon nodded and drained his glass in one gulp. He exhaled as the liquor burned his gut.

"The good Father got on the wrong side of a few powerful bishops and they hatched a plot to defrock him. I couldn't get all of the details but it seems Lazarus was booted out for fathering several children out of wedlock. Five women gave sworn testimony and the church had little choice but to send him packing."

Collins took a sip from his glass considering this new revelation. "Church politics," he laughed. "It appears our foes at the holy city are just as morally bankrupt as any other organization."

McMahon nodded and continued. "Lazarus dove into the

bottle pretty hard and wound up in some seedy tavern that catered to more than human clientele. I couldn't find all the details but he was turned that evening and supposedly lost most of his sanity trying to cope with his eternal damnation."

"What else?"

"As far as Lazarus, that's all we found, but Lazarus was dusted after he delivered the package and is off the board." McMahon looked worried. "Is there any truth to what that demon said? Did we just turn up the heat on a holy war between Heaven and Hell?"

"Yeah, Paul, it appears we did. But here's what I don't get. We get our orders from higher up on the less-than-pious side of the fence. Those forces knew what pilfering that little trinket was going to do. They had to know what would be unleashed. So why did Nicadaemus act so shocked? Ultimately our reporting chain filters up the same path. I think somebody higher on the food chain is breaking protocol and doing things on their own against the wishes of both darkness and light. Let's be candid for a minute. I'm happy with the status quo. I don't want to see total evil here because I'm not in the mood to have a Hell on Earth but at the same time I don't want another Garden of Eden either. I like the managed chaos of both sides fighting to the point where we're left to our dithers and can dabble ethereally as we please or don't please. I don't want either side gaining absolute hold over this realm, that doesn't serve our objectives in Washington or any other human center of power."

McMahon nodded in agreement. "If someone in our chain is going rogue there'll be Hell to pay, literally."

Andrew Collins grinned. "Our little trinket is stashed in the Vault. Three hundred feet down in a lead and depleted uranium lined bunker covered with twenty feet of steel rebar reinforced concrete. Unless God himself or an Archangel decides to come get it, that relic isn't going anywhere. As long as the shroud of darkness covers it, no one short of a high ranking power will know where it is. Fortunately for us mere mortals, the higher powers seem reluctant to do battle directly. Nor do they seem to want to get involved in the struggles of one tiny planet when the whole universe is out there for them to wage war over." Collins picked up the file on Erik knight and leafed through it quickly. He looked over at McMahon and frowned. "What about this guy? Is there any truth to all the rumors and tales about him?"

"I read the report by Special Agent Phil Penn after the Hopedale Mountain Incident. It raises a lot of questions on top of the reality we've been dealing with. Knight is part alien. The result of a genetic experiment put into place by a species that fought a battle here some ten thousand years ago. Knight is part Esper Soldier, an inhuman juggernaut capable of some amazing feats of strength and energy manipulation." The senator paused. "But it gets even better. Do you remember the destruction of Area 51? Remember all the freak weather patterns that were recorded in the area?"

Collins nodded. "Yeah, the electrical storms were cataclysmic and supposedly wiped out the surface of the base."

McMahon shook his head in disagreement. "No. Knight engaged in an all-out war against an invading force in that desert. In his alien form he generated enough power to level some massive alien war machines as well as generate two F-5 tornados. I heard stories that he also sent a blast of power into orbit crippling an alien battle cruiser."

Collins' jaw dropped, his face paled. "Why didn't we know about this?"

"Because at the time we were doing our best to cover our trail, the president sent Special Agent Knight to root out the underground operations in the federal government. It was the president's play to give the forces of Light an advantage in the conflict by having a non-ethereal player with inhuman power tilt the balance much as were doing now. In fact, you might say the forces of Light having unleashed Agent Knight brought about this turn of events and escalated the conflict."

McMahon shook his head. "I don't think the president is involved. He doesn't have the mark of a player. Maybe his actions inadvertently impacted the bigger game, but the president is simply a puppet to the human power brokers in Washington and the corporate lobbyists. He doesn't have any real clout in the larger game. He's a one or two term figurehead."

Collins considered the point and nodded in agreement. "Well said. The irony however won't go unnoticed ... a noble human act to clean up a corrupt government leads to an all out holy war." The House speaker exhaled, "So is Knight as powerful as the stories claim? And what motivated him to get involved in that kind of conflict? CIA coolers are usually 'Lone Wolf' personas content to work in the shadows."

"They abducted his pregnant wife with the intention of dissecting their child."

Collins nearly choked. "Are you serious? Aliens were really abducting people! Holy shit! That's extraordinary and terrifying all in one."

"Let me rephrase: We abducted his pregnant wife so we could study the child and at the same time we provoked an alien species to war." The senator paused while Collins paled. Sweat beaded on his forehead. "Knight and the alien species called Observers arrived at Area 51 at the same time. Knight was there for his bride and the Observers were coming to free a captive. The aliens were kicking our ass but good and the surface of the Groom Lake facility was leveled. When it looked like we were about to get the final kiss of death, Knight literally dropped out of the sky and engaged the entire alien force by himself." Senator McMahon leaned forward intently to emphasize his next words. "From what I was told, Special Agent Erik Knight literally pummeled through fifty feet of solid bedrock with his bare hands ... one titanic blow that registered on seismographs as far away as Anchorage, Alaska."

"Come on!" Collins chided. "That has to be bullshit! Nothing and no one has that kind of raw power—not even a mid-level ethereal being."

McMahon shrugged. "I'm just relaying the information as it was told to me. Let me add that Nicadaemus was very put out at the thought of Agent Knight becoming involved in ethereal affairs. The demon believed Knight could have a direct impact on the final outcome of whatever schemes are being played." The senator leaned back, "If I may be so bold to offer a hypothesis."

Collins refilled the senator's empty glass. "Please."

McMahon nodded. "Someone on our side broke protocol by establishing this splinter world government. We've been playing our part assuming that we're following the orders from our genuine superiors. But what if we're not? What if we're the puppets being strung along by a shadow puppet master? How long will it be before the real forces of power that control the universe step in and take matters into their own hands? If someone is pulling the pointed tail of our side, how long until he decides to take matters into his own hand and by doing so will that unleash the big guns or Big Gun on the other side?"

"You're talking a full-fledged Armageddon class event, Paul. You think some grade B player is looking to make an upward move by unleashing Earth's Armageddon early?"

McMahon shook his head. "I dunno. We're human. We can't contemplate what goes through the minds of an ethereal. Their ambitions and motives are unknown to us. Like you said, the stakes the higher powers play for are cosmic in scale. We're like some warring factions of micro bacteria to them. We only have a small glimpse into that realm. Somebody ... something is looking to trigger the ultimate war here on this planet. I suggest we get all the information we can about the little piece of holy real estate we're hiding in the Vault. We may be sitting on something more volatile than a nuclear bomb."

Collins handed his associate a Scotch. McMahon nodded and took a deep swig, savoring the burning sensation as the amber liquid singed his palette. "If we got hoodwinked into taking that trinket without the approval of our superiors, we're gonna need one million block sunscreen. Problem is I can't break ranks and ask higher up. We get our orders and its only one way communication. We're going to have to hope and pray that somebody in our power structure knows what's going on and is taking steps to solve the problem."

"Or accept the fact that our side just instigated the end of the world as we know it." McMahon shook his head. "I don't think praying will do us all that much good considering our allies but I'm certainly not beyond a few dark rituals to see who on our side of the playing field is paying attention to the events unfolding on this planet."

Collins laughed despite the situation's severity. "Duly noted. I'll poke around the beltway and see if anyone's trying to advance beyond their means. If it's a local occurrence, Nicadaemus will most likely be the ethereal handing out the punishment. If it's something larger, we're going to have some pretty heavy hitters paying us a call. The higher powers on both sides have to decide if this theft is worth turning a two thousand-year-old skirmish into an all out war."

McMahon frowned. "Nick was ready to take my head off! He was extremely agitated that we liberated that trinket. I smell a rat somewhere, Mr. Speaker, we better hope this mess cleans itself up."

Collins nodded. "An ethereal will have to come claim the prize. It's one thing to give an order through the unseen channels of communication, but if this relic is as valuable and crucial as we believe, the being that wants it will most likely come to claim it personally. That's when we'll know who's pulling the strings. The next time I'm contacted I'll pass the word along. For now let's keep it buried in the Vault and hope it's as well concealed as we believe."

Chapter 3. Holy Secrets

Vatican City, Rome

"**M**artin, let's put this off until later in the afternoon. We just landed…" Erik did the mental math. "It's eight in the morning here, really two in the morning for you and me." He placed a hand on his friend's shoulder. "You look exhausted, Counselor. You could use the sleep and I could use the time to meditate and clear my head. Going into this fuzzy won't do either of us any good."

"Mr. Denton, Mr. Knight?" A voice inquired behind them.

Erik spun. "Who's asking?" His voice was more forceful than he'd intended and the small man flinched.

"I'm Brother Anderson. I was told to take you directly to the Vatican suite so you could both rest and freshen up."

Martin jumped in, "Please forgive my cranky young friend. We're both a bit on edge after being cooped up in a flying aluminum tube for eight hours."

The skittish man smiled and nodded pointing toward the large glass doors leading out of Leonardo Da Vinci Airport. "I have a car waiting to take you to Vatican City."

"Excellent." Denton reached for his suitcase.

Erik grabbed his hand. "I've got it, Martin." He hefted the suitcase easily in his left arm while he slung his duffel bag over his right shoulder.

* * *

Martin was in a deep sleep as Erik stared out from the balcony overlooking the holy city. The spectacle was awe inspiring. Erik had a deep appreciation for the architecture and elegant design of the buildings. The reinstated CIA cooler stretched his legs and threw several combinations of punches in an attempt

53

to unwind. Erik launched a high side thrust kick followed up by a spinning back kick, imagining an opponent in front of him. The agent paused and performed a perfect side split. He held the position and executed several arm blocks and strikes. In an amazing display of muscle control he tipped forward, lifted his prone legs and body off the ground and executed a perfect handstand. He froze in mid air for several seconds then executed twenty inverted shoulder presses while maintaining a perfect line with his legs and torso.

Erik contracted and then flexed his powerful arms; iron hard triceps exploded propelling him up several feet. He executed a perfect back somersault with a twist landing in a fighting stance, his arms up in a defensive guard.

A faint tingling sensation traveled through the back of his head and down his spine. Someone was watching him. "Thank you Esper sixth sense." Erik did some stretching, moving his torso and head in several directions as his telescopic vision searched for the unwelcome spy. There! In the building directly opposite on the roof, a man with a spotting scope carefully watched him. Erik continued to make a show of stretching and loosening as he studied his observer. *It's the same weasel that picked us up at the airport. I knew there was something about that guy. He's no meek 'Brother'. He's a Vatican spy.*

"I'll bet our whole suite is wired too. I'll deal with that and the nosey little man later on." He entered the spacious living room, still brooding in dark thought. The detective drew the long curtains and closed each set of window blinds. He lay down on the long couch and forced his body to sleep for a few hours knowing the next few days would be more than challenging. *Focus on the case and on Martin. Don't let my internal issues cloud my judgment. Remember, I'm here for Martin.*

* * *

"Erik, we have company."

The detective opened his eyes. Much to his surprise he'd fallen into a deep, restful sleep. He blinked a few times, shook off the cobwebs, and glanced at his watch. Four hours had passed. Erik got up as the knocking on the door continued.

"Shall I invite our guests in?" Denton's hand hovered over the locked doorknob.

"Sure."

Denton peered through the peephole. "They look like police." Martin opened the door and two police officers introduced themselves. Each officer was a stark contrast to the other. One was a large, corpulent man of Greek ancestry while his thinner partner seemed to be of Scandinavian decent.

"Good afternoon, gentlemen." The large Greek began in a jubilant tone. "I'm sorry to disturb you so soon after your arrival but Bishop O'Malley is eager to make your acquaintance." The officer pointed toward his partner. "We've been assigned the duty of being your official escorts during your stay in the Holy City."

Martin smiled while Erik looked the men over suspiciously. The detective knew the Vatican had assigned them babysitters.

"I'm Martin Denton, CIA bureau chief and my stone-faced companion is Special Agent Erik Knight."

Erik nodded to the men. "Give us a few minutes to freshen up and we'll be on our way." He gestured toward Martin, and both men walked into the bedroom area of their suite. Erik closed the door and led Martin into the marble-laden bathroom. The detective turned on both faucets and the shower. Within seconds the mirror steamed over. Erik took his index finger and wrote on the film of moisture.

WE'RE BUGGED. EYES ON US. BUILDING ACROSS STREET!

The detective took a moment to wash his face and body while Martin did a quick check of the bathroom. The elder operative pointed toward a light fixture in the corner. A small black circle was visible inside the light cover. Erik nodded as he ran a brush through his hair and while gargling with mouthwash. Martin wrote on the large mirror.

WHY?

Erik shrugged his shoulders and took his towel, carefully wiping away the words they'd written on the mirror. Denton shook his head genuinely puzzled. Erik put on a fresh jersey and they headed back toward the living room area and their two escorts.

"Are you refreshed?" The slender officer asked.

"Much better, thank you," Erik buckled the belt that housed his Sentient Staff feeling somewhat better having his weapon on standby. The fact that he felt better armed disturbed him. Something was wrong; the detective felt it in his gut. He knew Martin felt it as well. His friend was doing his best to appear calm but Erik could sense his unease. The elder operative didn't need any more mystery or stress. He was here to investigate his son's murder. The bureaucracy should be rolling out the red carpet for him and bending over backward offering apologies and condolences instead of two uniformed babysitters.

"Let's not keep our hosts waiting any longer. We're here for a purpose. The sooner we get to it, the sooner we can get out of here." Erik headed toward the door, not bothering to wait for the other men. The two officers moved quickly to catch up.

* * *

Erik and Martin were escorted to a large opulent office in St. Martha's Chapel. The Greek officer, to his credit, was acting more like a tour guide than a babysitter. The officer clearly knew all the history and interesting factoids surrounding the holy city and Erik found the man's excitement contagious.

Several men joined Erik, Martin and the two police officers. Martin and Erik stood and exchanged greetings with the eight men. The leader of the eight, Bishop O'Malley, motioned everyone to a formal sitting area and began speaking as soon as everyone was settled.

"Mr. Denton, may I offer my sincerest apologies and deepest regrets for your horrible loss. The Holy Father's deepest sympathies and prayers are with you and your family."

Denton nodded, struggling to keep his composure. "Thank you, Bishop O'Malley. I'll relay your kind words to my family upon our return home. I didn't get all the details regarding the attack. Can you fill in the gaps before Agent Knight and I examine the crime scene?"

O'Malley shifted his position. His eyes darted toward his peers as if seeking approval or confirmation to tell his story. At some unseen gesture he answered. "We really don't know all that much, Mr. Denton. The Holy Father instructed his guards to check the lower chapel. They immediately returned and reported what they found and we called our law enforcement agencies and investigators. A forensic team analyzed the bodies and moved them to our mortuary. We did later learn that one of the brothers managed to escape through a little known passageway that leads to an old air shaft that was used to channel fresh air into the basement chambers before the dehumidifiers and fan systems were installed. Brother Finn is in our hospital receiving the best of care from our finest physicians."

"You said guards were told to investigate the chapel. I assume an alarm was triggered notifying the Pope of the theft."

O'Malley looked away momentarily. "Not exactly, but the Holy Father knew almost immediately and acted quickly."

Erik shook his head. "Video surveillance then. We'll need to see the tapes."

"There is no video, Agent Knight."

Erik frowned. "Okay, help me out, then. If there is no electronic surveillance and no alarm system of any kind, how was the theft discovered? Did somebody just happen to go down to the chapel and find this massacre?"

"As I said, Agent Knight, the Holy Father knew the relic was stolen. He sent his guards to investigate and that's when the bodies were discovered."

Erik knew they weren't getting the entire story. They were being fed bits and pieces of what really happened. O'Malley's deliberate obtuse responses to his questions were frustrating and the detective did his best to maintain his composure. "We're going to need to question the survivor after we've studied the crime scene."

"Brother Finn has been through an ordeal, Mr. Knight. I don't know if he'll be up for answering any questions."

The detective leaned forward. "Was he injured?"

Bishop O'Malley shook his head no.

"Is he in some sort of catatonic shock?"

Again the bishop shook his head.

"I'm not going to interrogate the poor man. I just want to know what he saw, and hear what happened through his own words. We can learn a great deal from a direct eye witness account rather than second hand recall." The detective countered with a cool, level tone. It was becoming obvious to both Erik and Martin the Papacy didn't want the men to do a full investigation. This was just a courtesy trip to soothe diplomatic lines and claim they had cooperated with US authorities.

"We're not looking to pry, Your Excellency, but if that survivor can help shed light on the identity of my son's murderer I'd sincerely be in your debt if we could talk to him. If you're afraid we're going to push him into revealing something you feel we shouldn't know, then have one of your people accompany us." Denton leaned forward. "My government and the representatives from Vatican City agreed that we were to have unfettered access to any and all information pertaining to these murders." Something happened to Denton's tone, there was an icy chill Erik never heard before. "I'm not as young as I once was, Your Excellencies, but I'll raise the gates of Hell if you even think about stonewalling me."

"I don't respond to idle threats, Mr. Denton! You cannot come here with your American swagger and bully an official of the holy city." One of the other bishops shouted clearly not used to anyone countering their will."

"You misunderstood me, sir," Denton snarled. "I made no threat. I simply stated my intentions, very clearly and concisely outlining my intended course of action should you and your peers attempt to block the investigation into my son's death. The next course of action is entirely up to you. You can cooperate as was the promise made to our government or Special Agent Knight and I can investigate on our own." Denton gestured toward the formidable cooler. "I don't think you really want Special Agent Knight turning the holy city upside down looking for clues.

O'Malley stared at both men. Denton's eyes were set like icy granite and Erik mimicked his gaze perfectly. Erik knew Denton was deliberately playing 'Bad Cop'. He had no intention or roughhousing over Vatican authority but the old man detected the barricades being erected before they even got started and decided the best way to move forward was the 'Wrecking Ball' approach. Erik had never seen Denton use it before and enjoyed seeing the normally stuffy and stalwart counselor throw down a verbal beating. O'Malley remained silent. They needed something else over the top. If an act of brute force and bravado was needed to snap the bishops out of their sense of secrecy he'd gladly provide the required shock and awe moment.

"Bishop O' Malley, how thick is the wood on this table top?"

O'Malley tilted his head puzzled at the 'Out of Left Field' question. "Its four inches thick made from common North American Rock Maple. It has no real significant dollar value. Why do you ask?"

The CIA cooler didn't answer, he simply raised his left fist and rained down a hammer blow that exploded like a thunderclap reverberating off the marble walls and high, domed ceilings. The large conference table crumbled under the sheer force of the blow. The eight bishops gasped as the thick wooden surface split in half and collapsed toward the center. Several books and papers slid into the long V-shaped canyon created by the two severed halves. Erik sat back in his seat, his eyes burning like two balls of lightning. The bishops looked over at the CIA agent with a mixture of awe and fear.

"What else is going on Your Excellencies? What are you trying so hard to hide? Don't make me break something else that may be of more significant value."

Martin took his cue and stepped in. "That won't be necessary, Special Agent Knight, the bishops were about to escort us to the crime scene." Denton looked over at Bishop O'Malley, the man's eyes were wide and his mouth hung open. "Right, Your Excellency?"

O'Malley looked over at Denton and back at Erik. He sighed. "I'll be blunt with you, gentlemen. I disagreed with the Holy Father and the cardinals regarding outsiders investigating this delicate matter. But as you say, we have agreed, or rather the Holy See has agreed and I am forced to honor that agreement against my better judgment and prejudices." The bishop sighed as he gestured toward his colleagues. "Take them to the basement tabernacle."

Martin and Erik were escorted by two bishops and their

police escort to a small service elevator at the far end of St. Martha's. A bishop tapped in a key code on a glowing number pad and the heavy elevator doors opened. Erik studied the mechanism as they entered. The metallic chrome finish was bright and unmarred, each number on the keypad bold and vibrant, and the keypad lock was new. The detective also observed several creases and indentations on the outer doors.

"The doors were forced and the keypad lock is new. I'd say this is how our murderer gained access to the basement." Erik whispered to his friend.

Denton nodded and made an exaggerated gesture with his eyes toward the ceiling. A panel had been replaced and the inner wall console seemed new as well.

Erik nodded in appreciation. Martin had his eyes open too. Erik often forgot that the elder man was one of the best field investigators in the firm.

The elevator descended five levels into the earth. The doors opened exposing a dimly lit stone and earth corridor with heavy wood buttresses and supports. There was a damp chill that marked all subterranean environments. Erik's heightened senses triggered. Something horrible had happened here. His danger sense rang like a five-alarm fire. The Sentient Staff too sensed a disturbance and began to hum and moan an eerie harmonic which the detective knew was some sort of warning alarm.

I know, he projected to the weapon, *be ready*. The staff purred in his mind then fell silent.

"Are you okay, Erik?" Denton placed a hand on his shoulder.

Erik nodded. "I'm good, Counselor, just making a few mental notes."

The party slowly moved down the dimly lit corridor. The subterranean hallway reminded him of a mine tunnel hundreds of feet beneath the ground rather than a basement hallway leading toward a religious room of worship.

"Is this an ongoing construction project?"

"No, Mr. Knight, it was decided to leave the hallway unadorned and purely functional rather than ornate. We believed it would ward off anyone seeking treasure."

The second bishop shot his companion a seething glare. The detective gathered there was more to this than murder and this confirmed his suspicions. Erik noted that Denton also picked up on the young bishop's faux pas.

"How long is the tunnel?" Erik did his best to diffuse the sudden tension and hopefully convince both men that the slip had gone unnoticed.

The young bishop was mute, clearly intimidated into silence.

"The tunnel meanders on a good way, Agent Knight."

They moved on in silence for several more minutes. Erik calculated they'd already covered enough ground to be on the other side of the street and well into the office complex the next block over. Only his Esper sense of direction allowed him to detect the slight changes in their direction and the angular shifts in the overhead buttresses. The detective leaned in close to his colleague. Martin appeared to be winded.

"How are you holding up, Counselor?"

Denton perspired but shook his head. "I'm okay, thanks. We must be halfway to Sicily by now. How long is this damn tunnel?"

"We're moving in ever-increasing angles, Martin. About every hundred feet or so, we change direction. Each change has been no more than twenty degrees. The positions of the beans and braces are angled to give the impression of a straight line but every few meters one beam and support is true to the overhead support lattice. The near dark helps to maintain the illusion. This reminds me of a maze. I half expect a wall to slide closed or the floor to drop out from under us."

"Let's hope not." Denton stumbled, catching his footing. "They're obviously hiding something down here—something of immense importance to set up such a labyrinth."

Erik placed a hand on his friend's shoulder, steadying him. "Indeed. We'll sort through it, Martin. We're not leaving until we have the answers we came for. You have my word on that."

Denton's smile was visible even in the dark tunnel. "Thank you, Erik. I have truly missed you, my young friend."

"Likewise, Martin." Erik pointed ahead to a large, well lit steel door. "Looks like we've arrived."

The older bishop produced a key from a concealed pocket and opened the heavy door. The hinges squealed with protest as the half-ton steel panels slid on rusted hinges. The bishop gestured toward the massive chamber. "St. Martha's basement chapel, gentlemen. This is one of the most holy, consecrated areas within Vatican City. Please tread lightly and with reverence. God is watching all of us."

Erik nodded as he stepped inside. He remembered his days going to Sunday Mass. The CIA cooler knew that an act of respect and reverence at this point would go further in gaining the trust of the bishops than any bullying or intimidation. He placed a hand on a nearby pew, dropped to one knee, and genuflected toward the massive cross mounted on the far wall. Martin repeated the gesture and both men slowly entered the chapel.

Erik took a moment to study the cavernous chamber. It rivaled any cathedral he'd ever seen. The detective tried to imagine the feats of technical and engineering skill that went into creating such a structure five stories underground. The walls were sheathed in heavy white marble and adorned with intricate stained glass murals. The detective noticed the Stations of the Cross positioned around the walls.

Light appeared to be radiating from the colored glass, casting rainbow hues on the pews and basking the white marble sheathing in a cacophony of color.

"Backlighting," Denton muttered in awe.

Erik looked on the floor and spotted the first indication of why they'd been summoned. A three-foot circle of dried blood stained the marble floor tiles. Dried blood splatters radiated out from the large dark red stain. In one heartbeat, the sense of awe was put aside and the detective snapped himself back to business. He tapped Denton's shoulder and gestured toward the crime scene. Denton focused on the dried blood.

"Another one here, Martin." Erik pointed several feet further into structure. "The blood trickles away from this central mass and towards the altar." The detective gestured toward several heavy droplets blazing a trail of death.

As Erik studied the second, larger blood stain, a chill enveloped him, and he sensed something dark. The only other time he'd felt such a chill was when he first encountered the Seelak warrior in the remote Hopedale Mountain. The detective looked toward the tabernacle. The polished stone top had been overturned and several statues had been forcefully tipped from their heavy support bases.

"Those statues must weigh half a ton, easy. Who could have done that?" Denton knelt down, studying the second blood stain. When he looked up at his friend, a tear rolled down his cheek. "I wish I knew which one was William's. They all must have died horrible deaths to have bled out so much. What kind of man would do such a thing, Erik? What kind of ghoul would kill in a house of worship?"

Erik shook his head. "I don't know, Martin. This doesn't make sense. Nothing adds up here." Erik knelt by the nearest pew and observed deep, fresh scratches in the wood. The detective could still smell the scent of the exposed pine. Keen Esper vision spotted the long wood shavings scattered along the length of the marble aisle. "Look at this!" He pointed toward the pews. "Every pew going back to the doorway has a series of deep scratches along the sides, like someone deliberately gouged them as he made his way toward his victims."

"To instill fear, I'd wager." Denton slid a gloved finger over the indentations. "Four separate grooves; possibly some kind of metallic claw."

Erik knelt down and studied the gouges. He spotted something inside one of the grooves—a black fiber. "Martin, get me an evidence bag from the kit ... I've got a fiber." Erik studied more of the grooves. "Several fibers. Get me some tweezers too. We'll gather up as much as evidence as we can for the boys at the labs. I'm sure our friends here would like a few samples as well."

Martin came back with the case he'd set down as they admired the chamber. Erik carefully removed and packaged several fiber samples. "It's not much, but it's a start."

The detective stood and made his way back toward the altar. Something drew his attention to a fallen cross mounted on a long pole. He slipped his hands into some blue, latex gloves and gently picked up the sacred object. Even though the gloves he felt the violent psychic feedback. He shuddered involuntarily and the object fell from his grip, clanging on the stone floor. The sound echoed off every surface.

"Are you okay?"

Erik shook his head and exhaled. "Yeah, I just picked up an impression from this cross. I need to hold it again." Erik bent over and tensed as he prepared himself for the upcoming violent shock. He firmly grasped the cross and hefted it in both hands. His entire being was awash with terrible panic and fear. The terror from the man holding this cross had been so powerful, the impressions imprinted upon the object. But there was something else, a sense of purpose entwined with the panic. Erik did his best to focus on that sensation above the background hum of terror. Try as he might, he couldn't get a lock; only brief flashes. In order to read the object, he would have to partially open himself up to his Esper half; something he hadn't done since the battle of Groom Lake.

Erik looked over at Denton. The old man did his best to keep his composure, but he could sense the waves of despair and agony radiating off his friend. Erik should have forced Martin to wait upstairs. The old man was already suffering a tragic loss. Seeing blood stains and splatters, some no doubt belonging to his own son, was more than any father should have to endure.

"Martin, you don't need to do this. I can work this while you interview our witness."

Denton shook his head. "No, Erik. I want to be here. I need to do this for my own sake. I have to find out firsthand what happened to my boy."

Erik nodded. "Okay, Counselor. It's your call, but the crime scene has already been disturbed. The bodies are at the morgue and it looks like somebody's done some kind of cleanup here. Nice of them to leave the blood splatters for us to study."

Martin looked at his friend. "You have that look on your face. The one that says you're contemplating something. Dare I ask what?"

Erik motioned for Martin to join him. Both men sat in a pew, their backs facing the two bishops and the Vatican policemen. "There are powerful psychic disturbances in here." Erik pointed back toward the cross lying on the floor. "Do you remember the Lisa Reynolds case about six years back?"

Denton nodded. "That was the first Seelak abduction. She's the girl you found in that mine shaft Pendelcorp had dug looking for minerals. It was filed as a kidnapping case originally."

Erik nodded as he looked straight ahead. "I found her locket at the Hopedale Park. It fell off her neck during the abduction. Her fear was so great that her emotional state left an imprint on that object. I was able to channel that imprint and follow the impressions back into the Hopedale Parklands. Martin, I was able to experience what she went through during her abduction to some degree before my change. With my current power level I should be able to get an idea of exactly what went on here by taking hold of that cross again. But I don't know if I'll get lost in the metaphysical riptide generated by tragic events. I don't know if I'll get totally swallowed up by what I'll experience."

"I don't pretend to understand how you can do the things you do, Erik. But if there's a chance you can shed some light on what happened here..." Denton paused, looking directly into Erik's face.

"You're right. Just keep talking to me. Give me a sort of anchor line back with your voice in case I get pulled in too deep." Erik smirked. "Shanda is so much better at this than I am. But I wouldn't want her exposed to the shit that's infecting this place."

Erik walked over to the large cross and carried it back to the pew. He closed his eyes. Remembering the transient state he needed to acquire, he took a series of shallow cleansing breaths and focused all his will on his empathic power.

The light around him faded but he was still in the holy chamber. He looked over at the pew and Martin was gone. He heard the savage hiss and saw a man shrouded in black. The first wave of fear savaged his body.

"Oh God, get away. Get back!" the detective screamed, his eyes were wide with fright as he cried out in fear. Yet somehow he knew the voice wasn't his own.

The dark being fell upon the brother that had reached out to him. Fangs tore into its victim spraying warm blood upon the cold white marble floor. The slurping sound as it fed on the dying clergyman, nauseated him. "In the name of all that's holy get back!" Erik screamed again as the vision inside his head totally took control. Again the voice didn't seem to be his own, but he shared the fear. Wave upon wave of abject terror coursed through his body nearly paralyzing him into a catatonic state of shock.

"I'm here Erik!" Denton screamed at his friend. "Tell me what you see. What's happening damn it!" Martin shook his friend, but the detective's eyes were vacant and lost. The psychic link had swallowed the detective's conscious mind completely, absorbing it into the horror imprinted upon the object. "Erik! Can you hear me?"

The detective was near catatonic. Terror and remorse riddled his voice. "It killed him. It fed upon his blood like some thrice damned ghoul. It just killed another, Brother Tom, my dear friend Brother Tom is gone. It's ... it's holding his beating heart up like a trophy, laughing hysterically as the blood sprays out from torn arteries. Tom's chest is spilling blood everywhere. Oh God no, he's still clinging to life, staring at his own still beating heart. Run Brother Peter, I'll keep it at bay! Tell the cardinals what's happened!" Erik wept uncontrollably as wave after wave of shear agony and torment flooded his body from the object. "Oh my friends how could this happen in this, the holiest of places? God why hast thou forsaken me and my brothers? What sins have we committed to deserve such torment?"

Erik leapt up from the pew and in one superhuman vault landed twenty feet away in the middle of the marble floor. He held the large pole cross like an axe waiting for his imaginary foe to strike. "It's coming for me. I won't go down without a fight!"

The detective's eyes turned into fiery blue embers and he leapt up holding the cross like a weapon. "Back to the stinking pits of Hell with you!" Erik slammed the cross down with superhuman force shattering the marble tile and snapping the heavy pole like a toothpick. He adopted a fighter's stance preparing to fight some unseen opponent.

The monk next to Erik in the vision fell. The dark being in the hood stood over him and began butchering the still-struggling body. The hybrid felt rage boil inside him. The sense of fear faded, replaced by a disgust and hate. The cloaked being looked toward the altar, not seeing the detective, oblivious to his rage. "You wanna fight!" Erik screamed at the dark murderer, "You got it! Fight me you bastard, I'm no helpless monk!"

The enraged detective swung his weapon with lethal precision, his eyes burning slits of rage as he prepared to fight the opponent inside his mind. The sentient staff crackled with aqua-blue energy and an aura of unbridled power surrounded the enraged hybrid.

* * *

Martin heard a loud buzzing drone. Something flowed like liquid chrome from Erik's belt, forming a long slender cylinder that settled into his friend's outstretched hand. Denton felt his stomach churn. "Oh shit! Why did he bring his staff? He'll blast us all to kingdom come!"

A sense of dread overtook Martin. The tingle of fear raced through his spine, exploding in his skull. His friend began to change. His skin took on a silver quality and his powerful human physique grew, threatening to burst through his clothing. If the power of the silver warrior was unleashed here, the whole facility would collapse killing them all and entombing them forever beneath thousands of tons of rubble. The enraged hybrid would undoubtedly survive the cave-in and keep fighting and blasting away at his unseen foe, oblivious to anyone or anything in the real world. Desperation gave the old man courage. He had to reach his friend's mind, break the hold the vision had on him.

"Special Agent Knight!" Denton screamed at the top of his lungs. "Erik! Erik! It's over, what you're seeing is past. You're seeing something that's already occurred! There isn't a threat here! You fire that weapon you'll kill all of us!" Denton wasn't getting through. "Erik, you're in some kind of goddamned nightmare! Snap out of it lad!"

Erik leveled the staff at his unseen foe. Lightning danced around the weapon's tip and, even several feet away, Denton could feel the radiant heat and static buildup. The weapon's eerie luminescence illuminated the entire chamber. The staff was about to fire a blast of indescribable power. The discharge would blow a gaping hole through the walls, obliterate several support columns, and bury them all. Denton closed his eyes awaiting oblivion.

"I am the Warrior!" The detective's battle cry echoed off every surface and reverberated for several seconds followed by dead silence.

Martin counted to three and looked up. "We're still here." The air was filled with the smell of ozone and he heard the crackle of untamed electricity. His friend was on his knees, clinging to his staff, weeping. The staff purred an almost comforting harmonic.

Martin made his way over to his friend as their four escorts approached the fallen detective.

"Erik?" Martin whispered. "Erik, it's me, Martin. Are you okay?"

Erik didn't move. His head was bent over, his body shivering.

* * *

Erik looked up at his friend, tear-stained eyes radiated agony and haunting pain. "Oh God, Martin, I'm so sorry. Your son ... he bought time for one of them to escape with his life. I saw what happened up to the point your son was killed." Erik looked down, he knelt in a dried pool of blood, the blood of Brother William Denton.

The shaken detective pointed. "He used that pole cross like a sledge hammer and cracked its skull. But the thing survived the blow. It got back up and..." Erik stopped himself short; Martin didn't need to hear this. The battered detective stood, using his staff like a cane. The weapon instantly adapted itself, forming a silver walking stick. The detective ignored the gasps from the Vatican police and bishops. "I want to see the edge of that cross."

Erik bent over and studied the cross. It was embedded in the subflooring. With a burst of superhuman strength, he hefted the holy symbol from the protesting timbers. Half of the cross was covered with a black ichor.

"Blood... it's some kind of dried blood." Erik studied the substance. "But it looks like it's been burnt or scorched." He looked over at Martin and the others. The police were studying him with concern and something akin to fear and awe. Martin sat alone in a nearby pew, his head in his hands. The realization finally hit the detective. He had relived his friend's sons last moments and relayed them to the grieving father like some horrible nightmare. Erik didn't know what he had said while in his catatonic trance, but he suspected he'd given his old friend a gory peek at his son's final moments.

"Oh shit! This is turning into one big cluster fuck." Erik looked back at the large suspended image of Jesus and rolled his eyes. "Hey ... a lot worse has been said and done here in the last week, so cut me some slack." He walked over and placed a hand on the counselor's shoulder. "I am so sorry Martin. I swear to you I had no idea it would play out like that."

Denton looked up through tear-stained eyes. "It's not your fault, Erik. I pushed you. I wanted to know, and now I do. He died a horrible death by some godforsaken psychopathic ghoul with a fetish for gothic flare."

"Why don't you head back to the hotel and let me wrap this up? You've had a hell of a morning so far, Counselor." Erik shrugged. "Actually, we both have."

Denton looked up at his friend and stood up slowly. "I'll be fine, Erik. Just answer me one question, please."

"Anything."

"Was his death quick? Did he suffer?"

"No Martin, from the impressions I got, he didn't suffer."

The old man sighed. "Thank God for that."

Erik gently patted his friend's shoulder and picked up the lab case. It was a blatant lie. But Erik could live with it. If he could spare his friend more suffering, he'd lie, even in this place. "I'm going to pull a few samples off that metal cross and then we'll take a look at the overturned altar and see what our homicidal friend was up to here. It might tell us what secrets our friends in Vatican City are hiding in this basement."

Denton pointed to a particular blood trail that was partially intermixed with his son's blood. "Let's get blood samples from all these spots too. Those splatters look markedly different than the others. Hopefully the lab can give us an idea of what kind of blood dries nearly onyx black."

Erik nodded. "Can you take care of that while I head over to the altar? If we divide and conquer, we can get out of here that much sooner. We still need to question the survivor. I can only imagine the tale he's going to have for us."

Denton nodded in agreement. "Erik, one more question."

"Fire away, Counselor."

"I don't know exactly what you saw in your head, or what you were fighting, but you were in the process of changing into your warrior self. You were one heartbeat away from using that silver lighting stick and blasting this whole place to kingdom come."

Erik looked down at his staff and then back over at his friend. "I'm sorry, Martin. I could have killed all of you. Trying to read that object was a stupid call on my part. I wasn't prepared for such a powerful onslaught. The sensations were more intense than anything I've ever experienced." Erik looked over at the shattered pole and now-damaged holy icon that lay on the fractured marble floor tiles. "I made a bad call, Martin. I underestimated the impressions imprinted on that thing and let myself get sucked into that negative wormhole. It won't happen again." The detective rubbed his hand through his hair. "Maybe getting back in the saddle wasn't such a good idea."

"No, Erik, this mess is my fault. I pushed you. I should have chosen the more prudent course. I let my self-interest cloud my judgment. That won't happen again, either. I need you here, Special Agent Knight. Your talents and abilities are wasted behind a desk at that health club. We learned a great deal from this little episode." Martin looked up at his friend. "We both just need to get the rust off our asses. We've been benched for too long. We'll get back in our groove. I know we will, but what I want to know is this. Did you hear me yelling at you? I tried to get through to you, but I couldn't. You were about to unload a king-size can of whoop-ass but you stopped. What finally allowed you to regain control?"

Erik looked at his friend as he considered the question. "I honestly don't know, Martin. I was about to give that thing a million-volt kiss of death but something inside me knew it was a phantom. Before I could let loose, I finally realized it wasn't real. The next thing I knew, I was on the floor." The detective placed a friendly hand on Denton's shoulder, "Maybe I heard you after all. Let's not jinx our good fortune by over-analyzing it."

Martin nodded. "Agreed. Let's get back at it, Special Agent Knight. We still have a great deal of work to do."

Erik half smiled and nodded. Martin's back-to-business tone still had his friendly undertone. "Yes sir." Erik nodded and approached the altar. The Greek police officer nervously shadowed the detective as did one of the bishops. Both men kept a safe distance but watched the detective's movements with great intensity as he investigated the overturned granite top.

"What were you looking for over here that caused you to topple the entire table?" Erik asked aloud. He spotted three exposed wires and knelt down to examine the exposed copper. "Black is negative, red is power and green is ground if I remember correctly—and if the Vatican follows the same wiring standard as the United States." He spotted an exposed sheet metal screw that was bent and half jarred from its housing. "I'm guessing the ground wire went here." Erik grabbed the wire and guided it toward the screw and housing … the wire length indicated his assumption was correct. The detective reattached the wire and took a dime from his pocket to serve as a makeshift screwdriver, securing the ground wire back in its place. He focused his attention on the other two wires. "And you two were connected to something…" he looked at the overturned granite slab. "On that, I'll bet." He walked back over to the large slab of polished stone and discovered a shattered mechanism on the table's exposed underside. "Bingo!"

"What are you doing, Agent Knight?" A bishop approached nervously.

"I'm investigating the murders, Your Excellency. What do you think I'm doing? That table has an electronic mechanism. I'm guessing there was something more going on here than murder. I don't recall electronic devices being standard fare on altar tables."

Erik studied the ruined plastic and metal box. "It's some

kind of button relay." The detective walked back to the altar, jumping up the four steps. "I wonder...." He held his hand over the red wire and could feel the pulse of electricity with his enhanced senses. "What will happen if I close the circuit?"

Erik held the two wires by the insulation and touched the exposed ends together. A loud clang occurred inside the wall directly behind the altar. Large chains that supported the massive suspended crucifix began to rise, lifting the tilted fifteen-foot cross from its previous resting position. A stone panel slid open exposing a heavy metal safe. The door to the safe was open and swung freely.

"Well now!" Erik looked over at the bishop. The man's jaw fell open. The police officer looked at Erik, then back toward the bishop. "Senior Field Agent Denton!" Erik shouted in a formal manner. "I've got something here."

The detective turned toward the bishop. "I assume you knew this was here."

"No, Mr. Knight, I was not aware of any such thing. I assure you."

Erik studied the man. His eyes were direct and there was no increase in his pulse. He was telling the truth. Why weren't they told about this? Surely Bishop O'Malley knew something was hidden here. Erik shook his head. This was the piece of the puzzle they needed to investigate.

"What's this?" Denton pointed toward the exposed panel.

"Just another mystery on top of the one we're trying to unravel." Erik pointed toward the opening. "Let's take a look."

The six men approached the open safe. The latch on the door was warped and twisted. The locking bar had snapped under some terrific pressure. Erik felt some sort of residual power emanating from the metal box—a power directly opposing the dread he'd felt coming off the bloodied cross. He gasped as his body absorbed the radiant energy.

"Erik, what is it?"

"Whatever was hidden in there was a source of great power, Martin. Nothing like I picked up from the cross—this is completely different. It's benign, almost passive but far more powerful. Something very special was kept in here, Counselor. Our friends upstairs have some more explaining to do. We definitely aren't getting the whole picture."

The detective wrinkled his nose and sniffed the air like a blood hound, his eyes narrowed.

"What is it, Erik?"

"You don't smell it?"

Denton frowned. "I don't have your bloodhound senses."

"It's a smell I haven't experienced since my Special Forces days in Colombia. We got ambushed by several drug cartel 'Mercs' with flamethrowers. Before we could neutralize the threat, three of our men were barbecued alive. I'll never forget the smell of charred flesh! I just got a hint of that scent." Erik looked at his friend. "There's something more happening here. We have a cross with burnt blood, the smell of burnt flesh, and now a hidden safe that appears to have been robbed. I'm getting a picture here and I do *not* like it one damn bit. Our holy rollers upstairs are playing us like chumps and I'd like to know why."

Denton nodded his head in frustration. "Okay, we'll grill our friends upstairs later. Right now let's check this out."

"This safe door was forced." The Greek officer noted. "But it would take some kind of mechanical or hydraulic apparatus to perform such a feat, or perhaps heavy explosives."

Erik shook his head. "I'd rule out explosives. There's no collateral blast force damage. Any kind of apparatus with enough power to pry this open would be too big for one man to bring down here, let alone remove single handedly. Plus, look at the handle—see how it's torqued and bent? Someone exerted an extreme amount of pressure to open this safe and I don't think any artificial mechanism was involved." Erik put on a fresh set of gloves as he continued to study the safe. "Look, here, Martin. There aren't any pry marks or any surface scratches on the metal."

Erik peered inside the ruined safe. "Holy shit!" He blushed. "Excuse me, Your Excellencies. This safe is lined with solid gold," Erik ran his gloved finger over a ridge on the safe's bottom. "There's at least an inch of gold lining the inside of this safe and on the door itself." The detective's brow wrinkled.

"What is it, Agent Knight?"

Erik looked at the Greek. "I'm sorry, sir. I never got your

name." Erik cursed himself, he knew how important relations were with the police and he'd always made a point of being cordial to law enforcement.

The Greek laughed. "Totally forgivable, Agent Knight. Your hosts have kept you busy. I'm Nicholas Tekaropolis. Please call me 'Neko'."

The detective took off his right latex glove and extended his hand to the officer. "A pleasure to meet you, Neko." The two men exchanged a firm handshake. The detective looked toward the other police officer and extended his hand.

"I'm Michael Severin, Agent Knight."

"Pleasure to meet you, Michael." Erik pointed toward the safe. "Have either of you ever heard of lining a safe with gold?"

"Only if it's the gold one is trying to protect and shelter, Agent Knight." Neko's reply lacked conviction, as if he wasn't certain of his assumption.

"I'm going to assume that this isn't some sort of 'Vatican practice' and the gold lining is for a purpose."

Michael Severin scratched his head, puzzled. "I have never heard of such a Vatican custom, Special Agent Knight." He looked over at the bishops. "Perhaps they would be the ones to shed light on your inquiry?"

"Please, Erik. My friends just call me Erik." Erik felt a familiar tingle, the once-lost sensation of working a case permeated through him. It was coming back slowly, the interaction and the deduction that seemed so elusive and awkward earlier was becoming second nature again.

"Gold is very dense, even more so than lead," Martin chimed in. "Maybe this gold lining was used to keep whatever was inside hidden away from detection, like a shielding of some type."

Erik snapped his fingers looking at his friend. "Like lead's used as shielding in a nuclear reactor or a protective bib during an x-ray. This gold lining could have been used to keep something shielded." Erik pointed toward Martin. "Brilliant deduction 'Holmes'." The two officers understood the compliment and chuckled.

"Why would the Vatican see fit to store a radioactive item here within consecrated grounds?" Neko glared at the two bishops. Both shrugged their shoulders.

"Good lord, you don't think there's radiation contamination in here do you?" Michael took two nervous steps back from the open safe.

Erik chuckled and shook his head. "If there were, Officer Severin, we'd all need decontamination protocols at this point. The detective's hybrid senses scanned the surrounding air for any radiant particles. "I assure you whatever was in that safe wasn't radioactive, but it did possess some kind of energy, that much I'm sure."

The officer crossed himself several times. "Thank you, Lord Jesus!"

Erik rubbed a hand across his unshaven cheek. "Martin, did you get the samples we need for testing?"

Denton nodded holding up a case. "I've got everything we need. Should we dust the safe for prints?"

Erik studied the safe. "We may as well, but even if our thief left fingerprints, I doubt they'll do us any good. He's either smart enough to do this job without leaving such an obvious trace, or he knows fingerprints won't help us."

Erik dusted the safe, mumbling as he searched for any evidence. "What kind of man can overturn a granite slab and pry open a heavy safe with no pry bar and no heavy equipment?"

"Uhm Erik." Denton hedged. "The only man I know capable of doing these things is investigating the crime scene."

Erik continued his examination but his hand flinched slightly. "I have an alibi, Counselor. I was back in the States."

Denton laughed, "I know that. I'm just implying that the feats performed here indicate the possibility of another hybrid on the loose. Maybe it's a Seelak/Human as opposed to your Esper warrior/Human DNA. That would explain the murderous tendency, the bloodlust, and even the enhanced strength."

Erik stopped what he was doing and looked over at his friend. "The feeling was different, Martin. The Seelak was dark but driven by hatred for a war fought and wrongs done ten thousand years ago. Its need to hunt was based on its genetic design and the need to feed off emotion." Erik shook his head. "What I sensed through that object was something different, darker on a scale I've never encountered. If this was a Seelak or a Seelak hybrid, I'd know. My Esper DNA is wired to pick up and respond to such a threat. I'm positive we're not dealing with a Seelak. Truth be told, I don't know what we're dealing with. If I believed in fairy tales I'd offer a hypothesis based on the available data, but I'm not ready to go down the road of make-believe just yet."

Denton pointed toward the safe. "Anything?"

Erik shook his head, pointing toward two evidence bags. "No prints but some more of those black fibers. To be honest, the imprint coming off this safe is so powerful it's interfering with my ability to focus. I've had to erect a mental shield just to concentrate on what I'm doing."

"Bad?" Denton stared at the seemingly innocuous safe.

"No, Martin, just the opposite in fact. I find myself half on the verge of falling to my knees and just surrendering to the tranquility and peace."

Denton sighed. "I'm jealous. I could use a little tranquility and peace right about now."

"Seriously?" Erik looked toward his friend and focused his telepathic power. He detected the pain and sorrow over Denton's lost son but also the guilt and regret over lost ties and contact. Erik closed his eyes and lowered his mental shield. He allowed himself to be engulfed in the palpable waves of peace and holiness emanating from inside the safe. He harnessed those impressions and gathered them like a man harvesting a crop. With a deliberate slow gesture, he redirected those impressions toward his friend.

Denton gasped as the first waves engulfed his body. "Oh my word! What's happening?" He fell to his knees weeping openly as the psychic bombardment saturated his mortal essence.

Erik felt the impressions consume him, drawing him into the unbridled ecstasy and tranquility. With great effort he restored his mental barrier and ceased the transfer to his friend. Erik walked over to Martin and offered his hand. He lifted his friend up and held him until the older man was able to stand on his own power.

"Erik," Denton muttered in awe, "that was beyond anything I've ever experienced. Good lord, man! How do you not allow yourself to get enraptured by that feeling?"

The detective's brow furrowed. "I don't know, Martin. It's appealing to lose one's self in the euphoria, but I'd be just as lost in bliss as I was when I got swallowed up by the dark imprint from that cross earlier." Erik placed a hand on his friend's shoulder. "I hope that eased your burden a little, Martin. I understand now what you're carrying and again, I'm so sorry."

Denton nodded. "That was just the jolt I needed. I'm an atheist, Erik, but I may have to rethink that based on the events of today. Anyway, when William told me he was becoming a cleric, I admit that I didn't take the news well. He had a job lined up with the firm as an agent and showed real promise. I hated the church for taking my son from me. I didn't think about his happiness or that he'd found his true calling. I wanted him with me following in my footsteps and maybe giving me grandchildren and some direct family. Since his murder, I've been feeling crushed by the guilt of my bigotry and selfishness." The old man turned toward his friend. "I didn't feel that when he was alive. All I felt was a sense of righteous indignation." Denton sighed but there seemed to be a great weight lifted from him. "He was happy and found a home, a place where he belonged and felt at peace. I really was proud of him and maybe even a little envious. I wish I would have told him so." Denton sighed again. "What kind of father abandons his son like that?"

"I'm sure he knew, Martin. The fact that you're here now, doing what you're doing, speaks volumes of the love you had for him. If Heaven is real, then your son is looking down at his father, and he knows, Martin." A tear ran down Erik's cheek. He didn't bother to wipe it away. "He knows his father came for him and he knows the pain you feel and he forgives freely." The detective turned away. "I'm sorry, Counselor, the emotions from that box and from what I read from you are wreaking havoc on me."

"You don't have to apologize, Erik. You've given me a great gift."

"I often wonder, Martin," the detective's voice softened, "if my own father is looking down at me sometimes and proud of the man I am despite my failures and shortcomings." Erik's eyes were vulnerable and his face betrayed a desperate longing.

"Erik, if there is a Heaven, your father is there. I know he's proud of you and probably bragging to anyone who'll listen about how special his son is and what an amazing man of character and principle he's become."

A second tear rolled down the detective's cheek and he shuddered in spite of himself. He took a deep breath, then exhaled, gathering his composure. "Thanks Martin, I needed to hear that."

"Erik, when I first met you, I instantly took a liking to you because you reminded me so much of William. You were a brazen young rooster determined to do things your own way on your own terms. Then when you changed and you acquired all these incredible gifts, I often wondered how you'd change. I wondered if you'd become arrogant and cocky like most men who acquire power." Denton smiled and shook his head. "You didn't. If anything you became more humble, more insecure about yourself and your humanity. You were always careful to not use your talents except when coming to the aid of somebody in need. That takes a special kind of man, Erik—someone like my son, William, who only wanted to help and serve others in his own way. I see a lot of you in him and I'm proud of the man you are as I'm sure your father would be. I know William would have liked you a great deal and you would have found him to be a kindred spirit."

Erik struggled to contain his emotions. "Martin, when I held that cross, I felt William's essence. I felt his courage, his decency and sense of justice. He willingly sacrificed himself to defend his brothers. Your son had your values, your sense of decency, Counselor. You did well with him, and he apparently learned a great deal because he carried those values with him across the ocean and lived them." Erik pointed toward his friend. "Your values, Martin. He had your values and your sense of justice. He was your son and I know he loved you and respected you." Erik's voice dropped. "I'll share something with you. I've always admired those traits and struggled to emulate them. I hope, and sometimes even pray, that my father was a man like you. I don't know much about my family, but since I've known you, I've always imagined my dad being a lot like you. I'd like to believe he'd have taken the time with me like you have over in the past to tell me when you think I'm on the wrong track and point me in the right direction even when I was hell-bent on my own course. I've missed that these last two years, the friendship and the guidance. You're a wise man, Martin, a good friend and a good father. Believe me when I tell you your son knew how you felt and knows now. As far as family goes, Counselor, we're not much, but Shanda, EJ and I always have a place for you in our home."

Denton nodded wiping a stray tear. The old man suddenly broke out in a fit of laughter.

"I think I missed the joke."

Denton looked at his friend and smiled. "I'm laughing at the irony, Erik. A devout atheist and a human/alien hybrid share a 'bonding moment' in a church while investigating a multiple homicide involving the atheist's son, a religious cleric preparing for the priesthood. Plus, no investigation would be complete without seemingly inhuman and, as of yet, unexplainable components." The counselor shook his head while blowing his nose in a handkerchief. "It doesn't get much more screwed up than that."

Erik was silent for a moment. He chuckled followed by a deep belly laugh, "Amen, Martin. When we bend the curve of normalcy, we make it a pretzel for sure!"

They laughed for several seconds drawing confused glances from their hosts. The two police had fallen back and were speaking with the bishops at the opposite end of the large chamber. The men looked over at their guests clearly confused by their sudden levity.

Denton shook his head. "Do we about have this wrapped up?"

"Just about. I'm gonna do God a small favor though." Erik's eyes burned with aqua blue fire. He approached the massive stone tabletop. The hybrid's arm and back muscles rippled as powerful hands grasped the massive bulk. The detective roared as he hefted the six-inch thick granite slab over his head. Erik's shirt seams split as powerful muscles flexed and tensed under the massive stone altar top. He carried the heavy burden over to the altar base and gently laid the three ton top back on its massive base. There was barely any impact noise as the heavy top gently settled against the four marble support pillars. The powerful hybrid delicately lifted the heavy marble statues and placed them back on their bases. One of the statues had been damaged and the detective carefully laid the broken piece next to the large base pedestal.

Erik spotted the crushed gold chalice—a cup he knew held the representation of Christ's blood. He picked up the crumpled goblet and held it in his hands. The hybrid focused his will channeling high energy plasma through his cells and into the golden chalice. His hands radiated blue power as searing waves of heat and energy dispersed throughout the chamber. Fiery blue fingers reshaped the damaged holy object. After several seconds the glow faded. Erik studied the golden cup, reformed and nearly flawless. He placed the cup on the altar and covered it with a white linen. He gazed up at the representation of Christ on the cross. He nodded and pointed to the repaired altar and the statues. "It's not perfect, but I hope you'll accept the gesture in the good faith I intended. Some nasty stuff went down here and if you're watching, we all could use a little divine blessing to get through this." The detective reverently knelt toward the cross then walked back toward his friend.

"That was amazing, Erik." Denton pointed toward the two police officers and the bishops. "I think our friends are in shock though."

Erik smirked. "They'll get over it. Hopefully this gesture will buy us some goodwill 'upstairs' and on this plain. We need answers, Martin, and we don't have time to be stonewalled by the bureaucracy here. Plus, I don't like the idea of any place of worship being trashed and robbed. The savage butchery that happened here makes me sick. It's just plain wrong on too many levels."

Denton raised an eyebrow as Erik walked past. The senior operative gathered their evidence case and followed. Erik turned back and winked. "Let's go talk to our witness, Counselor, shake some trees and see what kind of bad apples we can make fall. There's an unspoken truth here and it's time somebody started talking."

* * *

Our Lady of Perpetual Hope Hospital, Room 345

Erik, Martin, and their police escort walked down the hospital corridor. The two visibly shaken bishops retuned to report to Bishop O'Malley. Erik wondered how the staunch Vatican elder would react to their undoubtedly wild report. The detective spotted two men in simple black clothing guarding a doorway.

"I'm going out on a limb and guessing our witness is in that room and those two men have orders not to admit anyone."

"I thought we covered that earlier today?" Denton deliberately slowed their pace. The seasoned agent craned his head back at the police. "Neko, will we have any problems gaining entry?"

The burly cop shook his head. "Let me see how the diplomatic winds are blowing before Erik is forced to toss them through a wall or out a window."

Erik snorted. "I'd rather nobody gets hurt today, Neko. If you can smooth things over that would be most welcome."

Neko made his way toward the two men and engaged them in conversation. The police officer gestured toward Martin, Erik, and Michael motioning them forward.

"A good sign." Denton nodded to Erik as they approached the doorway.

"Let's hope so. We've had nothing but roadblocks since we've arrived."

"Mr. Knight, Mr. Denton, I've been instructed to give you ten minutes with Brother Peter." The guard opened the door allowing them access. As Erik walked in, the man forcefully laid a hand on his shoulder. "No more than ten minutes, Mr. Knight."

The detective nodded as he removed the man's hand, applying pressure to his wrist and bending it in a jujitsu lock. The guard grunted in discomfort as Erik continued to apply pressure forcing the man's hand back down. "I got the message. Ten minutes, no more." The detective released the wrist lock and entered the room.

Neko shook his head smiling. "The Vatican Bureau are bullies, Mr. Knight. They enjoy throwing their considerable influence around the holy city."

Erik shrugged. "I gathered as much. But we're not in the holy city right now and I have zero tolerance for bullies no matter who they are or who they work for."

Erik focused his attention on the lean man sitting on a large chair wrapped in blankets. The man held a Bible and whispered prayers with fervor. "Oh boy! Here's another twist in the pretzel."

Erik knelt down next to the brother, who babbled incoherently. "Brother Peter, can you hear me?"

The cleric continued to mumble prayers clutching the Bible. He looked up at Erik as if suddenly seeing him for the first time. "Death, death came for us that day. My friend let me escape. I fear Death is still out there, looking for me, waiting for me in the dark to claim my soul along with the others."

Denton leaned down, gently taking the man's hand. "Brother Peter, can you tell us what happened?"

Peter looked at the elder agent. "We only came to pray and reflect. The basement cathedral at St. Martha's always made us feel at peace. I knew we weren't supposed to be there but the feeling of God is so powerful in that place. Whenever we had doubts about our calling, we would go down to that chapel and just 'feel' the presence of God." Peter clutched the Bible tighter reciting the Lord's Prayer, seemingly lost in some private torment. "Peace, may peace be with you, peace, peace..." The mantra fell into a whisper.

"Brother Peter, were you aware of anything special hidden in that basement chamber? Some artifact or relic?"

The brother gazed back at Erik. "Shhhhh, it's a secret! We're not supposed to be down here. Father Mathews will be angry if he realizes we come down here. We must keep the secret. Kneel with me. Feel the presence of God."

Erik shook his head, curbing his frustration. "I feel Him, Brother Peter, but the darkness, the darkness clouds my peace. He's shrouded in black. How did he get in this place?" The detective changed tactics.

Brother Peter looked up, his eyes wide with fright. "We don't know! We heard him hiss. We turned and there he was. Brother Karl approached him, reached out to him in friendship, and was cut to ribbons. I screamed, panicked." Peter became agitated pulling his blanket tighter around his body. Pale, cold hands clenched the Bible and rosary beads tighter. "Our Father who art in Heaven … hallowed be thy name … Oh God stop this bloodshed! We only wanted to feel your grace."

The detective knelt down beside the raving cleric. "Peter!" Erik whispered. "I'm going to join you, don't panic. I'll protect you."

Erik reached for the terrified man's temple. Denton grabbed his hand.

"Erik, what are you doing?"

"We need to see what he's witnessed, Counselor. I'm going to find out just who or what was there by sharing his memory. Somewhere in that traumatized mind dwell the answers to our questions and possibly the identity of your son's killer."

Denton kept his grip on Erik's hand. "What about the cross? Did you forget what happened with the cross? You almost leveled an entire complex tapping into some negative energy. You go batshit crazy here, you'll kill hundreds. Your warrior alter ego and that portable lighting rod you carry could level the entire city."

Erik pulled his hand away. "I know. But I'm ready for this now, I can do this Counselor. The more time we bicker the less time we have to get to the bottom of this. We have about seven minutes and the clock is ticking."

Denton shook his head. "You're sure you've got this?"

"I'm sure." Erik looked over at Neko. "If I'm wrong, and things turn, yank my hand away and slap me as hard as you can. That should be enough to snap me back into reality."

The nervous officer nodded as Erik touched Peter's temple.

There was the odd sensation of reality shifting as the hospital room warped and then completely dissipated into a thin fog. Erik was back in the basement cathedral, only the perspective was different. He was reliving a memory.

"Run Brother Peter, I'll hold him off! The cardinals must know what's happened here?"

The hybrid felt the sheer terror and panic, the emotions washed over him, flooding his mind with horrible visions, drawing him into the action. Erik focused his will, pushing the emotions aside constantly reminding himself the events were history and he was reliving them not experiencing them. His conscious mind was able to keep reign over the chaos and panic. Erik watched the nightmare unfold. Peter tried the doors but they were jammed shut. THE VENTS! Brother Peter looked back. His dear friend was being butchered alive. The being turned, its hood partially fell and he could see his face. The being howled in pain as exposed flesh sizzled. It desperately reached up and pulled the hood up concealing the face once again. The dark-robed demon stood and approached Peter. He panicked and ran toward the old vent.

Peter's eyes briefly fell on his friend. He'd been disemboweled. Blood and organs stained the once pristine marble floor. Erik felt the wave of sympathy as Peter struggled to fit through the small shafts connected to the now unused ventilation chamber. The monk desperately climbed to safety but heard the angry hissing below. The being in black shouted vile threats and curses sending shivers down his spine as he painfully climbed the five stories to safety.

Erik spoke inside the cleric's mind, *You're safe now. You don't have to be afraid.*

Peter's eyes darted from side to side. *They're dead. They're all dead! What will I tell the father? No one will believe me.*

Erik radiated calm. *They know the truth, Peter. More than you do, I'm afraid. They will believe you. You can't keep punishing yourself by reliving this horror over and over again. Take my hand. Let me take you back. Let me help you escape this nightmare.*

Peter looked up from his curled position in the filthy air duct. *You will help me?*

Erik smiled. *Yes. I'm here to help you. You have my word.*

Who are you? Peter's brow furrowed.

My name is Erik Knight. Give me your hand, Peter. It's time for the nightmare to end.

Erik broke the link. Peter's eyes popped open and he looked around as if seeing his visitors for the first time. The cleric took the detective's hand, muttering apologies as his body shook with grief. Peter wept. A sob of agony and loss saturated the sterile room.

Erik looked down at the broken monk. The detective's breathing became shallow and he gently placed his hand on

Peter's shoulder. The monk tensed. His weeping ceased and his eyes were alight with sudden rapture. "I can feel His presence." Peter touched his chest, "In my heart I can feel His presence again, like being in the chapel!" Peter looked over at Erik. "You kept your word. You have taken away my pain and given me a gift that I can never repay. No one has ever given me so much. Thank you."

Erik nodded and sat on a nearby chair. The detective was pale. Martin looked over but Erik simply nodded and pointed toward the rejuvenated man. "Peter, are you up for answering a few questions? Mr. Denton here would like a few moments of your time."

Peter looked up at the elder man. "Denton…. William's Father?" he reached up, extending a shaking hand toward Martin. "Your son was my best friend. He gave his life to save mine. I feel awful about this, sir."

Denton leaned closer to the now remarkably calm cleric and clasped his outstretched hand. "Please, is there anything more you can tell us about what happened?"

"I'm sorry, Mr. Denton. I panicked. Everything happened so fast. No one seemed to know about the lower church, and we never asked our mentors about it. We went there because William learned of it from his readings and research. Your son was an amazing scholar. He drank up knowledge like a sponge. I've never seen anything like it. He could read theological texts and interpret the meanings from passages that even had our professors baffled."

Denton nodded. "He was brilliant." The agent focused back on the issue at hand. "And you have no idea what the man that killed him wanted?"

"None, sir. Like I said, the first time we snuck down there was after William read about the basement chapel in an old text at the Vatican library. That was about a year ago. We didn't believe what was in the book. One Saturday during our free time we followed the map William had copied into St, Martha's. We found an elevator in the back of the building. William had some kind of device that was able to bypass the code. I have no idea where he got it. I never bothered to ask. We stepped in the elevator went down the five levels."

Denton shook his head. "How in the hell did he make a cryptograph?" The old man shook his head. 'I'm sorry, please go on."

"William made many gadgets from odds and ends we brought him. He made a nice radio for Father Bill on his birthday out of old circuit boards we salvaged from some trash." Brother Peter took a deep breath and continued his story.

"We followed the passage. It was crazy. We seemed to be walking forever. We finally came to the chamber and William picked the door's lock with some tools. He was driven, like he knew the place was there all along. As soon as we stepped in, we all felt it. The presence of God permeated the entire chamber. The peace and tranquility brought us to our knees. We stayed there for hours, praying and meditating on the mysteries of our faith." The young cleric smiled. "We had found a piece of Heaven on Earth, Mr. Denton, and we swore each other to secrecy. Whenever we felt stressed or overwhelmed, we would all sneak away for a few hours, go to the hidden chapel to pray, and feel the presence of God."

Denton nodded and looked over at Erik. The detective nodded slightly. "Peter, were you aware of anything hidden inside that chamber? Or maybe William told you something about treasure or something of intrinsic value in that underground church? Any rumor or musing he may have shared with you?"

"No, Mr. Knight, we never felt the need to explore. We would simply kneel in front of the altar and then sit or kneel in the front pew meditating on our faith. William did scour through several other texts for more information on the hidden chamber but he never found anything else. No other text in the library mentioned the chamber and no other map of St. Martha's has the deep basements identified. It was a mystery."

"Did you or any one of your friends tell anyone else of this discovery? Did anyone else know what Brother Denton discovered?"

"No, Mr. Knight. William said we should not say anything to anyone. He wanted to read more on the subject. He believed if more people knew, they would want to come and experience the presence of God. We knew it was selfish to keep such a miracle to ourselves but we figured there was a reason those in authority kept the chamber a secret. If people started going down in droves, the cardinals would know what we'd discovered. If it was meant to be a secret, we might be in trouble. Worse, they might keep us from returning."

"You're certain William kept this to himself and never told anyone else, even someone he may have considered a confidant?"

The brother stared at the floor. "Brother William and I were the closest of friends, and we shared many secrets over the last several years. Believe me when I tell you he told no one else."

Erik nodded. He could feel the sense of loss welling back up in the young cleric. "I understand. You have no idea who or what attacked your brothers?"

"No, Mr. Knight, but I assure you it was a servant of the devil himself. Nothing else could be capable of committing such hideous evil in such a holy place."

Erik nodded as he glanced at the clock. Their time was just about up and it was clear that Brother Peter wouldn't be able to shed any more light on the murders. "Thank you for your time, Brother Peter." Erik gestured toward the clock. "Your caretakers are about to come in and escort us off the premises."

"Thank you, Mr. Knight," the rejuvenated cleric gestured toward his heart, "for giving me the inner peace I'd found in that chapel."

The door opened and the two burly men in black stepped in. They were shocked to see Brother Peter lucid and engaged with Erik and Martin. They weren't able to disguise their looks of alarm and concern. It was evident that the only reason they were given access to the patient was because they believed the patient was in no condition to offer them anything.

"Thanks for the time. We got just what we needed. I'll let Bishop O'Malley know how cooperative and helpful you both were." Erik made no effort to hide his sarcasm as he stepped out followed quickly by Martin and the two police officers.

Martin tapped Erik on the shoulder. "What did you see?"

"He saw the attacker's face. Now I have it." Erik tapped the side of his head, "It's up here now, in my memory and we can use that, Counselor."

Martin's face clouded.

"What's wrong?"

"William was too clever for his own good. That's partially my fault. I let him watch and help me as I dabbled in espionage electronics. He learned to build those gadgets from me. When he was thirteen I accidentally locked us out of the house. The rain was pouring down in buckets and my wife was out of town. I used a lock pick to get into the house and showed him how to work the tools. We made a game of it after that. I'd get several different padlocks and we'd have contests to see who could open them first. At that time, William wanted to be an agent, just like his dad. I'd forgotten all about those times. Hearing Peter's story brought back some memories."

"Hang on to them, Martin. William never forgot the lessons you taught him, so I know he kept those good memories alive as well."

"I hope so."

"I know he did, Counselor." The detective glanced back at the black-clad Vatican guards. One of the men was speaking into a cell phone, "We need to keep pushing forward, I'm sure news of Brother Peter's remarkable recovery has been relayed to our Vatican friends." Erik quickened his pace until they were outside the hospital.

* * *

Erik and Martin had put some distance between their police escort and sat on a park bench. Both men sipped from coffee cups as Erik stared intently at several dozen pigeons. The detective took a deep swig from his cup and broke the moody silence.

"We need to examine the bodies. I'm sure our Vatican friends will probably have another immaculate birth if I make the request. But you being the next of kin can gain access to see your son. They can't do much to stop that." Erik took another sip of his coffee and looked over at the two police officers sitting several benches from them. Neko was on his phone, no doubt making some kind of report regarding their whereabouts and activities. "Our hosts in the holy city seem hell-bent on keeping this whole incident a state secret. I'm confident they didn't expect us to discover the safe or get anything from Brother Peter. It's a safe bet the good bishop is getting minute-by-minute updates on everything we've done and discovered." He gestured toward the Greek police officer.

Denton looked over and laughed. "They're just doing their jobs and following orders. I can't really blame them. You've sure given them some pretty colorful stuff to report though." Denton tossed some bread crumbs and seed from the bag he'd purchased into the pigeon flock, getting some relaxation from feeding the multitude of birds. "I need to see him, Erik. I need to say goodbye to my son."

"Of course, Martin. I was wondering, perhaps, if you'd had enough excitement for one day and would consider waiting until tomorrow. We could make the formal request this evening since I'm confident we'll be escorted back to Vatican City for a debriefing." Erik helped himself to some birdseed and flung a handful at the flocking pigeons.

"Did you bring an agency phone?" Denton tossed another handful of crumbs and seed.

Erik nodded. "Yeah, it's in a case in my duffel bag."

"I'll make the request tonight. I assume we'll be invited for a dinner meeting and grilled appropriately as we're fed a line of bullshit to explain away what we've uncovered. I'll ask to see my son alone as a personal visit to say goodbye and to make the final arrangements. You can make a fuss about coming, but I'll be the one who tells you no. If I make the refusal it buys us that much more credibility. I'll have my phone on and you can use the tracer function and catch up with me later." Denton looked over at his younger friend. "I assume you'll have no problem losing our babysitters."

Erik snorted. "I don't think that'll be much of a problem. I just hope they don't get in too much trouble. I like them."

Denton nodded in agreement. "As far as babysitters go, I like 'em too. Not enough to trust them, of course, but I like them just the same."

Chapter 4. Prelude to a Holy War

Washington DC, Columbia Heights

Senior Senator Paul McMahon and Speaker of the House Andrew Collins sat nervously in the executive state room of the Starlight Bistro. Collins picked at his filet mignon while McMahon nervously sipped his third glass of wine.

"Twenty years, Paul, twenty years I've been taking instruction through that blue phone and never have I been ordered to meet anybody from the ethereal realm. The Eternals like to manipulate things from a distance."

McMahon's hands shook slightly, upsetting the contents of his wine glass. "I've only dealt with a few, lower-level mortal entities. I'll confess that seeing Nicadaemus personally dispatch Lazarus with not even a flinch was unnerving. I'm reminded just how small and insignificant we really are in their eyes. I'm wondering if we're going to live through this encounter."

Collins shook his head in disagreement. "If they were going to kill us I don't think a public restaurant, even one as shady as The Starlight, would be the venue. We'd be butchered in the privacy of our own homes and deposited in some deserted back alley lot." He took a bite of his steak, pondering the upcoming meeting. "Like I said before, there's something wrong. Somebody, somewhere is upsetting the evil applecart." Collins sipped from his wine glass. "We're about to get interrogated by a divine, dark attorney looking for answers. I don't think we'll be having dessert in Hell."

The senator placed his glass back down on the table. "That really doesn't make me feel any better."

A curvy waitress interrupted their brooding. "Excuse me, sir. There's someone requesting an audience with you both." The woman looked back over her shoulder nervously. "He has a very disturbing presence."

Collins nodded. "We're expecting him. Please show our guest over and have a bottle of 'Domaine de la Romanee-Conti' burgundy brought to the table."

McMahon raised an eyebrow. "A twenty thousand dollar burgundy? Do they even drink?"

"From what little I know, the Romanee-Conti wines have an appeal to our immortal friends—something special in the fermenting process. Our employers have a very expensive pallet."

McMahon nodded. "Never hurts to kick off a meeting with a good gesture."

Collins smiled. "My feelings exactly."

Andrew Collins felt a disturbing presence. He looked over his shoulder. Their waitress escorted a tall, thin man in an expensive Italian suit. The being's powerful, inhuman presence was undeniable. Collins felt immediately uncomfortable, unsure of what would happen in the next five minutes despite his earlier bravado.

The Eternal studied the humans momentarily as if weighing something of their stature. "Gentlemen, I appreciate you taking time out of your schedules."

Collins stood up and extended his hand. "The pleasure is ours."

Paul McMahon mimicked his colleague's gesture and the three men sat down at the spacious table. Their waitress brought over a silver container that held the chilled bottle of wine. The being studied the bottle and nodded in approval. He looked over at Collins. "You've done your homework, Mr. Speaker. I'm impressed."

The waitress poured a glass for their guest, her hand trembling, and then departed.

The ethereal took a small sip, then with a sudden motion drained the entire glass in two gulps. He smiled and exhaled. "An excellent vintage. Now, gentlemen, let's get down to business." The being leaned forward. "The order to steal the relic was not issued from our forces. Our line of communication was compromised."

Collins nodded slightly. "We figured as much when Nicadaemus paid us a visit earlier."

The being shot him an annoyed look. "Nicadaemus is a blunt instrument and often goes off half-cocked. However, this time, his concerns are valid. What you've done is further exasperate a situation that's been spiraling out of control for the last six years."

"May I inquire as to exactly what's going on? We can't be of much service if we don't know how bad our situation really is." Collins poured himself a glass of Romanee-Conti and then poured another for their guest.

"Thus our meeting this evening." The being took a sip from his glass, leaned forward, and disclosed some alarming facts to his two human colleagues. "I'll start at the very beginning. Some 10,000 of your years ago two species fought a war of extinction on your planet. This war spilled over from a conflict initiated on a home world some three hundred light years from Earth. The normal rules of creation and extinction set about in the beginning stated all planets that had intelligent life capable of free will that were embroiled in ethereal conflict must be kept isolated from each other. The Espers and Seelak did not become embroiled in ethereal affairs until they were extremely advanced technologically, far more than your race has achieved. When the battle of Light and Dark broke out on their world, it shook the very foundations of Heaven and Hell. The war was so great that their planet and star system were eventually destroyed by it. A small group on both sides managed to escape in a large spacecraft and they settled here upon Earth some 10,000 years ago.

"Their arrival here caused alarm on both sides. The battle for Earth wasn't ready to be fought and your species was still in its infancy. 'He' intervened..." the being gestured toward to the ceiling. The senator and the House speaker understood he meant Heaven. "Some type of malady rendered both sides sterile and a series of diseases began slowly decimating the alien populations. It was decided they would simply be allowed to live out their lives until both sides became extinct. Your species would be protected and the war the interlopers fought would simply be inconclusive with neither side gaining ground." The being paused, draining his glass and pouring another. He offered the bottle to both men before continuing. "The forces of

Light and Dark focused attention on other developing worlds as our eternal conflict continued. But one of our forces, a rather ambitious demon, possessed a Seelak and began hatching a scheme to slaughter the human species and lay claim to this planet. He was very influential and assisted the Seelak scientists in developing a breed of being so monstrous that once unleashed would not only wipe out the Esper race but then turn on the infant human species. The Espers fought one last desperate battle and, using the Seelak's own Netherspace technology against them, were able to prevail, but the final battle decimated both sides dooming them to extinction. These actions were not according to our plan and here's where things went awry. An Esper warrior, called Jakor, actually captured the Seelak demon and locked him in an eternal prison to be fed upon by the very monsters he'd created. He, along with several others of his species, were entombed in the hull of their spaceship to be prey for the creatures they'd spawned to kill both the Espers and the Humans."

"A rather harsh form of retribution," Collins remarked. The House speaker was stunned to learn humanity's untold history.

"Indeed, but what the Espers didn't realize was that the genetically engineered creatures wouldn't die once their food sources were depleted. They'd simply hibernate until a new source presented itself. It was feared that humans would eventually discover the ship and inadvertently free the creatures. The Espers created a mutagenic virus that would combine all the powers of Jakor, their mightiest warrior, with a perfectly compatible human host, and another virus that would carry the knowledge of the war and more importantly the ability to trigger the mutagenic reaction by handing this one being Jakor's primary weapon. If the Seelak creatures were ever released the genetic instructions on both the viruses would activate, causing the seeker to find the one being that was Jakor's genetic match and give him the weapon. The weapon would then detect its owner's genetic makeup triggering the transformation."

"Incredible," McMahon jumped in. "Absolutely incredible! Erik Knight was that perfect match, one man in billions of people throughout the world and throughout time."

"Erik Knight was never meant to undergo that change,

Senator. The process was supposed to be a stopgap preventative for something that would never occur. When the Seelak creatures finally killed the Seelak possessed by Molec, the demon was freed from the Seelak shell. As an ethereal, he was able to pass through the solid barriers and free once again to roam the earth. As I stated, we were busy on other worlds until man had progressed enough. When the time of the first Son came upon Earth, some two thousand years ago, we took interest again and focused some of our forces to the battle here. It was at that time that both sides realized what Molec had done and what the Espers had set into motion centuries before. Your God knew of Molec's actions and inspired the Esper's rather ingenious stopgap.

"We scoured this planet looking for Molec but he could hide his essence inside a human shell and become virtually undetectable. Eventually he was forgotten as the war for Earth intensified. As with most advanced species, the more man's technology progressed, morality regressed as rapidly. For the first time in a millennium we had the upper hand on a planet according to God's own established rules of engagement."

Collins leaned forward. "We greatly appreciate the history lesson, but I'm wondering how this ties to what's occurring now?"

The ethereal flashed a wicked smile. "You humans claim to know so much, but you fail to see the very danger right under your very noses. There's a human quality—patience, I believe you call it. Indulge me a few minutes more, Mister Speaker, and I'll tie up the history lesson with our current problem at hand." The being's eyes were viscous and his look sent a chill down both men.

Collins swallowed hard doing his best to avoid any further eye contact with the being. "My apologies." He leaned back in his chair. "Please continue." Collins looked at the being. "I'm sorry, I didn't get your name."

The being looked at him and smiled again. "Because I didn't give it, Speaker Collins. You don't need to know who I am as long as you know who and what I represent."

McMahon shot his friend a warning look. Collins shrugged. "Again my apologies. It was not my intention to offend, sir."

The being leaned in close. "None taken, yet." The ethereal picked up the wine and drank deeply, draining two thirds of the bottle. He wiped his mouth with a napkin, exhaled a deep sigh of satisfaction and continued his tale. "Now, the war was going swimmingly for our side. We had infiltrated and corrupted the church, instigated war and mistrust among the world's religions and most humans were becoming secular humanists of their own volition. Then we believe Molec and his forces made their first aggressive move to lay claim to this word, upsetting the balance and incriminating us in the process. Somehow he manipulated a company to open the crypt that kept his creations in slumber. A team of geologists and scientists broke into the prison awakening the hibernating terrors. The creatures slaughtered humans and terrorized the town of Hopedale. Much to Molec's chagrin, the forces of Light had kept Jakor's genetic match very close. The forces of Light believed we had freed the beasts and took direct countermeasures. They allowed the hybrid to be created. Instead of being killed after an encounter with both creatures, Erik Knight was healed and forever altered. He slaughtered both of Molec's creations leaving the demon angered and irrational. We were close to reclaiming him but he managed to elude us. The forces of Light now had a champion of immense power upsetting the balance and putting our plans for Earth in jeopardy. That power has continued growing inside him. Erik Knight is no longer human. He's more powerful and capable of more destructive force than any other being. His actions could single-handedly sway the war between factions. If the hybrid chose to fight on the side of Light, we would be defeated. The forces of Light are already convinced that we have broken the rules by allowing the Dark creatures to be freed from captivity. They look upon the creation of Knight as a justified counter to our perceived betrayal."

"May I ask a question?" McMahon leaned forward.

The being nodded.

"Knight became a CIA cooler, fighting terrorism and narcotics under the employ of Martin Denton. Denton isn't a player that I'm aware of. It seems Knight was effectively out of the picture and out of our hair. Why would Molec do anything to provoke him? If we lose to the forces of Light, won't he lose too? I'd imagine that his goals and your goals would be one and the same."

The Dark lord smiled again. "An overabundance of arrogance. I confess, those of us on this side of the conflict are afflicted with it. Even you humans drawn into politics, lured by the money and power believing that you know better how to run the nation than your opponent." The being laughed. "Like Lucifer during the great battle, Molec is not content to serve. He believes he can better manage Hell and the forces of darkness. Molec wants to accelerate man's downfall, unleash Armageddon, and destroy the last vessel of Light on this planet, sealing it forever in an eternity of darkness. I personally have no problem with the plan. I just don't think Molec can manage it. He lacks the power. If provoked too far, God will cast out Molec the same way he cast out Lucifer after the Earth was formed. But if Molec has the Ruby Crucifix of Christ, all he needs do is keep it and destroy the Vessel destined to wield the holy relic and this world is lost, by God's own rules."

"So by acting out and taking the relic now, Molec has, in effect, shown his poker hand to the other side and marshaled the forces of opposition," Collins chimed in fascinated by the story.

The being nodded in agreement. "Very astute. Molec, not deterred by his earlier failure, made another attempt to upset the balance and instigate a major conflict among the eternals. There was an incident just over three years ago instigated by surrogates from an underground rogue element of your human government. We didn't pay much attention to it until a certain human became embroiled in the controversy."

"Special Agent Knight," Collins injected.

The being nodded. "Special Agent Knight. This rogue branch of your government attempted to instigate an interstellar incident while at the same time abducting Agent Knight's wife." The being took another swig from the wine bottle clearly enjoying the vintage. "As far as the interstellar war went, we were happy Knight was able to intervene and keep Earth from being obliterated, but the plans being made for termination of his wife and the dissection of his child would have escalated our conflict for possession of this planet to a scale never before seen since the Esper War some 28,000 years ago. Molec was controlling those government forces, using his military stooges like puppets. His subterfuge would have worked if not for Knight's uncanny telepathic power. Molec didn't care about causing an interstellar incident and didn't care about the delicacy pertaining to the Observer juvenile being held prisoner."

The speaker did some quick math in his head. "My God! If those aliens came to Earth 10,000 years ago and you just said their war was some 28,000 years ago ... am I to believe they fought a protracted battle for 18,000 years?"

The being nodded. "Less the two decades it took them to find Earth. As I mentioned, the battle they fought was savage and titanic, worse than anything ever witnessed by mortal beings. The weapons and technology used were staggering. Species, like the Observers you Humans sought to engage have yet to become embroiled. They are simple seekers of knowledge and have no desire for power. Truth be told, the Espers were on that same path. If not for the Seelak, they too would never have become embroiled in ethereal affairs."

"The file I read claimed Colonel Ross wanted to create an army of hybrid beings using the child's genetics." McMahon took a sip from his own glass growing more intrigued by the tale being told.

"Colonel Ross was being possessed by Molec, an unwilling and unaware human host. When the hybrid defeated the Observers and the legitimate government forces were closing in, Molec influenced Ross to take his own life thereby allowing the demon to flee the host. Ross couldn't cope with the reality of what he'd done. The poor human actually believed he was freely committing the acts of brutality. Molec was able to manipulate him further into killing himself. Ross was a bitter soul and our demon capitalized on that bitterness to his own ends. Molec's plan was simply to harvest the child and slaughter it before it could become too powerful like its father and possibly fulfill its purpose. Your technology is far too limited to even begin the cross genetic splicing required to duplicate Agent Knight or his son."

"So Knight is somehow tied to the biblical end of the world."

Collins shuddered as the weight of this realization struck him.

"Erik Knight, as he is now, was never supposed to exist. His son was never supposed to exist. His life came to be only by Molec's first attempt to control the conflict on this planet. His son is a genetic impossibility and I believe a creation of the forces of Light but I have yet to prove that theory. The hybrid is an unknown element sired by the forces of Light but not sworn to uphold those values or virtues. He is the Son of the Stars spoken of in the Apostle Peter's unpublished writings. A being Peter said would never come to pass. The war for Earth is coming undone and if rules continue to be broken and Molec provokes both sides, Earth will become ground zero for a battle between the forces of Light and Dark. As proud as Lucifer is, he knows he cannot win such a battle. His hope is to win by the rules established in the beginning. We have abided by those rules so we may continue to exist and prosper to some degree and snatch a world here and there for our own. Earth was to be our greatest victory. If Molec is successful, it will signal the end of everything for this planet and possibly impact ethereal conflicts on countless other worlds."

Andrew Collins felt his gut twist in a knot. They'd been played by a second string ethereal into triggering a massive confrontation that could very well bring about the end of the world and the end of humanity. "What do we do? There has to be some way to diffuse this time bomb we've set into motion."

"There are forces of Light in Washington looking for leads to track Molec and the holy relic. It's only a matter of time before your involvement is discovered and you're both taken for your role in this scheme. Before you can be hunted down I suggest strongly you reach out and return what you've wrongly acquired. We cannot be associated with this thievery. The cost of being implicated is a war that will end all wars and make the Esper Seelak war look like two children fighting in a sandbox. I trust the relic is well hidden."

Collins nodded. "It is."

The being slipped the speaker a piece of paper. "I believe you know this man."

Collins studied the name. "Thomas Michael Henderson. He's a freshman pol from Iowa, an unassuming quiet guy."

"He's a human agent of Light and serves much the same role for them as you do for us. Reach out to him, tell him you know where the Ruby Cross of Christ is located and have every desire to see it returned. If he doubts you, and he will at first, tell him you spoke with Bartholomew." The being drained the remains of the wine and sighed happily. "Representative Henderson's father was embroiled in Molec's last plot. He knows a great deal about the activities going on in Washington and elsewhere. Heaven always has eyes upon him. Reach out to him, and Heaven will know. A being of Light will no doubt be dispatched to reclaim the relic. Cooperate and return what is theirs and we can hope things will go back to normal."

"I'll call him first thing in the morning, Mr. Bartholomew," Collins assured the entity.

The being turned. "Never let my name slip from your tongue again, human. Never, ever speak of what was discussed here today. You know certain truths because it was necessary for you to know. I strongly suggest that once the relic is returned you forget this conversation. Ethereal knowledge tends to get humans killed." The being called Bartholomew stood and quietly departed.

McMahon watched the tall being disappear. Muscles tensed and breath held until Bartholomew was out of sight. "Holy shit! Could we have fucked this up any more if we tried?"

Collins shuddered. He reached over and picked up the empty wine bottle. "I can only assume the higher ups don't find us at fault. We both know the price for failure. The fact that we're allowed to fix this mess means our lives are secure for the time being. I strongly suggest we reach out to Representative Henderson's staff first thing in the morning." Collins placed the empty bottle back on the table. "Best expenditure of campaign money I've had all year."

McMahon nodded. "He did seem to enjoy it. I'm going to have to watch myself around Henderson now. I totally misread him. I figured he was a harmless farm boy."

"That was probably his intention. I'll let our staff know to be extra careful around him now. Henderson is on three committees that control a great deal of discretionary spending, find out who appointed him. We may be able to get leads on some others."

"Well, after tomorrow, he'll undoubtedly know who we work for as well. In the end it's a zero sum gain for both sides."

Collins laughed. "Touché. I think our ethereal friends like things the way they are, balanced with no forward momentum, just like Washington and government—look busy while accomplishing nothing but convince everyone around how much you've done for them."

"That's our job in a nutshell, Senator. That's what a politician does best, keep the status quo." Collins stared lustfully at the buxom redhead clearing a nearby table. "I'm going to spend the rest of the evening with her, doing my best to forget this whole ugly mess. I'll call you in the morning."

McMahon winked. He had a special intern waiting for him at his apartment. "Until tomorrow, Mr. Speaker."

* * *

Vatican City, Rome

Erik and Martin ignored the summons from the Bishop's Council. Though Martin wouldn't admit it, the events of the day had worn on him both physically and emotionally. Neither man was up for a mental chess game with the Vatican at this point. They'd put their plan of action into play in the morning. Erik stared at the closed blinds pondering the visions he'd encountered from the pole cross and from the shell-shocked cleric, Brother Peter.

"Something wicked this way comes," he muttered. "This is not what I expected. But it ties into my gut feeling." He stared at his watch; it was eight in the evening. He picked up his agency phone and dialed a series of numbers.

"Hey babe? How goes things at home?" Erik closed his eyes savoring the sound of Shanda's voice. He could hear the loud music from her store in the background and then EJ giggling close to the sales counter. Even though he'd only been away a day he already missed the sounds of home.

"Yes, we've started the investigation." Erik didn't go into any details knowing their room was still bugged. But he provided their cover story for ignoring the bishop's summons. "It was getting to be too much for Martin. The loss and the jet lag have hit him hard. He's fast asleep. The poor soul is exhausted. He wanted to keep pushing but I knew he needed the rest. We'll pick up where we left off tomorrow and hopefully be on a plane for home some time later in the day."

Erik grunted a few times as Shanda talked and they exchanged light conversation for several minutes. "Okay babe you tell 'Lil Man' daddy will see him soon." Erik suddenly laughed aloud. "Yes, I promise I will find a Vatican gift shop and get you a souvenir." He paused for a moment. "I love you, Angel. I'll see you tomorrow, or the next day at the latest." He tossed the phone on top of the small table and leaned back on the couch. He closed his eyes and assumed a deep meditative state. Tomorrow was going to be another busy day

* * *

Erik heard Martin's light footsteps as he entered their living room area. The detective glanced at his watch. Three hours had passed. Erik's body required little to no sleep since his change but his mind enjoyed the peace and tranquility found in meditation. The past hours had refreshed his mental faculties. "You're up and about at a late hour, Martin."

Denton flinched. "Sorry, you startled me. I was trying not to wake you."

"No worries, Counselor. I wasn't really sleeping." Erik sat up and gestured toward a large armchair. He picked up a nearby hotel pad and began writing.

We need to talk, and I'm confident other ears are listening.

Denton nodded as he read. He picked up the pen.

Do a sweep. I've got an idea. I'll be right back

Martin left the room and Erik silently scanned their hotel suite. He found a small microphone hidden between the ruffles of the balcony curtains and another device under the lip of their coffee table. He casually crushed the eavesdropping devices and placed the broken fragments in a plastic evidence bag. Martin came back out of the room carrying a small black device with two blinking green lights. He walked around the room holding the box in front of him. As he approached the far wall, the lights flashed red and yellow. He walked toward the opposite wall and the device flashed again. There were listening devices inside the walls as well.

Erik pointed toward the plastic bag and Denton rolled his eyes. The elder agent turned a black knob and placed the device in the middle of the room. Erik's enhanced hearing picked up a high frequency static. "A white noise box?"

Denton smiled. "The latest tech gadget from our lab geeks. Not only will it scramble any audio sensor but if our friends have any video systems, they're about to get nothing but static as well."

"I'm impressed. I have to admit, our friends in the holy city are far worldlier than I'd have ever imagined."

Denton laughed. "The church has been around for a long time Erik, and they've lots of practice being sneaky."

The detective nodded. "So it would seem. I'd like to compare notes about the things we've experienced today. It's always helpful to bounce ideas and theories off somebody else before a large meeting."

"Good idea. I wasn't as much on the experiencing side of events as you were. I can give my gut reactions and my impressions of our friends on the police force and at the Vatican, but as far as the experiences you had, I'm only good as a sounding board and not much else."

Erik nodded. "A sounding board is exactly what I need right now because I have a theory and it's pretty farfetched. I'm very reluctant to bring it up tomorrow and I'm hesitant to even tell you. But I need to get it out there, ridiculous as it feels."

"Well it's just us now so fire away. I'm sure our nosey friends are quite distressed at this point."

Erik leaned forward. "Okay I'm just going to come out with it. I don't think our killer is human."

Denton raised an eyebrow. "That much I gathered already. Based on your reactions when you picked up the cross and the wreckage at the altar, I gathered our killer was something more than a run-of-the-mill human murderer."

Erik stared at his friend and tilted his head. "You seem to be taking this in stride."

Denton shook his head. "No, not really. I've just been nosing around the edge of things the last few years and have become aware of happenings that would drive a normal person insane. I've kept these things to myself because I feared if I brought it up my own life would be forfeit. I never expected my son to be involved with such things though, let alone be murdered by a non-human entity."

"Care to enlighten me, Counselor?"

"Remember when you were working with the government ferreting out the rogue leaders in Washington?"

The detective winced. "How could I forget? I've never seen such a cesspool of collusion and corruption. That investigation made me lose all faith in Washington and in our system. Each time, we thought we had all the rats trapped, there seemed to be another level of corruption even deeper, incriminating more people. Finally the President gave up and took what he had for a win and called me off. I was close, Martin, real close to finally netting some of the bigger fish. Somebody got to the President. I can't prove it, but in my gut I know that's what happened. Washington couldn't take the political heat from the headlines."

Martin shook his head. "I don't know, Erik. Initially when you told me about the investigation being squashed I agreed. But after seeing some of the political maneuvering taking place over the last several months I'm convinced there's something more involved. I intercepted some high level intel from Washington to our agency heads and the subject involved matters of state involving several high ranking committee members in the House and Senate. They were orders, or at least instructions, on certain courses of action to take in the 'War'. There was a series of symbols in the message that took me a month to crack."

"And…." Erik leaned forward.

"One of my friends is a Biblical Scholar and he told me it's a language he's only seen on a holy scroll, here, in a museum in Vatican City. It's believed to be a divine alphabet, the language of angels if you will." Denton paused letting his revelation sink in. "The coded message instructed our agency to pull resources off of projects and assign them cases I'd never heard of. Some of the assets were people in my direct chain of command and I know one of those agents was a key player in ferreting out the Washington corruption. That kind of repositioning on our chessboard requires coordination through proper channels and goes through my office. This obviously didn't. I waited about a week to see what would happen and sure enough I got a phone call from Washington informing me that three of my assets were being reassigned and it was all above my level of clearance. When I pressed, I was told I didn't have a need to know and was advised to drop the matter."

Erik rubbed a hand through his long hair and shook his head. "So you're saying some angel upstairs didn't want the pot stirred in Washington? That's one hell of a stretch to make based on an intercepted message, especially with you being an atheist and all."

The old man sighed. "I know, but I started snooping around and asking questions, probably more than I should have. Each time I mentioned the strange script to the higher ups they got very uncomfortable and nervous, like I was raising a taboo subject. I'd never seen seasoned staffers sweat and look so uncomfortable and tell me I'd be better off dropping the subject. Every federal document gets scanned and stored somewhere. I stayed late a few nights and ran some 'EYES' database searches for documents with similar script. I programmed the spectrum scanner functions in the search to look for typographic variants, word and letter patterns in documents, and even a few other encryption ciphers I knew of to conceal data. I was stunned when I actually got several hits. I started examining hard copies of files too. The different ways the symbols were hidden are absolutely brilliant. The documents were all from three high-ranking congressmen and one senator. The symbols were all cleverly hidden inside text or watermarked very lightly and barely visible to the naked eye. If someone wasn't specifically looking for these symbols, they could possess these papers and never know the markings were there." Denton paused a moment to compose himself. "I started doing some background research on these men and I couldn't find any common thread or any activity linking them together besides that script on some highly classified correspondence materials."

"Did you save the images? I'd like to get a look at these symbols. Maybe one of my sources outside the agency can shed some more light on them. There has to be some meaning behind them. If we can decipher those messages, we may have a clue to who's behind the Washington conspiracy."

Denton frowned. "That's the problem, after two nights of snooping and building a case file, I was going to take all the data to an associate who has a source at the Archeological Institute in Seattle. She was going to take the images and have them analyzed.

Erik rolled his eyes. He knew what was coming.

"A very tall, lean man paid me a social call one evening. He knew all about me, Erik, all about what I was doing and all about my history with the firm. He told me if I valued my career, and more importantly my life, I'd stop snooping where I wasn't supposed to. I got the sense it wasn't a threat, but more of a warning. His tone was amiable and even borderline friendly. He advised me to enjoy my final years and live in peace, that digging into these symbols would only cause me more trouble and aggravation than I could tolerate. The next morning when I arrived at work, my computer had been wiped clean. My case files had been emptied, and my retirement paperwork was on my desk filled out awaiting my signature." Denton shifted his position on the couch. "I got the message." Denton looked over at his friend, "I have this dreadful feeling that my snooping somehow led to William's death. I feel responsible. If I hadn't poked my head into affairs that weren't my concern maybe he'd still be with me today."

Erik sensed the wave of despair. The detective knew the debilitating effect such emotional guilt would have on his friend. "Martin, if there's some connection between what's going on in Washington and what happened here, it has nothing to do with you. You said yourself you didn't have any leads or evidence. You wouldn't be given a 'friendly' warning then retired if the plan was to kill William all along. They would have leveraged your son in the warning to force you out and that didn't happen. Why block you out and then provoke you with something so horrible? 'They' would know something this drastic would only serve to pull you back into active status and into this investigation whether officially retired or not. I don't think." He paused to look his friend in the eye. "I know for certain, the two events, though seemingly related, are just an ugly coincidence."

Martin smiled. "Thanks Erik. I think I needed to hear that from an objective source. You wouldn't lie to spare my feelings would you?"

Erik flashed back to the fib he'd told his friend in the sub-terranean church. "No Martin. On something like this I'd be totally on the level. I'm telling you I'm certain there's no connection."

The old man frowned. "I'm starting to believe in the super-natural. A sense of darkness and evil in a church, you seeing a hooded figure cloaked in black, and the alphabet of angels. It's enough to make a man believe in God. I don't mind admitting I may have been wrong all this time. What a disturbing way to have a revelation."

The detective nodded. "Would it help if I said better now than later."

Denton chuckled. "Yeah, now I can spend the rest of my days repenting."

"Well, since you're in the mood to accept the existence of supernatural entities, you won't mind me telling you I suspect some type of vampiric being is responsible for your son's murder."

"A vampire? Come on now!" Denton nearly choked on the word.

"I know how bizarre it sounds, Counselor, but the smell of charred flesh in the chapel combined with what I saw in Brother Peter's memory, then factor the superhuman strength required to perform the feats in the basement chapel. We've just ruled out the entire human population. I know how messed up this sounds but I'm just throwing it out there as a possibility." Erik sighed. "And I also saw this being drinking blood from an open throat wound. Well, at least that's the impressions imbedded on that cross. Whatever killed your son and the other two men wasn't human." The detective forced the words out of his mouth knowing how crazy they would sound. "The data we've collected does seem to point to a vampire. As effed up as that sounds, it's the only conclusion I can draw based on the current facts."

"I hate to throw water on your theory, but how could a vampire exist inside a church? Don't they go poof or something when exposed to crosses and such?"

Erik frowned. "Yes, they're not supposed to be able to exist in such a holy place. I suspect we'll get some interesting results from the black fibers we recovered. Also if the relic inside that safe was as holy as we suspect, how in the hell..." Erik rolled his eyes at his own words, "Pardon the pun, but how in the hell did a Dark being survive an encounter with it, let alone steal such an object without being vaporized." Erik shook his head. "I don't know anything about this stuff. Shit! The only thing I know about vampires comes from the movies. Maybe the movies have it wrong. Perhaps our Vatican friends can shed some light on this tomorrow."

"Let's hope so. I know I wanted your help investigating my son's murder, but I never imagined it would evolve into such a bizarre mystery. Let's take stock of what we do have: We have impressions you picked up from a religious relic and images from a 'Jedi' mind meld with a distraught cleric along with his story, which does support your hypothesis by the way." Denton shifted uncomfortably in his chair, "The only physical evidence we have are the fibers, the dried blood stains and the wrecked safe. We found no prints or any other trace of physical evidence that can place someone else at the crime scene. I'm not doubting your word or your abilities, Erik. I'm simply looking at our situation from an outsider's perspective."

Erik shook his head, laughing.

"What's so funny?"

"You mixed up your franchises, Counselor. We can't have you upsetting the science fiction fandom. Every geek with a toy phaser or light saber just got offended."

Confusion clouded Denton's face. "I'm totally lost."

"The term is 'Vulcan mind meld' from Star Trek. 'Jedi' is from Star Wars." Erik smiled.

"Well I can't go around butchering the genre; I'd cause a disturbance in The Force." Denton grinned wickedly, "I got that one right. Can we get back to work now?"

Erik nodded. "By your command."

Denton's jaw dropped. "Please don't. You're gonna give me a headache."

Erik got back to business "I agree with your assessment

with one exception, the black dried blood is the key. I think that will prove somebody else was there and tie back to our somewhat unorthodox hypothesis. We can speculate till the cows come home but we can't do anything more until we have the lab results. There's a story to get, Martin, and we'll get it tomorrow.

* * *

Erik stepped out of the shower and wrapped a towel around his waist. He could hear Martin on the phone and knew they were being summoned to the Vatican Council. Erik anticipated an escort rather than a mere phone call. The detective could ignore any edict from the religious authority, but Martin was representing the United States Government and even though he was soon to retire, the elder agent still had to maintain a diplomatic posture. Erik dressed quickly tucking his sleeveless t-shirt into his pants. He grabbed a dress shirt from his closet and made his way to the large common area. Martin had opened the heavy drapes and was admiring the morning view of Italy.

"This is really a beautiful place, Erik. I'd like to visit Italy for a few weeks once this is wrapped up. I've always wanted to travel and see the world at my leisure instead of chasing terrorists, drug dealers or spies across the globe at a breakneck pace." Denton sighed. "William would have been a wonderful tour guide."

Erik placed a comforting hand on his friend's shoulder. "I'm sure he would have, I can relate to your sentiment, When I got booted from the CIA I was resentful and angry. But I enjoy the slower pace and the less complicated life. I'm home at night and no one is trying to kill me. It's boring, uneventful yet satisfying at the same time. Retire and enjoy the peace."

Erik waited for his friend to reply but he didn't. The old man was intently staring at his arm. Denton's eyes were wide with shock.

"What's wrong, Martin? You look like you've seen a ghost?"

"Your tattoo." Denton pointed. "For the love of Pete, your tattoo has those symbols I saw on the papers." Denton moved closer studying Erik's artwork.

Erik frantically gestured toward the walls.

Denton examined the ink work. "The noise box has been on all night. I don't need the Vatican hearing me groan, fart, snore or slurp my coffee in the morning."

Erik held his arm out examining his tattoo. "Where?"

"These marks right here, they're carefully hidden behind the barbed wire etching but I recognized them. God knows I've seen them enough in my head. There are three distinct symbols within the pattern. The artist was very clever. Just like the people who sent the symbols on the government documents." Denton looked over at his friend. "I hate to say this but you've been branded."

The detective stared at his arm. "Son of a bitch! Why?"

Denton's brow creased. "They knew."

"I don't follow you, Martin." Erik buttoned his shirt, gazing at his friend.

"They knew I'd call you. They know we're friends and they knew once I was told William was murdered I'd want to investigate and 'They' knew I'd bring the best field agent I could get my hands on to help." Denton sat on the couch. "They wanted you here for some reason, Erik. Our friends in the Vatican wanted you here, to see you for some reason. Those symbols on your arm mean something and my gut tells me our friends are keeping a great deal of information from us."

The detective absently rubbed his arm, his ice-blue eyes burning. "I'm running out of patience with all these mysteries. Let's cut through this bullshit and get some answers." Erik looked back at his friend. "'They have some explaining to do."

* * *

Bishops' Council Room

Erik and Martin were escorted into a large chamber nearly fifty feet across. At the end of the chamber stood a solid white door with a pearl handle. The door was a vast contrast to the paneled wall and ornate furnishings decorating the chamber. Their escort gestured toward the door.

"The Archbishop and his council are inside, Mr. Knight."

Erik looked at their escorts. "I gather you're not escorting us in."

The guard shook his head emphatically. "We are forbidden to enter. Only the most holy may enter that room."

Erik tilted his head and shared a puzzled look with Martin. "I assure you, we are far from the 'most holy'. You're certain this is right place?"

"I am certain Mr. Knight." The escort pointed again. "They are waiting, sirs."

"Well, let's not keep our hosts waiting any longer." Erik boldly approached the door, twisted the pearl handle and pushed it open. The detective paused and gasped aloud. He heard his friend's audible shock as well. The entire room was monochromatic white. The walls were solid white and the ceiling matched perfectly. There were no windows, decorations, or any other type of contrasted furnishings to break up the endless ivory sea. Erik needed his enhanced senses to determine where the walls ended and the ceiling began. The illusion created by the color scheme made the large room appear cavernous and without end. The overhead lighting was of the purest ivory and perfectly matched the surrounding walls. Similar lights were carefully placed inside the walls to further confound the senses.

Erik projected a telepathic wave into the room. The feedback instantly registered in his hybrid senses. "The walls are opaque, made of a plastic material. It's the lights behind them that give the illusion. The entire chamber, including the floor, is made up of some clear membrane backlit by several hundred identical light sources blended perfectly into one dizzying mass of light."

"Light effects or magic, this place is incredible," Denton mumbled. "I'm feeling dizzy, Erik, I have no sense of where the floors meet the wall or where the ceiling is ... it's almost like being in the dark but it's pure light ... I'm literally blinded by the light."

Erik chuckled and placed a guiding hand on his friend's arm. "I think that's the general idea, and that was a bad pun, Counselor."

Martin nodded. "As soon as I said it, I realized. This place is incredible. I get no sense of scale, everything blends together in an endless sea of white. It's almost painful to keep my eyes open."

Erik barely noticed the bishops, he'd been so enamored by the room. They sat at a large table illuminated just as the walls surrounding them were. The flat surface was nearly invisible.

A voice broke their observations. "Come in, gentlemen, and close the door behind you."

Erik turned, closed the door and was stunned to see that it too was backlit. Once closed, the door was swallowed into the endless white morass perfecting the illusion.

Bishop O'Malley sat at a large marble conference table, to the right of a man that Erik judged to be in his late eighties or early nineties. All the men wore matching white tunics that again were perfectly blended with the walls and lighting. The visual effect made their heads appear to be floating in air. The old man's tunic was slightly different than his colleagues as was the large ornamental pin fastened to the ornate embroidery on his heavy robes.

The old man gestured toward two empty seats, barely distinguishable from their surroundings. "Gentlemen, please make yourselves comfortable. We have much to discuss about a great many things."

Erik and Martin walked toward their hosts, their colored clothing a ridiculous contrast to the pale surroundings. The detective seated himself as he continued to study the eerie chamber. His enhanced visual receptors had compensated for the unusual lighting and he was now able to clearly discern the outlines of the table, chairs and even the separate light panels illuminating the room's massive walls. The ceiling overhead was twenty feet high and the far wall was easily fifty feet away. The detective knew he'd taken several steps from the door to get to this large table and judged the room to be at least seventy feet wide. Erik could now detect that the walls were curved and they were inside a massive oval-shaped room similar to the Oval Office in the White House, only dozens of times larger. It was obvious the room had some significance but he had no idea what. He suspected they would learn that truth shortly.

"A most impressive room," the detective commented.

"The lights are of a special frequency and illumination that keep out unwanted ears and eyes, Detective. I'm sure men in your line of work can appreciate the need for precautions and certain rooms that those in the spy trade would call 'secure'. But we're not here to discuss the nature of our conference room. Rather, we must ascertain information and answer questions you may have."

"Starting with what you know about the being that killed my son," Denton boomed, asserting himself. Erik knew the wounded father wanted answers regarding his son's case. Everything else was secondary, including illusions and diplomacy.

"I assure you, Agent Denton and Detective Knight, we will attempt to unravel all of the mysteries you've unearthed. Your angst is understandable given the circumstances, but you must understand our need for secrecy. I've been given permission to enlighten you and forever change your lives."

Erik stood, reached into his pocket and tossed a plastic evidence bag directly toward the old man, then took his seat again. The light illuminated the fragments. "I believe these belong to you."

The old man picked up the bag examining the destroyed electronic eavesdropping devices. He looked over at the brash detective. "Our holy bureaucracy is very nosey and often uses less-than-appropriate means to gather intelligence." The old man placed the bag inside his tunic. "You live up to your reputation, Detective. Your police escorts have provided us several accounts of your unorthodox feats." The old man smiled warmly for a brief moment. "And I'm sure God does appreciate the repairs you made to his special home as does the Holy Father and all of us in this chamber."

Erik nodded, there was something about this old man—something special, that he couldn't put his finger on. The man didn't talk as much as he whispered. His words, however, blared like trumpets. The room they were in and the old man's demeanor were unsettling.

"Martin Denton, I am so sorry for the loss of your son. William was a fine young man and was on the road to becoming an impressive biblical scholar. We didn't realize he'd found the Chapel of Eternity. We knew he was reading several of the old tomes, but we believed all references to the chapel were removed from record."

Martin nodded slightly. "He was a smart young man. Sometimes too smart for his own good." Denton's eyes locked on to the older man. "What was kept down there? Who would resort to grotesque mass murder in order to obtain it?"

"If I may Archbishop," Bishop O'Malley interjected.

The old man nodded in agreement and leaned back in his chair. O'Malley bowed his head briefly in a gesture of reverence before turning toward Erik and Martin. "What was taken was the greatest holy relic on this planet. An instrument that was to be used to end the plague of evil unleashed during the final days of Man." O'Malley looked directly at Erik, "Have you read the Bible, Detective Knight, specifically the Revelation to St. John?"

Erik shook his head. "I'm familiar with that part of the Bible, though I'm far from scholarly." He looked around uncomfortably considering the company. "I know it pertains to the end of mankind, the second coming of the Son of God to Earth and the final expulsion of evil from this world. If I'm not mistaken, it refers to the cleansing and ultimate accounting of all souls. Those left alive after..." He searched his memory recalling the decades old lessons from his stepfather, "the Rapture, I believe is the correct term. Those souls not taken to Heaven during the Rapture will endure several torments, a literal Hell on Earth. After that torment the second coming of Christ will serve to drive away the evil, the Virgin Mary will slay the dragon and a new age will begin." The detective closed his eyes summoning his enhanced powers of memory, picturing the specific passages he'd seen in his youth.

"As he sat on the Mount of Olives, the disciples came to him privately, saying, 'Tell us, when will these things be, and what will be the sign of your coming and of the close of the age?' And Jesus answered them, 'See that no one leads you astray. For many will come in my name, saying, "I am the Christ," and they will lead many astray. And you will hear of wars and rumors of wars. See that you are not alarmed, for this must take place, but the end is not yet. For nation will rise against nation, and kingdom against kingdom, and there will be famines and earthquakes in various places.' Matthew

24:3:13." Erik wasn't sure if he'd cited the proper passage.

The Archbishop nodded. "'At that time shall arise Michael, the great prince who has charge of your people. And there shall be a time of trouble, such as never has been since there was a nation till that time. But at that time your people shall be delivered, everyone whose name shall be found written in the book. And many of those who sleep in the dust of the earth shall awake, some to everlasting life, and some to shame and everlasting contempt. And those who are wise shall shine like the brightness of the sky above; and those who turn many to righteousness, like the stars forever and ever. But you, Daniel, shut up the words and seal the book, until the time of the end. Many shall run to and fro, and knowledge shall increase.

"'Then I, Daniel, looked, and behold, two others stood, one on this bank of the stream and one on that bank of the stream. And someone said to the man clothed in linen, who was above the waters of the stream, "How long shall it be till the end of these wonders?" And I heard the man clothed in linen, who was above the waters of the stream; he raised his right hand and his left hand toward heaven and swore by him who lives forever that it would be for a time, times, and half a time, and that when the shattering of the power of the holy people comes to an end all these things would be finished. I heard, but I did not understand. Then I said, "O my lord, what shall be the outcome of these things?" He said, "Go your way, Daniel, for the words are shut up and sealed until the time of the end. Many shall purify themselves and make themselves white and be refined, but the wicked shall act wickedly. And none of the wicked shall understand, but those who are wise shall understand. And from the time that the regular burnt offering is taken away and the abomination that makes desolate is set up, there shall be 1,290 days. Blessed is he who waits and arrives at the 1,335 days. But go your way till the end. And you shall rest and shall stand in your allotted place at the end of the days."'

"'Behold, I am coming quickly, and My reward is with Me, to render to every man according to what he has done. "I am the Alpha and the Omega, the first and the last, the beginning and the end."'" The old man smirked and nodded slightly.

Erik nodded his head. "Daniel 12:1-13 and Revelation

22:12-13, give or take, I apologize it's been several years since
I've studied biblical verse."

The bishops stared at the detective dumbfounded and
O'Malley tilted his head. "You are modest, Detective. You're
more scholarly than you let on. You clearly know the Bible passages and there are many scholars who share your understanding of St. John's prophesy. Now that we have an accounting
of the subject matter we can begin our discussions. What you
don't know, Mr. Knight, is that the Holy Scriptures omit ref-
erence to the instrument of ushering in the new age after the
plagues and false prophets befall mankind. That instrument is
the Ruby Crucifix of Christ, a cross forged from the very wood
of the large cross the Romans used to crucify Jesus. The wood
forged into that holy relic was saturated with the blood and
tissue of the Son of God. This object is endowed with incredible
power from the Lords of Light."

"And that's what was locked inside that safe." Denton
shifted in his chair. "And why my son and his companions
were slaughtered."

O'Malley nodded. "Sadly, yes. Only a select few know the
secret location. Your son and his accomplices were trespassing
on sacred ground. Sadly, they paid the ultimate price."

The detective frowned contemplating O'Malley's remark.
"If I interpret the meaning behind what you've just said, Bishop, you're blaming William Denton and his friends for their
murders by claiming they should not have been where they
weren't supposed to be. With all due respect, your logic is
flawed. If they never were supposed to know this place existed
and you posted no sentries or warnings of any kind outside the
chamber doors to discourage potential trespassers, you share
a measure of responsibility as well. The 'Curiosity killed the
cat' mentality doesn't apply in this case. I would also add that
your efforts to expunge all references to the subterranean chapel were less than diligent if a young cleric was able to find the
location with some rudimentary reading and research. Frank-
ly, considering the light show you have here and the level of
sophistication you demonstrated in bugging hotel rooms, you
seem well equipped to keep out eavesdroppers. I'm appalled
at the lack of security at the basement chapel. If this object is

as priceless as you claim, and I have no reason to doubt your word, why not have a more elaborate system of protection?"

The old man gestured around the room. "The security in this chamber is not to thwart human eyes and ears, Detective. As for the holy chambers below St, Martha's, we feared that palace guards and proactive security precautions would only draw attention and announce that we were protecting something of intrinsic value. We felt by hiding the relic where we did and removing all references to it would increase rather than decrease security," countered the Archbishop. Erik felt the weight of the man's words despite his hushed tone.

He nodded considering the elder cleric's rationale. "I understand your reasoning but I don't agree with it." The detective stopped himself. Now wasn't the time to question their security protocol or their apparent lack of protection for such an important and powerful object. Erik wasn't totally prepared to accept everything that was said at face value but he'd withhold his conclusion until after their meeting. "Forgive my blunt reply, Archbishop. Now isn't the time to argue over security tactics. We need to find out who stole the relic and who killed Brother Denton and his friends." Erik considered the Archbishop's words: *Not meant to thwart human eyes and ears.* The theory he'd presented Martin seemed more credible.

The Archbishop nodded. "Our most Holy Father Church is very secretive, Detective Knight, and I have no doubt your efforts on our behalf were somewhat hampered by the Church's desire for secrecy. The Church, like any other government, has its state secrets. I trust you understand and respect that."

"I do." Erik nodded.

"Please, tell us what you've uncovered." The Archbishop assumed control. "Also, before we begin, I am aware of your ability to probe the thoughts of men. I trust that you will respect the bounds of decency and not probe the minds of anyone here during these deliberations. I have no intentions of lying to you, Detective, but the idea of someone plundering my thoughts uninvited is most disturbing. All men have secrets, even men such as us. I imagine you would not appreciate someone probing your thoughts and pray that you will accord us the same courtesy."

Erik tilted his head slightly but did little else to reveal his shock. The Vatican had done their homework regarding him. "I don't go where I'm not invited, sir."

The Archbishop nodded and smiled. "Splendid, let's begin." The old man gestured toward Erik and shot him a disarming smile.

"As you already know, you were robbed. The murders seemed to be an afterthought. What disturbs me most was the severity of the killings. This wasn't simple murder to cover a crime. This was more in the line of vengeance killing, or even a perverse desire to maim and torture. The victims were slaughtered." Erik paused allowing the bishops a few moments to digest what he'd said. "Then we have the wanton destruction and vandalism caused by the perpetrator. The destruction appeared motivated by anger, like a finishing touch to some sort of revenge vendetta, a way to rub salt in an open wound." Now he was going to challenge their beliefs by describing what he'd seen and the means he went about seeing it. Erik hoped the Archbishop's earlier words were an indication they wouldn't be laughed out of Vatican City.

"As you're all aware I possess some rather unique talents. One of those talents is the ability to see images embedded in physical objects, a kind of psychic echo detection. I witnessed some of the events that occurred in the Chapel of Eternity by examining a large cross that had been handled by Brother Denton."

The Archbishop nodded. "Yes, we received some colorful rantings from Michael and Neko regarding your particular exploits."

Erik laughed. "I'm sure." The detective continued wondering how best to broach the unusual conclusion he'd arrived at with Martin and his plan to unearth the identity of William's killer. "I saw men literally ripped apart by a single man shrouded in black. I felt the abject fear and terror from each man as they perished and the heroism of Martin's son as he gave his life to save his friend, Brother Peter. I assume you already have reports on the condition of the bodies when they were discovered."

The Archbishop and Bishop O'Malley nodded slightly

confirming the detective's findings.

"Then we have the unusual darkened blood on the cross Brother Peter used as a weapon. The blood is markedly different from any other blood smears and stains that I've encountered, excluding some extraterrestrial blood. The blood samples we provided you and the ones Special Agent Denton had sent to our satellite offices should unearth some of the mystery surrounding our lone killer, and that leads to the next mystery." Erik looked directly at the Archbishop. "One killer, one being, was able to topple those huge statues, overturn a six thousand pound stone slab and rip open a heavy duty corrugated steel safe and not only enter the chamber unseen but leave unseen as well." Erik glanced over at Martin. "As my colleague addressed during our investigation, only one person he knows of is capable of performing such feats, and I have a solid alibi for my whereabouts."

The bishops appeared uncomfortable, each man looking around nervously, glancing at O'Malley and then the Archbishop.

"Are you implying our perpetrator is an alien hybrid like yourself?" O'Malley finally spoke.

Erik shook his head. "No. If this was an Esper or Seelak I'd feel the alien presence. What I felt was evil, gentlemen, an unmitigated evil and more importantly our deceased and Brother Peter share the same opinion." Erik took a deep breath before continuing. "I saw the conflict through William Denton's eyes. I felt the fear and dread he had. It was so strong that the emotions embedded themselves on the large pole cross he used as a makeshift bludgeon. The feelings of dread and terror nearly consumed me. I saw that hooded specter feed on one of the brothers before ripping him apart." Erik looked at the Archbishop. "I saw what it did to Brother Denton after he attacked it. What is the Vatican's position on vampires? Because as far as I can tell, based on the evidence at hand, some being with vampiric powers and tendencies is responsible for what occurred under St. Martha's Chapel." Erik gestured around the mysterious white room. "I assume this room was built to keep out the darkness or evil if I may be so blunt."

The bishops remained silent so the detective continued.

"This also poses another riddle. Forgive my assumption because I really have no knowledge of the evil undead. I thought vampires and the like weren't able to exist in a holy place like a church or someplace special, dare I even say sacred as a chapel containing the most holy relic on the planet. Why didn't this vampire go 'poof' or is that simply fiction?"

Ten silent seconds passed and Erik's question hung in the tense atmosphere. "What are you people hiding? You just said minutes ago you were going to astound us with some deep dark truths and answers." He turned toward the Archbishop. "Was what killed Brother William a vampire or some kind of being with similar abilities? If so what other kinds of 'creepy crawlies' are running around at night preying on humanity? What's out there that requires a room of this type?"

The Archbishop nodded slightly and leaned forward. "Yes, Mr. Knight, vampires are real, as are demons and ghosts." The old man paused expecting the detective to scoff or laugh. "I see you have an open mind. Good."

The detective smiled. "Archbishop, if you have studied me, then you know I'm not fully human. I've learned to accept the unbelievable since I'm living proof that the strange things people mock can be true."

"Well said, Detective Knight. We have been at war with evil for several centuries and I fear that the forces of Light are not faring so well right now. Humanity is being seduced down the path of darkness with the sins of greed, lust, and avarice at a pace we cannot combat. Our church has been infected with men who claim to serve God yet wind up performing great evil instead. We have been caught flat footed the last decade, unable to adjust or cope with humanity's rapid descent into secular humanism and worship of technology over theology. We cannot combat the internet and the perverse aversions found in cyberspace. We are fighting a losing war and humanity is descending, happily, into the bowels of Hell. Departed souls of the warped and wicked are set free to plague mankind and terrorize the innocent. Evil beings inhabit the darker places of civilization while penetrating the areas of human power and leadership by buying political influence with money and power. We have lost the war for the heart of man and are rapidly losing the soul of mankind as well."

The Archbishop glanced at O'Malley. "Evil beings should not have been able to approach, let alone enter such a sacred hall. How this was accomplished is a mystery we need to solve."

Erik snapped his fingers. "The garb! The black garb was covering him head to toe. When the hood fell off and exposed his face, his flesh sizzled. Somehow that black garb he wore offered him the necessary shielding. We found black fibers in the chapel. Once they're analyzed we'll know what kind of fabric was used."

Another bishop shook his head. "I don't know of any fabric spun on Earth that can offer an evil soul the kind of protection required to enter that chapel, let alone handle the holiest relic on Earth."

"Then perhaps you'd best consider an 'other worldly' material, because it's obvious some type of fabric exists somewhere that allowed a Dark being to enter your facility, kill my son, and rob you blind," Denton interjected, frustrated at the lack of progress made in their investigation.

Erik placed a comforting hand on his friend's shoulder. "I'm confident our techs at the lab will give us some kind of lead, we'll follow up later today on our end and hopefully the people studying the samples we provided you will have some answers as well. At that point, we can compare notes and see where we are with the evidence." Erik looked back at the Archbishop. "Let's focus on the 'who' and the 'when', right now."

"I don't follow, Detective."

"You said this relic is of pivotal importance? I'm assuming that having it stolen at this point in time is significant. What events occurred recently that would lead the other side to such a drastic move? I presume this is a drastic move. Also let's address the 'how' as to how did your enemies find the relic? Who tipped them off? How many people in Vatican City knew about the existence of the chapel hidden below St. Martha's? That's our suspect pool to help us locate a rotten apple inside Vatican City."

"Are you accusing someone here of being an agent of evil, Mr. Knight?" A bishop asked, clearly offended.

"I'm doing what you should be doing, Your Excellency,

asking the relevant questions that need answering in order to solve this riddle. I'm not pointing a finger at anybody—yet. We have a great shortage of facts, gentlemen, and right now as we speak, whoever took your relic is either going to sell it for a huge sum of money or was merely a pawn in a higher scheme and paid handsomely to perform this high risk deed. One doesn't simply decide to rob a place such as this. It takes time and careful planning and a great deal of information. Now let's go back to why stealing this object now would be relevant. What's going on now that would spur the forces of darkness to commit such a wanton act and who has the power and ability to pull off such a theft and commit the kind of vandalism we discovered?"

Erik and Martin both stared at the Archbishop.

The old man nodded. "I will tell you more of the war and then you will understand why the relic was stolen and the role you, yourself, may play, Mr. Knight."

Erik leaned back in his chair, his instincts told him he was about to hear some life-changing information and he braced himself for it. "Please." Erik gestured toward the Archbishop, "Enlighten me."

"We know all about you, Detective—your ancestry, your lineage and we know the history of the Espers and Seelak as well as the war they fought on their home world thousands of years ago. All was written in the Apostles' Scrolls. What wasn't written or preordained was your existence. You were a stop-gap measure, designed for an event that was never supposed to occur. We understood the Esper/ Seelak problem had been resolved some hundred centuries or so in our past. But the forces of darkness interceded and allowed the hideous alien constructs to be freed. The very act of releasing those creatures is what led to your creation and your destiny."

Erik nodded slightly, doing his best to hide his shock. The Vatican knew all about other worlds and the existence of aliens—things they once denied in their teachings. "I'm aware of my history, sir and the history of that half of my lineage."

The Archbishop smiled slightly. "I know, Detective, but you need to realize we know as well." The old man sipped from a small white tea cup. "You were never supposed to exist, at least not in your current form. We—or rather the forces of Light—allowed the Esper's corrective measure to be implemented, since it was our forces that gave them the inspiration for the idea. As I stated earlier, you were a failsafe mechanism that was never meant to be used. When the Seelak creatures were unleashed and you failed to stop them, we had to allow you to change, even knowing that doing so could bring about a catastrophic acceleration of the war for this planet. Our choice was either to allow the Seelak creatures to breed and continue to feed on humanity or allow the Esper stopgap to be created and risk an escalation of our current conflict. We had no choice. The Seelak had to be stopped and as the Hybrid, you were the chosen weapon to do so."

Martin gasped while Erik's stomach churned.

"There's a war going on, Detective, all around you every day, unseen by most. It's a war we're losing at an alarming pace."

"Good versus Evil," Martin injected awestruck.

"Very astute, Mr. Denton, Good versus Evil. The battle has spread into politics, other religions, big business and technology, every facet of human existence is ripe with soldiers on both sides manipulating and coercing the events of mankind in an effort to gain the upper hand for the ultimate prize."

"Earth and the billions of souls that inhabit it," Erik added in a dread-filled monotone.

The Archbishop nodded slightly. "Earth, Detective, and the right to forge it on a path of prosperity for good, or a literal Hell here on this plain of existence. The Ruby Crucifix has the power to banish evil and usher in the second coming of Christ, but only one being, a son of Adam and the stars, has the power to wield and control the forces contained within the cross. Anyone else attempting to wield such power would be eradicated and his life and soul vaporized into oblivion. Only one being human or ethereal has the power to wield this most holy of objects. Do you understand me, Detective?"

Erik shook his head, denying what the religious elder implied. "No. No, I'm not buying it. I'm not some holy prophet in your war. I'm just a man, albeit with mixed DNA but I'm far from a Lord of Light or prophet worthy of anyone's consideration."

Denton's face paled, practically matching the room's ivory white. "The markings in your tattoo, Erik. For the love of God, the markings on your arm! Is that why you have them?"

The Archbishop tilted his head. "Markings? May I see them?"

Erik hesitated. He'd instinctively covered his tattooed arm with his hand, shielding the art work. His arm tingled and throbbed.

"Erik, you have to show them. If they can read those symbols…." Denton paused, letting his words hang in the air.

Erik closed his eyes, then nodded. "All right." He stood and unbuttoned his shirt, the tingling sensation in his arm increased as he tossed the garment on the table. The bishops gasped as they saw the Angelic script burning white hot beneath the dark tribal band artwork etched in his flesh.

"By the Holy Father! Look at that! The symbols! Celestial, Son and Adam!" Bishop O'Malley croaked in shock.

"My God, they're glowing like a white star," Martin gasped. "Erik, does it hurt?"

The detective shook his head. "No, they just tingle a bit, but there's no pain at all."

"Erik Knight, you have been chosen by the Lord of Light, marked as a soldier in the coming days of darkness. You've been selected by the Eternals of Heaven to be their standard bearer." The Archbishop looked at the detective with a sense of awe and amazement. "Do you understand your role and reason for being, Mr. Knight? You're the one being that can end the encroaching darkness. You can unleash the power of the relic and make this planet a garden paradise once again."

Erik put his shirt back on and buttoned it, not liking what the bishops implied. "I'm just a man, albeit a hybrid man, but still a man. I live a quiet unassuming life now and I'm happy. I'm not a saint. I'm not a holy warrior, and I'm far from what Heaven would want in a soldier. This is a mystery we can figure out later. Right now we're here to figure out who killed Martin's son and why."

The Archbishop leaned forward. "I understand your reluctance and can feel your shock, Detective, but you must understand the magnitude of this revelation. You're a key to the bigger mystery surrounding the Ruby Crucifix. Your existence is contrary to the original plan established for this world, and now the forces of Light have seen fit to bring you into their fold. This is a moment of religious doctrine that will have our scholars busy for years."

"Where in any doctrine are the Espers or the Seelak?" Martin chimed in. "Or any of this? I know I'm the least person qualified to comment on religion, but I don't recall anything in scripture that covers aliens, a war of the type you mentioned, or the existence of such a relic. What I know of Christian teaching is in direct conflict to this. Until recently, the Church taught that the Earth was the center of the universe and barely 6000 years old. Was this just some lie to control the masses?"

"Nothing so sinister, Agent Denton. When the holy words were written down, it was decided then that much of what the Apostles said would not be accepted by people. The concept of Christ rising from the dead, the miracles he performed on Earth, and his ascension into Heaven were enough in themselves to challenge credibility and believability in the minds and hearts of men. Imagine if the Bible spoke of alien worlds, great battles being fought outside our realm of knowledge and comprehension. At the time the Bible was written, we'd have been mocked and sullied, possibly even stoned for making such outlandish claims despite such wild tales being absolutely true. Even now, mankind's arrogance has difficulty believing in anything greater than itself. Faith and belief are at an alarming shortage. In the age of the internet, computers and flat screen television, religion and faith are considered archaic. The forces of Dark have outdone themselves getting God banned in the schools, in the courts, and almost everywhere else. Even now in these modern times putting up a Nativity scene at Christmas is considered an abomination. Secular humanism is rapidly supplanting any organized religion and the advent of technology and pornography has dominated the souls of mankind."

The Archbishop paused and took a deep breath. "I apologize, I'm meandering. We gave mankind what we thought it could handle at the time according to those we serve. Worlds of higher intellect were kept apart by great distances so that each could develop separately and worship in their own way.

Each planet that evolves and develops is eventually embroiled in ethereal conflict. God wants the souls He nurtured to share His paradise. Those cast out in the beginning wish to steal as many souls as possible and even dominate some worlds turning them into Hell planets condemning the populations to eternal torment."

Denton shuddered. "I don't pretend to understand any of this, but if God is all powerful according to your mythos why not simply eradicate all the evil in one fell swoop and establish whatever He desires. Wouldn't that be the easiest solution rather than all this subterfuge and secrecy?"

"Free will, Mr. Denton. Each advanced species must find God on their own and choose to worship him freely. Each soul is free to choose the Light or the Dark path. Since Lucifer made the choice not to serve and was cast out of paradise, each species is given the opportunity to choose God, or not. We establish forces on these planets to assure that the ethereal rules are followed and evil does not run roughshod over souls that don't choose the darker path. If the forces of Light and Dark collided unchecked on each world, there would be no mortal life forms left alive to claim for either side. God is all powerful, but Lucifer and his armies are immortal. Once a gift is given, it cannot be taken away. Lucifer has the gifts and powers of the Heavenly Hosts and he uses them for ill; his free will." The Archbishop gestured toward Erik. "And you have your powers, Detective, given to you freely and expanded upon so you can participate in the upcoming war. Your expanded powers also helped you vanquish the Observer threat several years ago and will allow you to stand against the darkness in the upcoming conflict."

Erik sighed not ready to accept some bizarre religious prophecy, especially from a religion that was responsible for the suicide of his stepbrother so many years ago. The detective steeled himself forcing the revelations to the back of his mind. "Let me be very clear, I am not interested in your war. I'm interested in finding William Denton's killer. Whatever this tattoo means, or the markings hidden there, I'll unearth once we've solved that mystery." His tone cracked like an angry whip

The room fell silent. The Archbishop took a moment to gather himself. "We all want to find William's killer, Detective.

Someone as astute as you must see the link between what you are and the reason for the holy relic's theft at this time. We believe your very existence, contrary to the initial plan for this world, is what triggered the events that have come to unfold before us like a dark road."

Erik pointed toward the old man. "Are you implying I'm responsible for William's death? That's absurd! I didn't know him and have been half a world away." Erik glanced over at Martin and the senior agent nodded his support for his young friend.

"We're giving you the 'Why' to your original query Detective. Why was the relic stolen? The Holy Father and the Papal Council all believe because the forces of Light allowed your transformation to occur. Had you simply died in the hospital all those years ago after your combat, the forces of Dark would not have felt threatened and would not have felt compelled to commit the wanton act that occurred in our chamber and the relic would still be safe within our custody. You upset their current advantage, Detective. You and your lineage should not exist. Because you do, you are a threat to the forces of Dark looking to keep their dominant foothold on this world. Stealing the relic halts the second coming and keeps Earth sliding toward the morass of evil and darkness. "

"You can't blame Erik for the change then, Archbishop … you should blame God."

"Heresy!"

"Blasphemer!!!"

The Bishops' Council exploded at Denton's accusation. To his credit the elder agent didn't recoil or back down. Denton pushed forward and stated his case to the stunned holy men.

"If Erik is part of a divine plan by the forces of Light, as you claim, then God wanted him to be what he is. You just said your boss forced the change rather than letting Erik expire from the wounds he sustained battling the Seelak constructs all those years ago. If that's true, then your boss…" Denton pointed toward the ceiling, "…is the one responsible for the theft and the deaths that occurred here, not Erik. Detective Knight would just be a pawn on God's chessboard, as are all of us. If the forces of Light are as involved as you claim, how much free will do any of us really have? Were we compelled to come here? Was Erik compelled by some outside force to clean up the mess in that lower chamber? If free will is important, and I'm just taking you at your word, Archbishop, how much of it do we really have? I've seen similar symbols to the ones on Detective Knight's body in my own agency. They've been cleverly disguised on staffing orders, requisition documents, and even some classified materials pertaining to clandestine operations throughout the world. In fact, when I began digging, I was given a friendly warning not to pursue the matter further and then forced to retire. If your forces are in Washington and in Boston, I'm betting the other side is just as embroiled and embedded. I may even go so far as to hypothesize that some of your faction on both sides are part of the shadow government we've been working to uncover the last several years."

The Archbishop nodded. "You would blame God, Agent Denton."

Denton's face burned with anger, a rage that could split rock. "Yes, I would. I'm pointing the finger where logic and the facts dictate it be pointed. Let God come here and tell me I'm wrong." The old man looked up. "Well!!! Am I wrong? Did you let my boy die?? Was his death part of some grand plan?" Tears rolled down Martin's cheeks. "Answer me you son of a bitch, I'm here, in your face, asking you point blank … or are you going to be silent and cowardly, hiding behind the skirts of these sheep? What kind of God lets an innocent boy die for nothing?"

Martin glared at the ceiling, his hands balled into fists, tears streaming down his face. "Just tell me why." His voice cracked. "Just tell me why you let my son be butchered like a side of beef."

Erik stepped up and pulled his friend into a hug. "It's okay Martin, we'll find out, I promise you." The detective helped his friend back into his seat and poured him a hot cup of tea from an ivory kettle. The holy men were still in shock over Martin's outburst, half expecting God to make a statement in HIS own defense.

Erik took a moment to compose himself. His mind reeled at the revelations. Good, Evil, Heaven, Hell, Angels and Demons— all real, and even more bizarre than any cleric, or layman, could ever comprehend. The forces of Light and Dark were constantly battling for worlds across the universe in a titanic game of chess with endless galaxies as their board. Even with all his incredible power, Erik felt insignificant at the thought of beings moving across galaxies fighting and warring to gain human and apparently non-human souls. He saw to his friend's wellbeing before facing the bishops. "I'm not interested in your holy war, or your prophecy, or your stolen relic at this point. I'm interested in who killed a young cleric by the name of William Denton. Your story, as fascinating as it is, will have to go on the back burner. I'll accept it as the rationale for 'Why' the relic was stolen. Your story means William and his colleagues were simply in the wrong place at the wrong time and our killer decided to butcher them out of spite." Erik glanced at the Archbishop. "I assume you have a list of everyone who knew of the chapel's existence. That's your suspect pool. Somebody gave up the location and usually such a betrayal involves money or blackmail. We'll have to run financial reports and check bank transactions for everyone on that list. If you find any anomalies in the bank records, you'll have a logical place to start looking for your leak. Also have your people examine social patterns. Has anyone on that list broken routine, met with new people, or requested an extended leave of absence?"

"Are you implying that a man of God could be suspect in such heinous actions?" A bishop challenged.

Erik looked toward the lean man and nodded. "Yes, I am. It's the most logical place to start looking. If everything checks out, then look at people they're close with." Erik looked at all the men, his eyes scanning each bishop. "Secrets are only as good as those who keep them. If the men and women on your list weren't bought or coerced, then the next thing to determine is whether they shared more than they should have with somebody?" Erik paused, his voice dropping a full octave. "Prudence is often set aside during pillow talk, gentlemen."

"Men of the cloth are holy and celibate, Mr. Knight. We are above such things" A bishop added his tone indicating his outrage and indignation at the detective's implication.

Erik tilted his head and smiled a wicked grin. "Tell that to all the altar boys who were molested in Boston. I'm sure they'll find great comfort in knowing the abstinence of your clergy. My stepbrother didn't find much comfort in that fact while he was being molested and brutalized."

The room fell silent. Each bishop looked away, unable to stare at the detective as he made his brutal counterpoint.

"I'm sure that was a great comfort to him as he took his own life because no one would believe a priest was capable of such things, including his own overly fanatical parents. So please, take your self-righteous indignation and stick it where the sun doesn't shine. You're no better or worse than anybody else. But, perhaps you have the cornerstone on hypocrisy." Erik's words were daggers cutting deep wounds in the bishops and Archbishop.

The Archbishop cleared his throat and took a sip of tea. "I am sorry for your wounds, Detective. I can tell the hurt is deep and the scar unhealed. It shames me to admit that you are correct. We are not perfect. We're merely flesh and blood, like you. Some of us gave into darker urges and committed terrible, unspeakable things, but some men deliberately entered the priesthood from the darkness to throw our church in disarray and cast the net of doubt on all. As I stated earlier, we were caught flat footed, unable to react to the rapid pace our enemies schemed. We failed our faithful. We failed our God and we failed your stepbrother. I can't undo the past, Erik. I can only assure you that everything possible is being done to vet out the weeds hiding in God's garden and purge them. I understand your bitterness and am grateful you put aside your hatred to help us unearth Brother Denton's killer. It's my hope that you will also consider extending your myriad skills in helping us find any potential leak that may exist within our hierarchy. But believe me, son of Adam and of the stars, you are part of a much bigger plan and whether you want to or not, you will be forced to choose a side in the upcoming conflict. I don't possess the clairvoyance of a prophet but that much I know. You were created for a purpose, Detective, and it isn't solving petty mysteries, battling aliens, or playing spy across the globe. Your purpose is bigger than you choose to believe. You are the warrior, a soldier of Light, Erik. In a time when darkness falls across the world, you are the chosen guardian against the encroaching evil. You will have to make a choice, fight on the side of Light, or allow darkness to lay claim and waste to this world, establishing an eternal Hell on Earth." The Archbishop pointed toward him and, again, Erik felt the weight and subtle power behind the frail man. "Sometimes, Detective, we simply have no choice. When the time comes, my heart tells me you will do the right thing for the right reason. I can only pray for you."

Erik shook his head. The Archbishop was a very determined soul. "I don't know what to say. I didn't come here to get involved in a war of such epic proportion. I didn't come here to get involved in any theological cataclysmic happenings. I can't even fathom the things you're claiming and I haven't considered faith, religion or God since the death of my stepbrother. My days of being a warrior are past. I'm a husband, parent, gym manager and PI when a case lands on my desk. Right now, that's enough for me." Erik looked over at Martin. His friend was silent with sorrowful eyes. Martin should be somewhere dealing with his grief surrounded by family and friends, not getting sucked into biblical conflicts between warring factions and being told his son was partially responsible for his own death. "I ask again, Archbishop, can we please get back to the matter at hand." Erik glanced at the bishops, they were still ruffled at his sharp rebuke. He needed to move past that moment. He silently cursed, why didn't he just swallow his venom and hold his tongue. This wasn't the time to address those wounds. "Let me offer my apologies, I should have chosen my words more carefully. I let my private life and my personal feelings interfere with my job. That won't happen again. I know only a small fraction of priests are responsible for the crimes I mentioned and on the whole most are solid, holy men. But you're correct, Archbishop, some wounds don't heal. Might I suggest we adjourn for a while? I know Mr. Denton would like to see his son. Can some arrangement be made? I believe he's been extremely patient and reasonably restrained all things considered. After Mr. Denton has taken care of those most important personal matters, we can continue our investigation."

Bishop O'Malley nodded, accepting the olive branch offered by the detective. "An excellent idea Mr. Knight." He gestured toward two underlings. "Get three clerics to escort Mr. Denton to our holding facility. He is to be granted access to his son's body. Contact my undersecretary to coordinate a time when we can discuss Brother Denton's final resting place with Mr. Denton as well." O'Malley looked over at the elder agent. "Your escorts will be here shortly." The cleric turned toward Erik. "I'll have my staff print a list of people who knew about the Ruby Crucifix and its location. If you and Mr. Denton would like to work with our staff to run through banking records, we would welcome the help. I refuse to get caught flat footed again."

Erik nodded as he headed toward the ivory white door. "We'll do what we can, Archbishop. May I make one more request?"

"Indeed, Detective, if it is within my power to grant."

"I'd like an artist brought in, if that's possible—a really good artist. I have a picture in my head of our killer and I want to get that picture on paper so we can put out some feelers and hopefully get a lead on him." Erik paused. "Or it … if we're considering the alternatives."

The Archbishop nodded. "Father Donlan is a most gifted artist, I'll have him summoned here."

Erik nodded and smiled. "Thanks."

Erik and Martin were escorted out of the white room to a nearby lounge area.

"I think we're going to be here another day or so, Martin."

The old man nodded in agreement. "At least. Hopefully we'll get somewhere when we get back." Denton studied his friend. "How are you holding up? I honestly didn't ask you here to get bombarded with all this 'Chosen being of Light' revelation." Denton shifted in his seat. "I have to admit though, seeing those symbols glow on your skin made my flesh tingle. I've been in some pretty deep shit in the last thirty-five years, Erik, and have never once felt in over my head. I don't mind admitting that I'm feeling that way for the first time in my career." Denton frowned shaking his head.

Erik curled his fingers into a tight fist. "Martin, I'm right there with you. I thought after the Observer incident nothing would faze or surprise me." The detective chuckled. "This little revelation from our Vatican friends disturbs my calm. I promised I wouldn't read their minds, but I left my senses open to their mental pathways and the Archbishop believes what he's saying. There's no sense of deceit in any of them. There was a sense of shame and embarrassment when I brought up the clergy abuse but even then, what the Archbishop said had the ring of truth to it. They've been behind the power curve in whatever's going on between the two factions. They can't seem to adjust their tactics to compensate for the world changing around them and they're quite flustered."

"So what's our plan going forward?"

Erik shook his head. "We do just what I said. Review the names and review the financials and hope the money trail gives us a few suspects. After we get our picture of the man or thing that murdered William, we'll send an image to the agency and have it run through every database our EYES system can access. If that comes up blank, I have a source we can try. But my gut tells me our murder suspect is someone familiar to Vatican City." Erik balled his right hand into a fist. "You don't hire someone to perform a job of this nature without him having intimate knowledge of the target area. This was an inside job, Martin. I'd bet my house on it. All we have are suspicions and theories right now. We'll know more shortly and we can adjust our plan of attack accordingly."

Denton sat back and nodded. "Agreed." The old man laughed. "I'm almost looking forward to retirement at this point. I admit I'm going to have to reassess my entire philosophical paradigm once this is over."

Erik chuckled. "No shit, you and me both."

Three men approached them. "Mr. Denton, sir. We are here to escort you to see your son."

Erik placed a hand on his friend's shoulder. "I can still be there if you want, Martin. You don't have to do this alone."

Denton placed his shaky hand over Erik's, his eyes heavy. "I've got this. Thank you though. I need to see my boy. We need to talk." A sob escaped him. "I need to say goodbye to my son."

Erik watched sadly as his friend was escorted out of the room. Despite all the intrigue, suspense, and terror they'd endured, the awful purpose of their trip came crashing down upon both men.

* * *

Salisbury, Delaware. Warehouse district

Speaker of the House, Andrew Collins, felt the overpowering weight of the being standing next to him. Bartholomew's aura of power seemed wan compared to the intense presence. The being was easily six and half feet tall with annoyingly perfect skin and hair. Despite having the appearance and build of a powerful man, his face seemed childlike and innocent if not for those eyes. The eyes threatened to burn though the speaker every time they studied him. Collins couldn't endure the weight of that stare for more than two seconds at a time.

"The facility is six hundred feet below this warehouse. We'll have to take the elevator." Collins pressed the button silently hoping he'd be spared the awkward silence waiting for the elevator to arrive. The door opened and he smiled with relief, waving the being inside.

The large entity carefully studied the metal box and gently probed the walls with long slender fingers.

"It's an elevator."

The being turned. "Elevator," he repeated, cautiously stepping inside.

The doors closed and the metal box began to descend. The sudden motion alarmed the being and it tensed, arms raised and eyes burning with unknown power.

"It's okay," Collins soothed. "You're in no danger, I promise you. The elevator is taking us down to a storage area where your relic is being kept."

The being looked down at his chaperone. His gaze burned through the human. Collins felt his mind being probed and knew he was powerless to resist the intrusion. "I'm not lying, I assure you."

"You speak the truth, for now." The reply was icy and cold.

An involuntary shudder raced down the speaker's spine. "We were both deceived." Collins attempted to placate the being.

"I was told this. I will not harm you, human. Your fears are pointless." The being held up a silver case. "I've been told only to take back what is ours. Other matters will be sorted out by higher powers."

Collins managed a quick smile and relief washed over his body. "I'm relieved and I too believe you."

The rest of the descent was spent in silence. After two uncomfortably long minutes the elevator stopped and the doors opened, revealing a dimly lit corridor. Collins stepped out, gesturing down the large hallway. "This way."

The divine being followed in silence, eyes scanning every detail. Collins could only imagine what kind of data his guest stored inside that inhuman brain. There were several items he'd rather be kept secret and having this being studying every nook and cranny of his private stronghold was unnerving. After a brief walk they arrived at a heavy vault door. Collins immediately knew something was wrong. The guards protecting the relic were missing! The massive door had been forced open, hanging by a single warped hinge.

"Oh shit, no!" Collins walked swiftly toward the vault, "No! No! No!" The broken, bloodied corpses of his two guards littered the floor. Both men had drawn their guns and the speaker noticed that one of the pistols had been completely emptied. Dark blood stains intermixed with their human blood. They didn't go down without a fight. The dead men looked withered, like dried husks of corn. "What happened to them? What sort of thing could do this to a man?" Collins went to the hidden shelf where he'd stashed the relic. It was gone. He looked over at the being of Light, literally terrified.

The being studied the dark blood, rubbing a sample between his thumb and index finger. He looked over at the speaker. "Nosferatu!" he spat in disgust.

"I swear to you, we didn't do this. No one could possibly have known the relic was here! The shroud kept its presence hidden..." Collins stammered, panicked. "I don't understand. What is a nosferatu?" Collins asked in a desperate attempt to buy himself time to figure a way out of this mess.

"Foot soldiers of Molec! They have been here since the beginning, cast out during the first war. They chose not to serve like their master. The Father took their beauty and made them malformed wraiths of death." The being of Light pointed to the corpses. "They have been drained of their life force and their souls have been consumed. They have been touched by the cursed undead." The soldier of Light looked toward Collins. "The blood of the Son has been defiled and is out of our reach!" The being's anger and frustration was palpable. "You will suffer for this. The higher lords will not endure this ignominy."

The speaker knew whatever bargain had been struck was now null and void. He glanced over at his butchered guards and then looked back towards the soldier of Light. The being had vanished as if swallowed by the air. "By the powers! We've just escalated the annihilation of mankind." He ran toward the elevator pulling out his cell phone. Collins waited impatiently cursing as the elevator slowly ascended. "Give me a bar damn you!" he yelled at his cell phone. After another minute of cursing, the cell phone registered. He dialed a number while pacing frantically. "Paul, we're in some deep shit! Get on our special phone and let our people know the relic was stolen from us! Right out of the damn warehouse! Our guards are dead and we've been compromised. Let our superiors in the Capitol know and get a team over here immediately. Oh and tell them our heavenly source blames the theft on someone or something called a nosferatu." Collins was quiet for a moment. "Yeah, it seems we have a mole in our organization. Listen Paul, we need to find this thing and fast ... and return it to the rightful owners because we've just lit the fire on a holy war of totally epic proportions. The being I was with was pissed and he just vanished like a fart in the wind! The forces of Light already know we lost their treasure and we are responsible. If the forces of Light go nuclear, we're all done for." Collins nodded a few more times. "Yeah, good idea, smart man!!! Call Henderson and let him know too! Odds are he's probably already been informed but he can serve as a barometer on just how bad the 'other' side is taking this. If you can convince Henderson we were victims too, we still may be able to keep this genie in a bottle."

* * *

Vatican City, Rome

Several bishops whispered amongst themselves, conversation tinged with desperate words, He tried not to listen but the words, 'Stolen', 'Escalate' and 'War' repeated among the hushed tones. Two other clergy sat in a far corner thumbing through a folder hastily scribbling notes. Two other bishops were talking on ivory colored cellphones, pacing to and fro, hands frantically gesturing as they spoke. The Archbishop wore a deep scowl, frail fingers clutched a small silver cross suspended from an ivory chain. He mumbled some kind of prayer as his right arm made the sign of the cross blessing the room. The Archbishop's stoic sense of calm was no longer evident.

Erik waited until the door closed and the room once again became a seamless sea of ivory. Once the door closed everyone took their seats. "My apologies, Archbishop, I'm not reading anyone but I can sense panic among all of you. I gather something significant has happened. And judging from the tense energy, I'm assuming the news isn't good."

"You are astute, Detective." The old cleric nodded. "We were informed by our sources in Washington that the Ruby Crucifix was stolen from those who stole it from us."

"Washington?" Erik's voice jumped an octave.

"That doesn't surprise me. It seems Washington is the nexus for all sorts of normal and paranormal criminal activity." Denton folded his hands, resting his forehead against clasped fingers. "So the trail for all of this leads back to DC, including my son's killer." The elder agent had been stoic and subdued since his return from seeing his son.

"That would be a logical assumption. If the relic made its way to Washington, we can assume that the perp is the one who brought it." Erik poured some iced water from a large pitcher and poured some for his friend. "Could you please give us a little more detail?"

"One of our operatives in Washington was contacted regarding the relic. He was told the relic was stolen by mistake."

Erik frowned. "Mistake? How do you steal something by mistake and commit acts of violence in the process? It would seem the activity here was most deliberate."

The Archbishop nodded in agreement. "Indeed. It appears the thief had a personal agenda in addition to robbery. We don't have many details yet. Our people there are still gathering information."

Erik nodded impatiently. "I think we figured that much out already. Did you learn anything more about who took the relic? What about who ordered the theft?"

"One of our soldiers was led to a warehouse outside of Washington, then taken a very large distance below the ground. His guide was the speaker of the House of Representatives. We also learned that the relic is stored within some type of shroud to keep its presence concealed." The Archbishop frowned. "I confess I am baffled at how anything can hide such a powerful object from the forces of Light."

"Andrew Collins, Speaker of the House is involved with this?" Denton exclaimed. "He was our liaison to the President during our investigation to uncover the rogue elements operating the underground government in DC." The CIA agent took a long drink of water and cleared his throat. "We kept him abreast of all our activity and gave him names of people we were investigating. That bastard was probably informing the very people we were trying to root out."

Erik nodded. "That explains why we were always a step behind in our investigation. But we have a name now, somebody we can dig into. If Collins is dirty we'll track him down and ring out whatever tidbits of information he's got. The speaker has a high profile in Washington. There aren't many rat holes he can hide in without having to surface for air once in a while. That's the price you pay for a powerful gig. Everyone knows who you are." Erik looked over at Bishop O'Malley. "Were you able to get a list of names for us to check and more importantly, did you find the artist?"

O'Malley gestured to a thin man sitting nervously in a corner. "The information is being compiled by my administrative staff and the young man in the corner is Father Donlan. He was a digital artist before he heard God's calling. He'll be able to recreate, on his laptop, whatever you describe to him." O'Malley studied the nervous young cleric. "The young man's talent is remarkable. He should be painting pictures for a gallery or museum."

Erik tilted his head. "That's a strange remark for a holy man isn't it?"

O'Malley laughed. "The Lord moves in mysterious ways, Mr. Knight. His call to each man is different. I suspect our young cleric will find his duty more focused in the arts than in shepherding the flock." O'Malley gestured toward the nervous priest. "Come forward my young friend. We have need of your God-given talents."

Erik studied the nervous priest. The man was thinner than a broom stick with flesh that was barely distinguishable from the ivory-lit background. Father Donlan set up his large laptop. His fingers rapidly danced along the keyboard.

"I'm just programming my digital pen and loading an updated color palette, your grace." The priest's face was buried in his work for several minutes before his head popped up from behind the seventeen-inch screen. "Okay, everything is all set, I've loaded a facial template program based on a similar system used by the FBI to digitally recreate faces since that's what I was told I'd be drawing." The young cleric looked directly at Erik. "We should be able to create a lifelike image based on the database of facial features stored in the software subsystem. If you'll come over here, Mr. Knight, we can begin the process."

The detective walked over smiling. "I have a better idea. If I could transfer the exact image to your mind could you draw it?"

The cleric looked at him puzzled. "If that were possible, yes. It would be like doing a sketch from my own imagination, I think."

Erik smiled. "Okay, I'm going to project an image to you. I swear to you, you won't feel a thing. You'll just see the image in your mind as clear as if you were recalling it from memory."

The young cleric looked over at the Archbishop. The old man nodded slightly.

"Okay. I've been given permission."

Erik focused on the vision of the hooded man in black, recalling the image from the terrified young man at the hospital. He let the image run through his mind until the moment when the hood fell, exposing the murderer, and an instant before his flesh began to smoke and sizzle. Erik took that still image and focused it to perfect clarity, then projected that single thought to the young priest. Erik heard the young man gasp.

"Heavenly Father!" The young man shouted. "I see it, as clear as day. I can see it! The image is in my mind as if I created it!"

Erik stopped projecting and looked toward the young man. "Can you make that image? That's the man who slaughtered Brother Denton and the others.

The young priest's face became fierce and determined. "I know I can, I promise."

"Excellent. Thank you for trusting me." Erik took a step back as the young cleric began working.

Bishop O'Malley nodded. "That was amazing, Detective. You have many skills and talents."

"Erik, please call me Erik," he extended his hand toward the bishop.

O'Malley clasped his hand, "Erik."

"Father Donlan, how long will it take you to compose your work?"

The young priest was totally absorbed. His digital pen danced across the screen one moment, then his hands tapped rapidly on his keyboard. "No more than four hours. The initial sketched layers are easy to draw, but I'll need more time to capture all the detail in the image. The picture is so clear in my mind that I dare not look away for fear of losing it."

The Archbishop nodded in approval. "Might I suggest we move to the administrative offices? We do no good sitting idly by for four hours." The old man struggled to his feet and began walking toward the invisible door. He looked back. "Come along, gentlemen, we have our own work to do with the list of names and financial records. Let me see if I can motivate Bishop O'Malley's staff to hurry things along." The old man smiled wickedly. "Idle minds are the devil's playground."

Erik and Martin chuckled as they followed the Archbishop. Erik looked back. The young priest was totally immersed in his work and the few remaining bishops were busy reviewing papers that seemed to magically appear on the large table.

"What are you gaping at, Erik?"

He turned toward Martin. "Did you see any papers on the table while we were sitting there?"

Denton shrugged. "I can't say that I did, but I wasn't really paying all that much attention to what was on the table."

Erik shook his head and followed his friend out the door. "There were no papers."

Denton rolled his eyes. "My friend, you have a habit of obsessing over minutia. We just learned about devils, demons, the end of the world, armies of Light and Dark inside a room so white you can't tell the walls from the ceiling or the floor, and you're going to contemplate whether there were papers on the table or not."

Erik raised an eyebrow. "I'd rather think about that than the other stuff."

The two walked on in silence for several steps. "Ya know, I don't think I saw any papers either." Denton elbowed his friend in the side. "Damn it, now you've got me obsessing over minutia."

Chapter 5. Molec

Washington DC, Columbia Heights

Burning red eyes studied the holy relic suspended inside a clear membrane of the strongest ectoplasmic material. The dark satchel had finally withered and burned away due to continuous contact with the powerful source of light.

A dark wraith gloated, "After so many centuries, we possess the key to unleashing the second coming. Only now it will sit in limbo for eternity and the forces of Light can search the entire universe and they'll never find it."

A voice as cold and hard as arctic ice disagreed. "Even now, God knows where this relic lay and could whisk it away with a stray thought."

The skeletal nosferatu bowed. "I beg forgiveness, Lord Molec."

The powerful demon turned to face his servant. "Only the rules laid down in the beginning protect us from eradication by the more powerful forces of Light. We need to move forward with the next phase of our plan. The forces of Light must know we've stolen the relic. The distrust between the warring factions will continue to escalate." Molec flexed his large onyx-colored claws, still gazing at his prize. "We need to move now! The son of Adam and the stars and his offspring must be ended. Once they are terminated, our hold on Earth is complete and we will have done what Lucifer has failed to do for over ten thousand millennia, wrest another world from the forces of Light."

Molec pointed toward the Ruby Crucifix. "Even my most powerful creation will not be able to contain the power of the Christ for long. We must move swiftly against Light's champions. Once they're gone, the relic becomes irrelevant, an object of untold power with no one alive to be the receptacle of such awesome might." The powerful demon laughed a hideous

141

sound that made his servant shudder. "Not only are the forces of Light scrambling after us, but I imagine my old master is most put out with me at this point and wishes to eradicate my essence back into the bowels of his own domain." Molec sighed and flames burst from his misshapen nostrils. "I will take the Earth and humiliate Lucifer, and then I will bargain with God for the return of his precious trinket. My price will be domain over Hell itself.

"My Lord, Molec, we have a problem."

The demon turned to face a woman of impeccable beauty and symmetry. Molec studied her form for several silent seconds imagining her with some horns and maybe some scales. A lusty groan escaped his throat, before her words fully registered. "What is it?"

"The hybrid found our Vatican sources. One of the papal undersecretaries just sent me a text."

Molec smashed his fist against his desk cracking the heavy mahogany top. "Damn his soul to Hell! If Knight gets his hands on those two worms, they'll squeal like stuck pigs!! Humans!" he cursed spitting a searing fireball that vaporized one of his lesser servants. A skeletal nosferatu moved in, grasping the empty air hoping to feed on the slaughtered being's soul. The gaunt wraith's eyes glowed fiery orange as its claws grabbed an invisible object. The being's hands captured something and a floating white orb materialized trapped in the creature's grasp. The baseball-sized ball of light seemed to flicker madly struggling in the creature's grip. With a slow perverse pleasure, the undead creature bit into the orb like a ripe apple and began sucking on the spiritual energy. The soul shrieked in agony as it was consumed. Little by little the orb's essence faded and the satiated Hell beast cackled with satisfaction.

Molec looked on nonchalantly as his servant cannibalized the soul. The demon studied the sultry woman. She had a perverse smile as she watched the wraith feed. "You're not disgusted by my servants, human? Have you nothing to say?"

The woman smiled a grin of pure evil as she unbuttoned her blouse revealing her firm body. She walked forward grabbed his large black hands pulling them to her breasts, allowing the creature to feel her soft, supple, flesh. She leaned in closer. "He should have stepped out of the way!" She placed her lips against his forehead gently licking his skull.

With one powerful gesture the demon ripped away the rest of her clothes forcing her on top of his desk, Molec looked over at one of his servants. "Don't stand there gawking at me. Tell our servant in the Vatican to kill those priests. I want them dead before Knight can interrogate them!" The demon turned his full attention to his human lover.

As the acolyte left, it heard the woman's screams shift from pleasure to pain and then to terror. It shook its head sadly, capable of remorse and regret. No human female could satiate a demon. Molec knew it and took his pleasure in torturing the seductress more for her arrogant audacity than he did in raping her. Human flesh tore so easily and the blood inside was so sweet.

* * *

Vatican City, Rome

Erik and Martin studied several pages of financial data. Two high ranking priests' bank accounts stood out from the others.

"The accounts are in the same bank," Erik pointed toward the letterhead, "and the deposits were wired from an untraceable account in Fiji. Every transaction was a deposit from some unknown source to both accounts simultaneously, right down to the minute."

"You're sure, Erik? Let's not accuse someone without being rock solid sure of our facts."

The detective nodded. "The Vatican secretary made a few calls on those deposits and the source can't be traced to any particular financial institution. That's not a coincidence, Counselor. While he was doing that, I went through some vacation records. It appears both of these men requested vacation at the same time over the last three years. I admit once or twice in three years isn't an anomaly but six times out of six requests along with untraceable deposits appearing two to four days after their return, deposited within seconds of each other at least begs a few questions be asked." Erik pushed the data back toward his associate.

Denton studied the figures one last time then tossed the

papers on the table. "I agree. Let's let Bishop O'Malley know we have two suspects."

Erik frowned. "If these priests are involved, Martin, they may know who killed your son. We may solve both mysteries at the same time. I know I promised the Archbishop I wouldn't probe anyone's thoughts, but if they go mute I'm thinking about just going into their heads and extracting the information we're looking for."

Denton shook his head, face set in stone. "That's not ethical. As much as I want answers, sifting through someone's mind like so much spaghetti makes us as bad as those we're trying to thwart. Let's stick to the tried and true methods of interrogation. I'm confident between the two of us and the pressure the Vatican officials will bring to bear will be enough to break our suspects. At least that's what I'm hoping for. I just want to get my hands on the man or thing that took my son."

Erik nodded. "We're on the right path, Martin. Let's take this to the Archbishop and O'Malley and wring some truth out of these two gentlemen."

* * *

The Archbishop studied the data Erik and Martin provided, listening carefully as both men presented their evidence. The old man shook with fury. "I personally recommended Father Bashir for service in Vatican City and Father Timulty is my dear friend. How could they do this? Why would they do this to us?"

Erik sighed. "I don't know, but let's find out."

The Archbishop pointed toward two of his guards. "You will escort Mr. Knight and Mr. Denton to the rectory suites. I want Fathers Bashir and Timulty brought here immediately. If they resist, toss them in irons and drag them here!"

"We just want to question them," Denton protested. "We aren't absolutely certain they're guilty."

"They broke their vows, Special Agent Denton. They should not be taking in any outside funds especially in these large denominations. Both these men have access to sensitive church data. If that data has been issued to our enemies, I need to know now. They are guilty! It's just a matter of determining just how deep their guilt and their sins run at this point." The old man's jaw clenched and his voice turned lethal. "I will have my answers."

* * *

Vatican Administrative Apartments

The guards gestured toward a large door. Erik could hear laughing and giggling coming from behind the door. "Women?" He looked at one of the guards.

"Women are forbidden here." The man hissed.

Denton turned toward his friend. "We need surprise now, Erik. This would be a good time for one of your patented acts of aggression."

Erik rolled his eyes, shaking his head. "I'll take care of the door..." He pointed to the guards. "You two rush in and gather our naughty lovebirds." Erik nodded and pointed toward the door. "Now!" His left fist smashed through the door. He followed up with a massive right cross knocking the door off its hinges, forcing the shattered barrier to collapse into the room. The guards rushed in to the sounds of screaming women and outraged men. Both priests had been caught with their pants down, literally. The two women they were with hastily threw on black dresses. To Erik's dismay, he saw veils on the floor. The women were nuns.

The detective shook his head looking over at Martin. "Well now, isn't this just a bad cliché."

Both agents watched as the guards apprehended and secured their suspects. One of the priests resisted and was cuffed across his head forcefully. "The Archbishop has many questions for you two." The guards forced their captives through the ruined doorway. Erik watched as the two young nuns ran from the small apartment. "You cannot hide from your disgrace! Pack your belongings, whores of Babylon, you will be expelled from this holy place!"

"Gentlemen," Martin did his best to conceal his anger, "we, along with the Archbishop, have several questions that need answers." He forcefully grabbed one of the priests by his shoulder in a grip that made the man wince in agony. Denton shoved the prisoner forward. "Move, now!"

Several other holy men watched in shock as the shackled priests were escorted from the rectory apartments to the courtyard. Erik saw several mixed looks, some of shock, some amused and a few others had looks of guilt followed by emotions that his senses detected without his asserted efforts.

"I suggest we go back through our files again, Counselor. We may have cast too narrow a net. Some of the raw thought waves I'm detecting indicate there are more dirty fish in this papal pond."

Denton increased his vice-like grip on the prisoner. "I'm sure our friends here will gladly share the names of their co-conspirators."

The turncoat priest groaned in pain as Denton shoved him forward again.

They had walked about ten paces through the courtyard when Erik sensed the threat. Danger was all around them! His Esper instinct took over, senses became hundreds of times more acute. "Martin! Ambush!"

The sound of gunfire echoed off several buildings. Erik tackled their prisoners, shielding them with his body. Slugs burned into his ribs and thigh. The hybrid's enhanced metabolism pushed the slugs out of his body and began repairing blood vessels and soft tissue. His powerful bone structure remained unscathed.

"Stay down!" he commanded, studying the rooftops of several buildings. He spotted another sniper raising his rifle. "Martin get down and roll!" The sniper fired and Erik could hear the angry hiss and the sonic boom as the bullet surpassed supersonic speed. The soft thump of searing lead tore into his flesh made him wince. He glanced around. One of the guards had fallen.

The hybrid pointed his hand toward the rooftop and focused. Angry blue plasma danced around his forearm building up to a critical mass. With a brief tensing of muscle, the searing beam shot toward the rooftop, burning a hole clean through a sniper. The charred corpse fell forward, dropping ten stories. The enraged human warrior fired several more burning pulses blasting several holes in ancient brick and mortar. Erik's body began to tingle as the spirit of his alter ego established dominance, a feeling he'd kept buried for years. He needed the warrior now, maybe not the full power, but he needed the skills and the aggression his Esper genetics contained.

A sharp hiss escaped his mouth as a bullet tore into his shoulder. He ignored the bloody impact as laser-sharp eyes bore in on the target. He brought both hands together, generating a blue orb burning with an awful energy searing the very ground he stood upon. He shot both hands forward unleashing the expanding ball of plasma toward its target. The energy engulfed the shooter and fifteen feet of structure, dissolving each bit of matter, flesh and mortar within seconds.

Silence dominated the courtyard. Erik risked looking down toward his allies. One guard lay dead, completely bled out and the other had a minor bullet wound. Martin was shaken up but not hurt. Erik looked at their prisoners. One of the priests had been hit, his skull shattered bathing his companion in brain matter and blood. "Martin, are you okay?"

"I'm just banged up a bit. What about you? I see blood all over you!"

"I heal fast, Counselor."

The smell of sulfur and rotten eggs assailed Erik's senses. The men gagged briefly. A whistling hot wind bent the thin trees in the courtyard. The surviving priest shrieked in fear. "Nosferatu! They've summoned the Wraiths of Hell! We're all dead men, our souls damned to eternity if that thing gets us!"

The hybrid's senses shrieked danger. A warning tore through his skull and a pulsing sense of dread tingled at the base of his spine. In the distance, a moaning wail like the growl of an enraged wolf dominated the stench-filled air. A burning silver orb raced through the sky. The hybrid extended his hand and the Sentient Staff settled in his grip. It too buzzed a warning of alarm and danger.

A tall skeletal man covered in black appeared in the courtyard. He walked slowly toward them. A bony hand pointed toward the fallen priest. Erik heard a voice in his mind that chilled his soul.

You have no sway here, son of the stars. I have come for the priest.

Give him to me and you will continue to live, for now. Deny me my prize and I will take your soul and feed on it for all eternity and take the priest anyway. Plus I shall kill your friend in a way that will cause him an eternity of torment.

"Don't listen to him Erik. We need that witness!"

Erik glanced at Martin. "You heard?"

"We all did." The remaining guard's voice was laden with terror. "How did a hell beast get here and how can it exist on consecrated ground?"

"Pppplease," the priest pleaded. "I'll tell you anything, just don't let that thrice-damned thing take me." The priest's face was pale with abject terror. "It will kill you all! You have to fight, if not for me, then kill it to save yourself and your friend!"

Erik looked down at the wounded guard. "Can we expect any backup?"

"I don't know, Detective. We don't have weapons capable of dealing with such monstrosities. Our best protection from evil is the very consecrated ground itself. No evil should be able to survive here." The wraith came closer and the guard gasped. "It will not hesitate to kill all of us. It will drink our life force until we whither like dying plants."

The Sentient Staff roared. Agitated energy crackled and danced upon the weapon's surface. Erik allowed his body to absorb some of the power to recharge then supercharge his body. He focused his breathing and willed his body stronger. He felt even more energy course into his limbs and torso. Esper senses flooded his mind with information. Enhanced neural pathways processed the stimuli and reacted. He radiated an aquamarine glow as more raw power coursed through his body. Every hybrid sense he had screamed of danger!

Erik looked down at his companions. "Get out of here. This is my fight now."

Before he could say or do anything, a beam of amber flame struck his body. The pain of a thousand bee stings and the scalding heat of a blast furnace ate through his flesh. The demonic force beam knocked him back over fifty feet. Erik's scorched body smashed through the brick and glass lounge of the Vatican rectory. His mind reeled and his flesh burned in agony. His soul cried out as the demonic fire threatened to consume him. Despite the pain he stood. The staff fed him more healing energy and increased in power. The weapon growled like an enraged wolf on the verge of attack. Warm blood cooled the cooked flesh hanging in charred tatters off his body. Exposed muscle tissue seared, burnt, and blackened from the blast.

Erik limped through the gaping hole and stepped into the courtyard. The wraith knelt over Martin, reaching for the terrified man. The old man's eyes locked on the demon, defiant, determined to face death head on.

"NO!" Martin's plight triggered an adrenaline spike. Erik raised his staff. The weapon roared, unleashing a burst of superheated plasma. A thunderclap shook the ground as the force beam slammed into the demonic creature driving it dozens of feet backwards. The wraith shrieked in agony as the battle-raged warrior continued firing. The staff growled louder as more and more superheated plasma engulfed the enraged hell creature. The ground around the beast burned then bubbled into a molten pool. The beast sank two feet into the liquid earth, its flesh and garment ablaze. Banshee shrieks of agony and anger shattered glass panes on every nearby building and sent chills through every living soul in the area.

Erik moved painfully toward his colleagues. He could feel blood hemorrhaging from the gaping burns on his torso. The smell of his own cooked flesh scorched his nose. He couldn't heal himself just yet. "We need to move now, Counselor, while that thing is distracted and sunk in the molten earth."

Erik's staff sounded a warning and formed into a circular shield deflecting another burning salvo of demonic power. The sentient shield howled a sound like a wounded puppy as it absorbed and refracted the demonic energy. The assault stopped and the shield changed back into its narrow cylindrical shape. The nosferatu was far from finished.

The creature had managed to crawl free from the molten slag, its flesh still ablaze but it ignored the hideous wounds. *You will all die!* The icy tone froze the men's hearts. Even the powerful hybrid shuddered as the deathly tone echoed through his mind. The creature charged, enraged. Hungry claws extended from beneath its burning dark cloak. Erik timed his counter. He unleashed a powerful right cross directly on the wraith's covered skull. The impact of his fist sent a shock wave through his body. His flesh seemed to recoil upon contact with the thing. The force of his blow snapped the wraith's head back and sent the creature airborne for over ten feet. The creature lay dazed but didn't stay down. It righted itself and large clawed hands cracked its fractured vertebrae back into place. Its flesh was smoking and its dark covering stopped burning. Erik could hear the exposed flesh sizzle.

"What the hell?" Erik muttered. "That punch would have dropped a gorilla dead in its tracks."

The creature leapt and floated forward as if the living Earth repelled its body. Hungry claws slashed at Erik's back as the creature sailed past. Erik screamed in pain as the claws cleaved his flesh to the bone. To the hybrid's horror he felt his own life essence and strength draining from his body, feeding his demonic foe. The wraith flew by again, faster, striking, another blow and cutting deeper wounds into his already bloody torso. The creature cackled and moaned as it banked sharply, relishing the newfound strength. Its body stopped burning and the creature no longer left a smoking contrail of burning flesh.

Your power is a sweet candied meat to me Esper hybrid. Soon all your strength will be mine.

Erik struck as the creature went by, but his blow glanced off. The creature was moving so fast, he could barely follow it even with his enhanced senses. It struck him again and again, each time taking a portion of his physical strength and energy reserves. Erik's counterstrikes grew slower and weaker. His body was shutting down as its very life essence was drained. His staff shrieked out a fearful warning and sent another trickle of power into its master.

"We have one shot at this," Erik whispered to his weapon. "A few more cuts and we'll both be out of power."

Your soul will be mine, son of Adam and the stars. I will feast on you for a hundred years, savoring the taste of your essence. After I kill you and your ape-like friends, I will take your wife and your child and feast on them. I'll rape your wife a hundred times before I kill her and I'll force your son to watch over and over and over again. I'll cherish with glee each time mother and child scream out your name, begging for you to save them. When I'm done, they'll both be cursing you for your failure.

Erik stood stone still, feigning helplessness, gathering all of his reserves. The demon fell upon him, arms outstretched hungrily. Erik swung his staff like a baseball bat turning his hips and applying all of his enhanced speed and strength into one desperate blow. The howling weapon cracked against the wraith's skeletal shoulder shattering the bones, sending the creature crashing into the ground, tumbling end over end for twenty yards. Desperation helped Erik find more internal reserves. The hybrid's eyes burned like two angry blue suns. Burnt flesh glowed with the same fiery blue nimbus as the battered warrior harnessed every ounce of his bioelectric power.

"You're not touching my wife or my son, you fucking hell beast! Give Satan my regards and you tell him I kicked your ass. You tell your boss I'll bring a war to his domain that'll shake the foundations of both Heaven and Hell itself if anything tries to lay a finger on my wife or son!!"

Erik looked heavenward and hissed a series of commands. The very sky darkened as electrons and static energy collided and gathered together. Thunder shook all of Rome as dark clouds covered the Holy City. The hybrid pointed toward its nemesis and screamed...

"ANARAH ANKOLAH!!!!!" His voice surpassed the thunder itself. The heavens opened and a searing lightning bolt three miles long streaked down from the sky. The thunderclap shook all of Rome as the bolt of unfettered power slammed into the enraged, broken nosferatu. Three miles of endless untamed energy burned its way through demonic flesh and tissue. The wraith felt its life force escaping and shrieked one last scream of pain and rage as the overwhelming power consumed it. The explosion from the impact turned the courtyard into a massive crater. Trees, benches, and bushes vaporized before the expanding wave of fire and energy. Erik willed his staff into a large shield, covering himself and his companions from the massive detonation. Whatever power existed within the hell beast had been released when the lightning bolt vaporized its flesh. The power of Erik's attack and the freed demonic energy transformed the large courtyard into a post-apocalyptic wasteland. The sides of buildings facing the courtyard were charred and several sections of stone and mortar had been either vaporized or collapsed from the final blast.

Erik's body sagged and he fell to his knees. The embattled hybrid warrior looked up toward heaven. "That goes for you too, minus the swearing and threatening ... leave my family out of this. They're innocent. You wanted me to shed blood for your cause?" He gestured toward the gaping wounds on his body. "I just did. I hope you're happy now." He turned toward his stunned friend.

"Martin, are you okay?"

The elder agent shook his head a few times to clear out the cobwebs. He studied the once-lush grounds. "My God, it's a smoking ruin." He noticed his friend's wounds.

"Holy shit! Erik, the skin on your torso—it's gone! You need a doctor!" He spotted the ripped flesh on his friend's back. "Jesus! Your back and arms, they've been filleted! We need to get you to the hospital now!"

"I'll be fine." Erik looked at the surviving guard and priest as he forced himself to his feet, an involuntary gasp of pain escaped his throat. "Are you two okay?"

Only the guard responded. "We're fine. Father Bashir appears to have soiled his vestments. You need both spiritual and medical care, Mr. Knight. A hell being has had contact with your essence and you must be cleansed." The guard looked up at Erik with awe. "You engaged a nosferatu in hand-to-hand combat and actually won! A single wraith has wiped out hundreds of men at one time, stealing their life essence and their souls. You saved us all, Detective. I am in your debt, as are all of us in the holy city."

Erik placed a filthy hand over the charred exposed muscle on his torso. "I appreciate the gratitude. I just hope nobody was in the courtyard when I let that thing have it." Erik studied the scorched buildings. "Or no one in those buildings was hurt."

"Your wounds, Mr. Knight..."

"My wounds are the least of our problems," Erik snapped. However the pain kept increasing and the detective had a difficult time blocking the discomfort. He took several steps away from the other men, holding his weapon tightly. "You saved our bacon, my silver friend. From now on you don't leave my side." The weapon purred at its master's praise. Erik willed the staff to shrink and take its customary place of concealment around his waist. He looked toward the center of destruction where the nosferatu had perished. Something had survived the incredible amount of power he'd unleashed. Erik limped over and discovered a section of tattered black fabric. Nearly a square foot of material lay by the scorched and molten earth. It had been singed and burnt but remarkably, a piece of it survived. The detective painfully bent over, ignoring the searing agony from that motion and picked up the material. It was dense but remarkably thin. He studied a few fibers, rolling them between his burnt fingertips.

"The chamber … This is made of the same fibers we found in the chamber."

Another searing wave of pain coursed through his body. Erik cried out in agony. "What the hell!"

"As I said, your wounds, Mr. Knight. The flesh may heal but your spirit has been attacked too, you need a healing cleric and several cleansing prayers." The guard yelled, still laying on the ground.

A wave of nausea shuddered through Erik's body and the edges of his vision began to fade. There were no more power reserves to call upon. He had reached the end of his endurance. "Martin." He struggled to force out the words. "I think I'm in some deep shit."

Erik collapsed into the dirt.

* * *

Bellingham MA, Newberry Comics

Shanda glanced over at EJ. He was playing with his trucks in the corner while she continued ringing up customers. She hated having to bring him to work, but the young boy enjoyed talking to people and playing with several of the unusual items in her store. Shanda's employees also genuinely loved him. EJ never wanted for attention.

Her body began to tingle. A feeling of dread swept through her body. She could sense the danger surrounding her husband. Erik was fighting for his life and his mental stress tore through the link they shared.

"Daddy! Daddy's hurt!" A tiny voice wailed in agony.

Shanda spun. In tears, EJ rolled on the floor, his arms wrapped around himself, hysterical.

"Daddy! Daddy!" he kept screaming.

"My God, he feels it too!" Shanda tried to move. Another sense of panic followed by a searing wave of unbearable agony assaulted her senses. She stumbled and fell, crashing into a display sending dozens of DVDs sprawling across the floor. "EJ, EJ," she cried, only wanting to reach her son.

The cashier nearest rushed to her aid and another employee scooped up EJ and brought him to her. Both mother and child huddled together, riding through a sea of panic and terror. Each knew that the feelings came from the man they loved over four thousand miles away.

Two women helped Shanda to her upstairs office as she cradled her weeping child. Shanda's assistant manager helped her get EJ settled under a heavy blanket on her couch. The child fell into a heavy sleep clutching a large stuffed animal. Her assistant, Carla, poured the frazzled young woman a hot cup of tea and sat down next to her boss and friend of ten years.

"Well, at least you have some color back in your face."

Shanda sipped from the hot beverage. "Thanks Carla." She kept looking over at her sleeping son.

"Do you want to talk about what happened down there? You scared me and the rest of our staff half to death, not to mention our customers."

Shanda pulled a blanket around her shoulders, shuddering. "Erik's in some kind of trouble. Remember a few years back when I was kidnapped?"

"Shit, how could I forget, I cried at your 'funeral.' That was awful."

"The link I share with Erik was blocked so he couldn't detect me, but he was able to break through it and hear me calling to him while I was in the Midwest and he was in Paris." Shanda looked toward her friend, her eyes wide with fear. "Something happened to him, Carla, something terrible and it sent shockwaves through our link so powerful that I felt some of his pain and fear." She took another sip of her tea. "I've been calling out to him and it's like I'm yelling in a canyon. All I hear is the echo of my own thoughts. I know he's alive. I can feel his life force but something is desperately wrong." Tears cascaded down her cheeks.

Carla reached over, picking up Shanda's cell phone. She tossed it over to her friend. "Then call him. You said he was with his friend, Martin. Maybe Martin will pick up his phone."

"That's breaking protocol, I have to wait until he contacts me."

Carla rolled her eyes. "Excuse me, babe. This is your man, and if he's hurt, screw protocol. You need to know what's going on!"

The two women stared at each other. "Call him, hun. If your gut says something's wrong, dial that number and find out."

Shanda stared down at her phone. "You're right. I have to know."

* * *

He floated in a sea of purple and green fog, but a force guided him. The essence was familiar. The mist cleared revealing a massive city floating effortlessly in a purple sky filled with amber clouds and a blue sun. He thought that odd. Sol was yellow and was bigger in the sky than this small burning blue orb.

My home, Erik. How I remember it. It was so long ago.

He turned to face a massive being of chrome, even bigger than when he made his transformation. There was a sense of familiarity and the burning blue eyes contained a soft intellect. He knew. *Jakor? Where am I? How is this possible?*

The large Esper warrior smiled, pointing toward a nearby bench.

Let us sit and talk, as your people say. We have much to discuss and I have much to tell you.

Erik realized that he was in his warrior form. The two titans walked toward the large bench. Jakor studied his human cousin with great interest. *I didn't think your hair would stay.* He absently stroked his bald scalp, running a finger over the heavy ridgeline on the top of his skull. *The mixture of our species had many interesting side effects.*

A massive winged reptile nearly twenty feet long swooped overhead and was soon joined by several others. Their songs were enchantingly beautiful. Erik looked up, captivated by the alien landscape. He felt a powerful hand rest against his shoulder.

You are unconscious, Erik, healing from your wounds. I applaud you, hybrid, engaging a nosferatu is a feat only suitable for a trained Esper Warrior.

Erik's eyes widened. *You know what that creature was?*

Jakor nodded. *Yes, I fought many of them before the forces of Light and Dark finally collided in one last great battle for our world. We had fought the Seelak for so long and after each battle, more and more beings of eternity took interest in the conflict. We had sided with the Lords of Light. The Seelak chose to ally themselves with the forces of Dark. Their expansionist desires of conquest and war seemed to draw the Dark while the Lords of the higher planes chose to ally themselves with my people.* Jakor sighed, a look of sorrow passed across his dire, fierce features. *I fear we were merely 'Ekoghtar' for them.*

I don't know that word, I'm sorry.

Jakor smiled, an expression totally alien for his face. *The human term would be 'Puppets'.*

Erik nodded. *I understand.* He looked around and pointed with his powerful forearm. *What is all of this? You said I'm unconscious but we're here in this place.*

You have the full untapped potential of your entire human mind, Erik. Yet you let fear and a desire to fit into some mold extinguish many of your gifts. I have taken it upon myself to create a home in a small unused portion of your subconscious mind. Since I am composed of mental images and chemical synapses existing inside your brain, it was only a small matter to manipulate a small unused portion of your mind and create this image for me to inhabit. Rather than disturbing you, I can spend your life here, in a memory of what my civilization once was before the higher powers took an interest. You live your life in peace without, as you said, the voice in your head, and I live my life here in this recreation of what once was.

Erik detected a hint of sorrow and regret in the giant warrior's thoughts. Jakor was not the simpleminded killing machine he'd imagined. *I'm sorry, Jakor, if you took offense to my thoughts or any of my feelings. Humans aren't wired for two sets of consciousness. Truth be told, I'd welcome the opportunity to converse with you time to time.* Erik studied the world existing in his subconscious. *And I'd love the opportunity to explore this fantastic city and hear all the tales you have to tell. I have some memories of yours but would welcome the chance to learn about the other half of my lineage.*

Again the silver giant smiled, placing a friendly arm on his shoulder. *I would greatly enjoy that. You are going to awaken soon, so I must tell you some things before your essence returns to reality. I know you don't want to fight in the war. I implore you to reconsider. The forces of Dark are gathering power, as they did on my world and the forces of Light will gather to fight them. There are rules governing these beings laid down by the All Powerful—He who rules All. If the war isn't fought by the rules, if one side breaks the compact of the All Powerful, both sides will spill into this world from the higher and lower plains and do battle. The power unleashed will destabilize and destroy this planet as it destroyed my home. Earth will be nothing but scattered dust and rock floating in the cosmic waste of space.*

The powerful Esper warrior flexed his massive arm. *I fear that we have brought this battle to Earth. It is my belief that a minion of the Dark hid away on our worldship, hiding inside a Seelak. This evil grew slowly and spread its influence throughout the Seelak population. We brought evil to your world ten thousand years before the Son of the All Powerful came to be. We gave the forces of Dark a hundred-century head start. I have had much time to reflect about what occurred on this planet. I believe the Eternals of Light and Dark both agreed that we should be exterminated. I believe the higher powers suspected we infected this world and it needed to be cleansed.*

Why would the Dark forces want their Seelak destroyed, if they had the upper hand why not fight to keep the advantage?

Jakor nodded in approval. *You're thinking like a warrior. Good. Keep that part of you open. All of my instincts and abilities are yours, inherent in the chemical combinations within your brain. Access that information and use it. You will benefit from my experience and will be able to combat the soldiers of Dark without sustaining such damage. Keep your weapon close. It can combat the forces of Dark and it will allow you to battle all the manifestations of evil. You may discover that evil cannot always be seen or confronted by means in which we are accustomed. The Sentient Staff can sense evil and is compelled to counter it.*

Erik nodded. *That explains why the staff came to me on its own volition when the wraith made its appearance and why the weapon was extremely aggressive.*

The staff has intelligence programmed into its bio matrix. It is aware of you, your lineage and its purpose. Trust the weapon. You regard it like a man does a canine companion. I understand the relationship as does the staff. It is good to see the weapon has bonded to you. It will serve you well as it served me over the centuries.

Jakor opened his hand and a large berry materialized from the very air. A large creature dove toward him with breathtaking speed. At the last possible moment the great beast stopped suddenly, landing feather-light on the ground barely two feet away. Jakor tossed the fruit and the flying creature swallowed it in one gulp. The creature leaned forward and the great Esper gently stroked its hide with firm movements. Erik heard the beast purr like a content kitten. *To answer your question, evil does not always cooperate with evil. Not all the Dark forces are loyal to the Dark lord. From time to time, a creature of high enough demonic stature desires to rule and will begin the process of gathering its own forces and launching a campaign to overthrow the Castouts. As far as I know, the forces of Light, save for the original rebellion, have never strayed in loyalty.*

Erik gently reached out and touched the massive creature. It looked at him and nodded slightly and continued to purr contently. *Are you saying that some other dark force besides Lucifer and his minions are behind the death of Martin's son and the theft?*

Jakor smiled, gesturing toward his self-made empire. *I can only guess. My exposure to the world is limited to your stored perceptions, but from what you have observed, I would make such a presumption. Darkness has nothing to gain from violating the terms of the war on this world. They were winning playing by the rules, breaking them would serve no purpose and lead to more unwanted interference from the higher powers of Light.*

Erik stood, he looked up at the alien sky and back over at the amazing city. *I never wanted this. I never asked for these powers and abilities. I never asked to get dragged into any of this. I have a wife and a son now, I live a quiet existence and I'm reasonably happy.*

No one ever asks for such things. Destiny and fate seek out champions. We are free to ignore the calls to battle but beings like us, warriors, feel the call to arms, the need to serve a higher purpose in the scheme of all things. I believe you had said earlier that you missed action and stimulation. In your heart and mind I can tell you hunger for it as I did. You are a warrior of Light, hybrid, willed into creation for a special purpose by the Creator of All. Now I have a revelation that you will no doubt find painful and disturbing. But know I speak the truth.

Erik turned as Jakor stood, standing even taller than himself. *That sounds ominous.*

Jakor nodded. *Your child is also a product of the forces of Light, willed into creation not by the joining of you and your bride, but allowed to occur contrary to the plans for this world. Your child should not exist.*

How can you know this?

Because you're no longer genetically compatible with your species, Erik. You are unique in the universe, not designed to procreate, designed to serve a single function and not destined to continue. Your son is a genetic impossibility. Only by Eternal interference could there be offspring from your coupling.

Erik shook his head in denial, emotional pain cascaded throughout his body. He sat back down, cradling his head with his powerful chrome hands. *My son, my little boy. You're saying he's not mine?*

On the contrary. He is most assuredly yours. He is of you and your mate, I am saying that the genetic combination cannot occur naturally. Your son should not exist but he does. Therefore it is only reasonable to conclude that another force aided conception. You need to ask yourself why.

Erik looked up, his burning eyes filled with sorrow. *We've been trying to have another child, and we can't... for such a long time we've tried. What you're saying explains a lot.* Erik's voice broke. *We can't have any more children, because of me, because of what I am.*

I am sorry. I sense the pain this causes you. I confess I don't understand it. I was not naturally created, but a product of science and genetics. It pains me that the part of you that comes from my species has caused this lessening of your humanity. I don't think Sennet had considered the ramifications of his great experiment. Our desire was to thwart the potential threat caused by the Seelak. We did not look beyond that objective. Jakor made a gesture with his hand and the giant creature took flight. *You are a warrior, Erik Knight, Hybrid. Your genetics and the fact that you were selected among billions of humans indicate your martial tendencies. You've trained in human forms of combat, fought as a warrior in human wars and military actions. This is what you are. You've been bred and chosen for a great purpose, to participate in the battle to preserve this planet, a continuation of the purpose you were selected for by the genetic virus we created. Your son was created for a purpose, Erik. I don't know what that purpose is, but the forces of Light never act without reason. You may not be able to create more children, but you have a son, a gift from the eternals, cherish him and nurture him. He has been given life, and all will be made known to you in time.*

Erik felt something pulling him away. Some force lifted him away from Jakor and the Esper paradise.

You are waking. Please remember what I have told you. I will be watching here, from inside your mind.

* * *

Vatican Hospital

"Erik, Erik can you hear me?"

The familiar voice drew Erik's essence like a beacon. His eyes fluttered and he slowly became aware of his surroundings. He looked up to see Martin and Bishop O'Malley leaning over his bed.

"Thank God." Bishop O'Malley made the sign of the cross. "You had us worried for a while."

Erik struggled to sit up. His waist was wrapped in bandages and his flesh had the scent of fragranced oils. The room had the heavy smell of incense reminding him of the smoke and candles used in church ceremonies.

"What happened?"

"You collapsed after your battle. You scared the dickens out of all of us. Our holy friends here carried you to the hospital and performed several healing services while you were out. Your skin regenerated shortly after we brought you here but we couldn't wake you up." Denton looked at Erik's pants and belt draped over a nearby chair. "Your little chrome friend over there's been buzzing and purring every few hours and believe it or not, you were making some vocalizations back to it in your sleep."

"How long was I out?"

Martin glanced at his watch. "Almost twenty hours." Denton slid a cell phone toward his friend, "Your wife's been calling. Somehow she knew you were critically wounded. It appears both her and EJ experienced the shock from your battle. She sounded terrified, Erik. I wish I could have given her some positive news. It was hard to say 'there's no change' over and over again."

Erik nodded. "Our link." Erik tapped the side of his head, "She knows I'm okay now. She'll sense it. But I need to call her anyway." He picked up his phone and the two men prepared to leave, allowing him some privacy. "Martin, before you go, what about Father Bashir? Did you get any answers from him? He has to be involved. Our opponents wouldn't have come after us like that if our priest friend didn't have some incriminating key to this whole mess."

Denton shook his head. "The Archbishop has men interrogating him in that white room. Bashir is more afraid of whatever was behind the attack on us than anyone or anything here." Denton cringed as he recalled the terrifying demonic presence. "I can't say as I blame him. That thing terrified me. I've tried to grab a few hours' rest but I keep seeing that thing and hearing that hideous voice inside my head. I may never sleep well again."

"We need to find a way to make him just as afraid of us, Counselor. We need answers, not more questions, and we don't have time to waste bantering with a reluctant captive." Erik took a deep breath and tossed the covers off his body with one flip of his arm. He rubbed a finger over his bare chest and shoulders. "I'm oiled up like a greased pig at a barbecue."

Denton looked down the hall, closed the door to his room, and stepped back toward his friend. "Erik, they were really concerned about you. They performed some very intense spiritual rites over your body while you were unconscious. How do you feel? Really? You took one hell of a beating."

Erik smiled. "I'm fine. Truth be told I was a little concerned myself. I hit that creature with enough force to stun a gorilla and it barely fazed the damn thing. It fed off me like some satanic leech, sucking my strength and energy every time it cut me. I was getting progressively weaker while it was getting stronger from my own energy. It took all of my remaining reserves to kill that thing. If you can kill a demon or wraith, or whatever kind of hell spawn ghoul it was. I'd never have believed such a thing existed." Erik shuddered as he recalled the sensation of having his vitality leeched. "It's an experience I'd rather not repeat." The detective forced his mind away from the demonic entity. "I'm going to call Shanda and EJ, grab a shower, and then I'm going to have myself a little chat with our turncoat priest. We've been stumbling around this whole case unwilling to accept what the facts are telling us. It's time we made our adversary a bit uncomfortable and turned the tables on our opponents. Father Bashir is the key and I intend to use that key to unlock this mystery. If they're looking for a fight, Counselor, I just may be inclined to give them one. "

Denton's eyebrow raised. "I'm confused. You were adamantly against getting involved before. Why the sudden change of heart? Do you really think this is our fight? I have to confess, even with your talents, I think we're a bit overmatched when it comes to taking on Heaven and Hell."

Erik cracked his knuckles. The sound echoed off the sterile hospital walls. "I didn't pick this fight, Martin, but a friend of mine reminded me that sometimes the fight picks you. You heard that thing. It knew all about me. It knew of my wife and my son and it threatened their lives. Sometimes you have to throw down, Counselor." Erik's muscles rippled and tensed and his aqua blue eyes burned with fury. "This is one of those times. I have a special friend in my head and he's made me privy to several combat techniques which will be most effective against our dark friends. They got the jump on us and they drew first blood. I intend to even the score."

"Erik this isn't a personal vendetta you can embark on like a solo special op."

Erik nodded as he grabbed a towel. "I know. I need more intel on our opponents and our allies in this war and I intend to wring that information from our reluctant padre and our Vatican hosts. I'd bet huge money he knows who killed William and I intend to get that tidbit from him as well. We're going to start behaving badly, Martin, just like the swashbuckling Americans we're supposed to be. We're scrapping the rulebook on this one! Agreed?"

Martin nodded. "I'll let Bishop O'Malley and the Archbishop know you'll be interrogating the witness." Denton paused before he closed the door. "Give Shanda my best." Denton pointed toward the closet. "I brought over some clothes. Your shirt and undershirt were a complete loss."

Martin closed the door and Erik stared at the cell phone. He tossed it on the table. He knelt on the floor, assuming a lotus position, then closed his eyes and focused on the most important woman in his world. He gently reached out to her mind across the thousands of miles separating them.

Shanda, baby. Can you hear me?

Her mental essence embraced him like a warm blanket. *Erik. Thank God! We were terrified! What happened to you?*

Oh babe, it's a long story. There's some crazy stuff going on over here. William's death was just the top layer of a rotten onion. I promise I'll explain everything to you when I get home. This is important. Don't let EJ out of your sight, not even for a minute. And keep your telepathic senses acute to any kind of presence—alien, human or just unusual.

Okay, but now you've got me worried. Are we in danger?

Shanda I don't honestly know. I don't think so, but I don't want to gamble with your safety. I'll know more in a few hours and I'll contact you again later. Do you remember "Little John" from the gym?

Yeah, he's as big as a house. EJ calls him the happy giant.

Yeah, that's the guy. I'm going to have him look in on you at the store a few times just so I'll be a bit more at ease.

Erik what aren't you telling me?

Babe, Martin and I were just exposed to a world we never knew existed. I fought something that wasn't alien and it wasn't human. It had supernatural origins. I plan on gathering the rest of the intel we need to find William's killer and be on a plane for home as soon as I can. I have to cut this short. I'm expected back at the main hall. Please tell EJ I'm fine and I love him.

I will, please be careful Erik. You nearly gave me a heart attack.

I'm sorry, Angel. I had my guard down, but not anymore. I'm about to go 'Bull in the china shop' as you're so fond of saying.

Erik could sense her eyes rolling and felt her concern deepen.

I know it won't do me any good to tell you to please be careful and to tread lightly. But please be careful. She paused. *And try to tread lightly.*

I'll try. Take care, hun, and I love you.

I love you too, Erik. Don't forget my souvenir. It better be a doozy after what you put me through. Shanda's essence faded but Erik relished the sensation of his wife's presence still lingering in his thoughts.

Erik glanced at the wall clock. It was after two. "Home is six hours behind. John should be out and about unless he worked a double at the warehouse." He picked up his phone and dialed.

He waited patiently and was rewarded.

"Little John, it's me, Erik."

"Hey Dude! Where the hell are you? Alyssa gave some line about you rolling with the Pope in Rome?"

"Yeah I'm overseas, 'rolling with the Pope' ... well maybe the Archbishop and his boyz, Alissa wasn't teasing you. Bro, I need a favor."

"Name it and you got it!" Erik smiled. His friend was eager to help out.

"You know where Shanda's shop is, right?"

"Yeah, right off route 140 in the big plaza. Her place is right by the cinema."

"Bingo! Can you stop by there a few times today and tomorrow and let yourself be seen talking to her and playing with EJ for a few minutes? If anyone has eyes on them, I want them to realize what they're up against. Can you do that for me?"

"Yeah, no problem. Are you expecting trouble? I can carry some hardware."

"No, John, I'm not expecting anything, and yeah just keep the hardware concealed. It never hurts to be armed. I'm just being cautious. There's some shit going on here and I don't want to be worried about my family. Having someone I trust nearby would greatly ease my sense of calm." Erik grunted a few times as his friend assured him, he'd keep eyes on his family. "I owe you. Hey the Italian place next door to Shanda's store—you tell the manager, Antonio, to take care of you and put it on my tab."

"*Do what ya need to do. I'll watch things here.*"

"Thanks, John. I should be home in a few days."

Erik ended the call and headed for the shower. He had a busy afternoon.

* * *

Washington DC, Columbia Heights

"Dokarth is the oldest and most powerful of the nosferatu!" Molec's onyx hands steepled in frustration as he leaned back in the large plush chair, "and the hybrid human simply vaporized him?"

"Yes, sir, the report we received from our spy was very detailed. Supposedly the grand courtyard in Vatican City is nothing but a twenty-foot deep crater and what's left of Dokarth is just a few scattered cinders somewhere in the center."

"What about the child?"

Molec's underling flinched. Our specter isn't in the child's room anymore. It's in the side yard hiding in a pine tree. The child is able to see into the Ethereal Realm. Our spirit beings are not hidden from his gaze. Also there is a low level Seraphim watching the home. It flies over the property several times each hour. It is aware of our agent's presence but is simply watching for now. Any aggressive action taken would be immediately countered and we would tip our hand to both the Lords of Light and Dark."

"The child must be neutralized if our plan is to unfold and we are to seize this world for our own and the souls that live here. A single Seraphim Angel isn't a threat. We can kill it easily and spill the child's blood before any forces of Light can respond."

"What about the hybrid? If we kill the child, the father will become battle raged. His Esper side will undoubtedly be unleashed and he'd hunt us down like a bloodhound. The Lords of Light would aid him and he would force a confrontation, sir. We would be exposed and our efforts to take this planet brought into the daylight."

"We would have already won the war. We have the holy relic." Molec pointed toward the ectoplasmic sphere. "And we'd have killed the vessel destined to wield it. The second coming would never occur and we could open a portal and flood this planet with demons and spirits loyal to our cause. Light would be banished and humanity would become a slave race and food source." Molec studied the ruby crucifix. Even trapped within its cosmic prison, he could feel the holy essence penetrating this most powerful of containment chambers. Nothing on Earth or in the Heavens save for the hand of God and the chosen being could handle and contain the power coursing through the object. "Once we control Earth and our forces are here, killing the hybrid will be a simple task for Legion or another higher demonic power." Molec flexed his arms and cracked his knuckles. "I would even entertain battling the Esper myself. It's been over ten thousand years since I fought an Esper Warrior. I don't think this cheap human copy is as fierce as his legend."

The underling nodded in agreement with his master, deliberately keeping his facial expression blank to hide his skepticism. "What are your orders, Master Molec?"

"I want the hybrid eliminated. We can't send any more forces to Vatican City. The Lords of Light are on their guard. They will, no doubt, blame Lucifer's forces for this unlawful attack, which will only benefit us." Molec laughed as he drank from a priceless bottle of wine. "When he leaves the protection of the Holy City, we'll have an ambush waiting for Heaven's guardian. I want to see just how far I can push this warrior and just what the limits of his power are." Molec drained the bottle and wiped his mouth with fine linen.

"As you wish, Master Molec."

Molec's burning red eyes sparkled. The essence of pure evil radiated off his charcoal black face. "I don't make wishes, I make demands! Am I clear, human?"

"As you command, Master Molec," The lean human bowed and left the demon to sulk over his loss.

Chapter 6. The Price of Betrayal

Vatican City, Rome

Erik approached the door to the Vatican meeting room. The hot shower and the chance to speak with Shanda gave the embattled detective some small semblance of recovery. Several questions still needed answering and Father Bashir was the man who undoubtedly had those answers. Erik hoped he'd spilled his guts and Martin and the bishops had everything they needed to wrap up this ugly episode. But his inner senses told him to expect the worst. His escort paused as they approached the large door. The man bowed to the two guards and Erik was allowed admittance.

Heavy tension thickened the air. The detective took his seat, nodding once toward Martin. Father Bashir was in some type of burlap smock and his wrists were secured with crude wrought iron chain. The turncoat priest looked miserable and the two men interrogating him were visibly frustrated.

Erik poured a glass of water. "I take it Father Bashir has had a change of heart now that the imminent threat to his life has passed."

Bishop O'Malley's face wrinkled with frustration. "It appears that way."

"The good father promised to spill his guts if we saved his life," Denton remarked dryly. "It appears his word isn't reliable."

"Bashir is a liar and a crook!" One of his guards spat angrily.

Erik stood, his arm shot across the table like a striking cobra grabbing the priest. Erik held the captive up by one arm, his fist clenched in the rough smock. The rogue priest's legs dangled over the table, knocking over glasses and scattering papers. "You listen to me, padre, and you listen good. I could go into your head and take every last thought you ever had and leave your mind nothing but a decayed vegetable. Is that what you want?" Erik heaved the terrified priest across the room like a rag doll. The stunned captive skidded across the floor slamming into the far wall with bone jarring force. The bishops cried out in shock but the detective ignored them and stalked toward the captive.

He grabbed the struggling man and hefted him into the air. "I'll give you one last chance to spill it before I take your thoughts from you."

"Do whatever you like, hybrid … nothing you can do would compare to the horrors I'd suffer if I talked."

"Please, Mr. Knight," the Archbishop cried out, "brutality is uncalled for."

Erik shot the bishops a look. "We don't have time for games, gentlemen. While we pussyfoot around with Father Bashir, trying to coax any tidbit of information, your enemies are busy planning their next move. It would be nice if we had some reliable intelligence."

"We know who we're facing already, Detective. We gleaned that information from one of our holy emissaries in Washington. We just want confirmation of a few facts from Bashir before he's imprisoned."

"I cannot talk and I will not talk." Bashir insisted struggling under Erik's iron grip. "There are worse things than prison, Archbishop." Bashir looked down at the enraged detective. "There's no manner of torture you can put upon my body that could be any worse than what they would do to me."

Erik sensed the priest's abject terror. The man wasn't going to talk no matter what he did. "I believe you, Father Bashir. I'm convinced." The detective lowered the renegade priest, grabbed the wrought iron chains and snapped the links effortlessly. He gently ripped the iron bracelets off Bashir's wrists and tossed them on the ivory floor.

"What are you doing?" The priest rubbed his wrists made raw by the rough manacles.

"I'm letting you go." Erik's lethal baritone echoed off the empty walls.

"What!" the bishops exploded.

Erik raised a finger. "How far does the protection of the Lord of Light carry outside Vatican City?"

"The blessings and protections are only upon the consecrated holy ground, Detective."

"So any dark and evil creepy crawlies can be lurking pretty much right outside the gates?"

Bishop O'Malley nodded understanding the detective's approach. "Yes, that's quite possible, Detective. There is no protection outside the Vatican gates from evil. The rules of the Ethereal Beings apply even to Rome. This scant two-mile parcel of land called Vatican City has the special blessings and protection. Outside these walls is the same as any other neutral territory."

Erik nodded. "Well Father Bashir," Erik pointed toward the door. "Good luck, out there on your own. I'm sure whomever you work for has acolytes watching the holy city. I'm sure your employer..."

"Molec," the Archbishop injected.

Erik looked over and smiled. "Molec, will want to interrogate you upon your release."

Bashir went white with fear. The priest visibly trembled. "You can't do that. You have to lock me up here, in the protection of the city."

"Bashir, we don't have to do any such thing." The Archbishop's voice was as chilling as the nosferatu Erik fought earlier. "I don't want the expense of feeding you, nor do I want you contaminating the city's penance chambers. Penance is for those who truly regret their sins and I sense you have no regret and your soul is totally owned by the darkness. We cast you out, Bashir. Go now and take your chances with the hell spawn you serve."

"Please, I beg you. Don't do this." Bashir wept openly. "I will tell you everything I know. Just please don't send me out there. I know they're waiting for me."

The Archbishop leaned forward. "You have one chance, Bashir. I'll give you ten minutes to tell us your tale. You'd better have nuggets of gold or I'll see you tossed out onto the street naked as the day you were born."

Bashir sang like a canary, confirming Molec was behind the

opening of the Esper Worldship, instigating the Observer incident, and caused several other world calamities in an attempt
to disrupt the normal conflict between Light and Dark. The
disgraced priest implicated several nuns who whored themselves out to weak-willed priests and senior Vatican staff sharing whatever intelligence they could gather back to the arch
demon and his servants. Bashir implicated several members of
the US Senate, Russian political hierarchy, Chinese politicians,
and several other powerful world leaders. The terrified priest
implicated terrorists groups and radical political action committees all having ties back to Molec's underground organization.
After thirty minutes of nonstop talking, the bishops, Erik and
Martin sat dumbfounded.

The Archbishop openly prayed to God for guidance and
blessings. He turned to Bashir's guards. "Lock him in a cell and
have three of our elite guards posted. No one goes into see him
without being accompanied by Bishop O'Malley. If they're approached and O'Malley isn't with them, they have my personal
orders to kill."

Something struck Erik's memory. "Wait, Bashir, one last
thing!" He turned toward O'Malley. "Father Donlan's picture,
do we have it?"

"Yes, on the table in that large white envelope. In all the
ruckus, I confess to having forgotten about it."

Erik opened the envelope and studied the picture. It was a
perfect reproduction of the image he projected to the nervous
priest. The young priest had captured the look and even the
dark feeling of the being that committed the atrocities. "This
man, do you know him? Is he an agent of Molec, too?"

Bashir made a show of studying the picture carefully, but
Erik saw the look of recognition. Bashir looked at the detective.
"He is not Molec's creature. Father Lazarus serves his own call-
ing."

Erik's jaw dropped. "*Father* Lazarus? Are you saying a
priest killed those young men and tore up that basement chapel?" Erik glanced over at Martin. How could they have been
so wrong? The sense of evil inhabiting the chapel was overwhelming and the images he'd seen were horrific! Surely a
priest wouldn't be capable of such horrid acts? Erik shook his

head. Bashir wasn't telling him the whole story. There was a piece missing. The detective hoped it was a very big piece.

Erik looked to the Archbishop and his council. They were visibly disturbed by Bashir's revelation. Each holy man studied the printed image and nodded. The detective turned back at Bashir. "Okay, you've managed to shake us up. I'm assuming our culprit isn't just a priest, I'm guessing something happened to him that made him more." He paused to rephrase. "Or possibly less than human. Would you care to elaborate on what you know about this man?"

Something in the disgraced priest snapped and he cackled a dark, sinister chuckle rich with irony. He looked over at the bishops. "They know who he is. They who sit in false, pious judgment of me know Lazarus. He was betrayed by the church hierarchy, here in the city before it became its own independent state. The Bishops' Council didn't want him serving and ruined him, disgraced the man, and drove him into the arms of darkness." Bashir pointed an accusing finger toward the stunned Archbishop. "You know the tale old man. I can see by the look of shame on your face, you know the tale of Lazarus, the holy man whose own colleagues betrayed him for being too pious." Bashir spat on the white floor. "Lazarus killed your son, Martin Denton, and the very people you ally yourself with created the beast. You're siding with those directly responsible for your son's death!" Bashir laughed another hideously vile cackle, "Tell them the story, Archbishop. Tell them the tale of the betrayal. Tell them how the church drove Lazarus to become the accursed night crawler that craves the taste of flesh and blood. "

The Archbishop pointed toward the door. "Get him out of my sight, now. I want the basement fires lit and fed constantly. We'll sweat the sin from Bashir's soul and burn the arrogance from his tongue!"

Martin leaned close. "It appears our turncoat padre struck a sensitive nerve."

Erik nodded, never taking his eyes off the Archbishop. The old man's hand trembled. His face shifted between righteous anger, hidden shame, and back again. Bashir wasn't lying, that much his hybrid senses knew. "Another untold truth. The church seems as secretive as any political organization in DC."

Denton nodded slightly. "It certainly looks that way. But now I know who killed William." Denton's eyes were frosty. "I know who to hunt down." His brow wrinkled. "Or what to hunt down. The lines are kind of blurry right now."

"Easy Martin. When it comes to confronting Lazarus, let me do the heavy lifting." Erik placed a friendly hand on the elder agent's shoulder. "Lazarus' power levels are super human. He's not someone or something we should take lightly. Let's get the whole story from our church allies before we hunt this thing down."

Erik and Martin waited until the priest was dragged away, loudly swearing and cursing his captives. Erik was about to speak but the Archbishop waved him off with a gesture.

"Take five guards and round up everyone Bashir mentioned. Call Mother Superior Agnes and inform her she has a den of whores inside her walls. Give her the names and let her round up those harlots. Throw them all in the basement cells with Bashir. We'll sort out that mess later."

"We don't have enough room, your grace."

"Double or triple bunk them. I am not overly concerned with their comfort, Bishop O'Malley. I want them imprisoned and the leak of Vatican intelligence plugged."

"I'd strongly suggest you screen all of your staff, Archbishop. I got the impression when we escorted Bashir out of his cozy love nest there were more guilty parties than we have names. By now everyone knows a battle was fought here and the side of Light prevailed." Denton pointed toward Erik. "They know we have Bashir and they know Timulty had his brains scattered across the courtyard. Any fool with eyes can see the aftermath of Erik's confrontation and God only knows how many other souls heard the words of that wraith in their heads. The evil rats know the jig is up and they'll be fleeing Vatican City in droves."

Erik nodded in agreement. "Martin's right. The impressions were loud and clear as Timulty and Bashir did their 'Perp Walk'. Several priests gave off impressions of panic and guilt. You need to do a thorough housecleaning and apprehend anyone trying to leave the city without a valid reason."

The Archbishop nodded. "A prudent suggestion. Bishop O'Malley, inform our guards at the gate that anyone attempting to leave the premises be detained for questioning. I'm going to report to our Holy Father and recommend Vatican City be put on lock down until we can sort the guilty from the innocent." The old man rose slowly and was escorted to the door. He turned quickly. "Bring Agent Knight up to speed on the fabric he discovered, and the results of the blood tests." The old man sighed. "And tell him the story of Lazarus. If that abomination is behind the murder and theft, then we need to find him as soon as possible. It's time we dealt with that disgrace as well. Lazarus has been a loose cannon long enough and we've let him run freely out of some sense of shame. That too ends today. What he did to our chapel is beyond the bounds and I want to send his decayed soul where it belongs—to Hell! We're at war my brethren, and it appears the rules of Eternal Engagement have been violated and we've all been played for suckers. We need to adapt and get in the game before Molec wrests this world from either side. We'd better start behaving more like soldiers than pampered holy men."

"Someone put a bee in the Archbishop's bonnet," Denton whispered as be picked up copies of the lab reports from the Vatican and his CIA source in Rome. Denton slid both folders toward his young friend. "This makes for some interesting reading and corroborates our undead theory."

Erik skimmed through the pages shaking his head in disbelief. "Low hemoglobin and iron count, no white blood cells, and abnormal blood platelets. The other samples from the victims tested as normal human blood." The detective tossed the report back on the table and looked at Bishop O'Malley. "What about the fabric?"

O'Malley took a deep breath. "We gave your sample to one of our more knowledgeable clergy and he knew the fabric. It was mentioned in some of his earlier readings. It's not a naturally occurring fiber on this planet."

Erik raised an eyebrow. "Okay. So what planet does this mystery fiber come from?"

"We don't know. It shouldn't exist here. How it got here, we simply don't know."

Erik lightly banged the table, shaking his head in frustration.

O'Malley ignored the detective's outburst and continued. "They are called talithum fibers. It's a material designed to mask both holy and evil essence. This is how Lazarus was able to enter consecrated ground and move about with no ill effect. He was shrouded in a garment of pure talithum fiber. I can only assume he put the cross in a sack of the same substance to mask its presence. This also explains how a creature as vile as a nosferatu could penetrate our grounds without being vaporized."

Erik rubbed his fingers across his unshaven cheek and chin. "So they've made a protective stealth suit." He looked over at Martin, "Do we know anything about this mystery fabric's chemical composition? Is it a natural fiber, or some kind of synthetic material?"

"The DaVinci Science Department in Rome ran the fabric through a mass spectrometer while you were in the hospital and I'm afraid to say they couldn't identify any familiar components." Denton slid another report toward Erik.

Erik picked up the report and studied it. He let his mind absorb all the data. He planned on questioning Jakor when he was alone. Hopefully his warrior counterpart had some experience with this type of fabric during their protracted conflict. "Bishop O'Malley, the Archbishop mentioned rules of conflict. Do the rules allow the use of foreign substances such at this? Can you elaborate on these rules and the players? It would help to know all of the pieces in play on this chessboard."

O'Malley shrugged his shoulders. "I am not versed on the rules of Ethereal conflict, Mr. Knight. The Archbishop or the Holy Father will have to answer your question."

Erik nodded. "Okay then, tell us about Lazarus. I'm sure Mr. Denton wants to hear the tale as much as I do."

Bishop O'Malley tilted his head forward. "It's not a tale we're proud of, Detective."

"I'm not going to judge, Your Excellency. But Lazarus appears to have touched a delicate nerve with the Archbishop and he's now our prime suspect in William Denton's murder and the murder of his two friends. I'm going to do the Archbishop a very big favor. I'm going to hunt Lazarus down and anyone affiliated with our renegade priest/vampire/ghoul or whatever the hell he's become."

O'Malley began the story. "In the late 1800s, the Church was very powerful and exerted a great deal of force and influence in the world. The methods of the Church at the time were often strict and intolerant of those who did not share its views. Lazarus was a product of those beliefs and practices and came to the Vatican in the early 1900s as an upper middle-aged cleric, ripe with his staunch conservatism. There were rumblings of change inside the hierarchy as Vatican City was being contemplated as an autonomous entity. The members of the Papacy and the College of Cardinals considered sweeping changes to make the Church more inclusive and less rigid in certain teachings and practices.

"Lazarus was a loud voice of dissent against these changes and his voice carried a great deal of weight and influence among many of the other clergy, even those at the highest level. Lazarus' knowledge of scripture and church law was borderline supernatural. But more important the man was a natural born Orator. "

Denton shook his head. "Politics."

O'Malley nodded. "Sadly yes. Lazarus began an active and vocal campaign against the council's ruling members and to the dismay of the Papal leadership, he was beginning to sway people to his position and there was momentum to elevate Lazarus into the College of Cardinals. If that occurred, he'd be in a position to influence the Holy Father and his council against the progressive movement the cardinals were trying to bring about."

"So the Church destroyed one of their own," Erik surmised.

O'Malley nodded. "Yes. Several local women of ill repute were paid to say that Father Lazarus had been carrying on intimate relations in direct violation of his oath of orders. Lazarus was able to refute those accusations but his image had been tarnished. Despite that, it was not enough to end his influence. A few weeks later the Bishops' Council paid a young woman to come forward and claim that Lazarus was the father of her bastard child. She told a compelling story of Lazarus forcing himself upon her in a confessional. Since the Bishops' Council was the church body that heard these matters, Lazarus was as good as finished. Despite his pleas and spirited defense, the Council expelled Lazarus. As the shamed priest was escorted out of the Vatican he swore vengeance upon the Church."

"That gives Lazarus motive, but not the means. How was he turned? I can't imagine there's a vampire on every corner in Italy." Erik looked over at the Bishop. "Or is there?"

"No. Lazarus spoke out vocally at local parishes against the changes being discussed in the Church, shouting down the local priests and deacons. We received enough complaints from local parishes that we sent our guards to find Lazarus and drive him out of Rome for good. Lazarus was expelled forcefully from a church and physically beaten by the guards. They stripped him bare and dumped his body in a refuse pit outside of Rome."

"A rather harsh punishment for speaking out against the religious establishment." Denton sipped a glass of water shifting uncomfortably in his seat.

"By today's standards, yes. Dissent wasn't tolerated back then, Mr. Denton. You were either a true son of the Church or you were a rebel. Lazarus chose to be a rebel, and his honeyed tones and words were able to sway many commoners and spiritual leaders to his cause. The Church deemed him a threat and acted as was appropriate during those times." O'Malley sighed before continuing his tale.

"Lazarus was wild with anger and humiliation. He fled Rome and found shelter in a nearby farming community. The shamed priest began speaking out against the Church and painting the papacy and all holy officials as corrupt and vile. He also took a liking to a local vintage of wine fermented by the small family vineyards." O'Malley sighed again. "That was his undoing. He got drunk one evening and fell to temptation. A young prostitute offered him the pleasures of her body and Lazarus, in a drunken stupor, accepted. He had her several times before he passed out and when he awoke, he found himself in a basement chained to the floor. He cried out for help but was there for several days. On the third day, the girl who seduced him entered his cell and gave him food and water. She mocked him, a fallen priest, one of the most holy now speaking out against his keepers. She tormented him for many days, countering the speeches he made against the devil and evil. At that point, Lazarus realized he'd been set up. The woman he bedded was a vampire and she'd brought a priest into her lair for all her brethren and sisters to torture and feed upon."

Denton gasped. "That's horrible!"

O'Malley nodded. "Indeed. They tortured Lazarus, raped, sodomized, and humiliated him in every conceivable manner. They told him over and over again that the Church had ordered this and condoned it. Lazarus cried out to God for mercy and release, begging God for forgiveness but his cries went unheeded. For several days and nights this went on. They fed on him and tortured him. Before Lazarus' body finally succumbed to the torment, he cursed God, the Church, and everything holy for his betrayal and abandonment. Before Lazarus died they turned him. In one final act of defilement, they made him one of them, an undead, a living mockery, a holy man turned into the very thing he'd decried all of his life. Lazarus would be a walking undead affront to the God and the Church he spent a lifetime serving."

Erik shook his head in stunned disbelief. "How utterly tragic. He was betrayed by the very thing he believed in and the forces of darkness used that against him."

"Lazarus was freed and returned to Rome and began attacking churches and holy men in outlying parishes. We sent soldiers to stop him, but they were all butchered like cattle. Lazarus made no attempt to hide his identity. He wanted us to know who committed the atrocities. We searched for his lair as he slept but never found him. The attacks continued on and off for five decades. Church men were attacked and innocent parishioners slaughtered in the dark hours. Lazarus told people who fled he was punishing us for abandoning him and condemning him to his unholy fate. Finally one evening he attacked a church with an aggressive pastor, who drenched Lazarus in holy water and oil. He shrieked in agony and fled into the night. The weakened vampire was caught hiding in a barn to avoid the sunrise. We locked him in the basement of an old convent just outside Vatican City until we could decide how best to interrogate him and finally dispose of him."

"I imagine he wasn't too cooperative." Erik leaned back

assessing the incredible tale.

O'Malley nodded. "When a human is turned, Detective, the soul is diminished and something else shares the shell of flesh, something unholy. Lazarus, or what was left of him after the transformation, went completely insane. He had become what he despised most of all in the world and he was condemned to suffer with that change for all eternity, a literal Hell on Earth for what was left of his human soul. Whatever beef Lazarus had with the Church, he didn't deserve such a fate. We tried to reach the human part of him and even tried to exorcize the demon within him, but it was impossible. His body had changed and there was nothing we could do. Even if we could have driven out the demon, Lazarus' soul was half destroyed and his body was already dead. No matter what we said, he was beyond reason. His hate for the Church and its body fueled his irrational rage and the beast dwelling within him only made the hatred that much worse. It was decided that he would be put down and spared further suffering. We couldn't have him spreading more chaos and blood across Italy."

Erik's eyebrow rose. "I gather that didn't go too well since he's still out and about causing mayhem."

"On the third day of his captivity, we went to drive a stake through him. When we approached the building, the door was open. The two guards were dead and Lazarus was gone. He could not have escaped alone. We had been keeping him weakened with holy prayers and oils. Someone or something aided his escape. We believe the nest of hell spawn that turned him heard of his capture and decided to keep their travesty alive." O'Malley poured a glass of water, drank deeply, then wiped his brow. "Over the next several decades we'd heard stories of atrocities committed around the world by Lazarus to churches in Spain, England, America and Brazil. Lazarus always left thirty small silver coins as his trademark to announce himself to the world, to let us know he was still out there wreaking havoc."

Denton tilted his head trying to comprehend the message.

"Judas betrayed Jesus for thirty pieces of silver," Erik explained. "He's taking the betrayal theme a bit far." The detective frowned. "Did Lazarus leave his calling card in the chapel?

We didn't come across any coins. Did you find any when you first discovered the crime scene?"

"No. Had we found them, we would have known who committed the atrocity."

Erik ran his fingers through his long hair, forcing some stray locks from his face. "He was hired then—just a stooge. If Lazarus' grudge against the church is as bad as you're making it, our unseen adversary, Molec, used him as a patsy to steal that prize. From what you've told us, I gather Lazarus isn't a great intellect, even though he's a persuasive speaker. If he's hell bent on leaving money as his calling card, he probably has little regard for it and therefore can't afford the wealth it would take to acquire the specialized stealth weaponry he used to infiltrate Vatican City. The fact that this nosferatu creature had a similar covering ties Molec and the clandestine forces of both planes—earthly and ethereal—to this crime." Erik looked over at the bishop. "Unless these wraithlike creatures are running around going 'bump in the night' as well?"

O'Malley nodded. "No, the nosferatu all serve Molec and from what we know, they are kept on short leashes. Your hypothesis pretty much agrees with what our sources in Washington told us. But it's nice to have the facts all laid out and tied up in a neat bow. Now what do we do about this? I'm sure the Holy Father and his staff are coordinating something with our forces in an effort to recover our treasured relic and hunt down Lazarus. Lazarus can lead us to the relic and possibly to Molec."

The detective shook his head, staring at his friend as the realization came to him. "Martin, I have a funny feeling we aren't going to find Lazarus."

A cacophony of emotions played across Denton's face. The old man's hand balled into a tight fist. He too came to the same conclusion as his mind processed the facts. "No loose ends! Son of a bitch, you're probably right!"

O'Malley tilted his head. "I'm afraid you gentlemen lost me."

"It's simple, Bishop O'Malley. If you paid someone to do a job for you and they botched it by committing multiple murders, thereby potentially exposing you and your operation, are you going to risk having that person run around freely? If you had employed someone like Lazarus, would you trust him to keep your business relationship confidential after the stunt he just pulled here?" Denton paused giving the bishop time to digest his scenario.

O'Malley's face paled. "They killed him as soon as they got the relic, to keep him from talking, just in case we apprehended him."

"As soon you called me and I called Agent Knight, Lazarus was living on borrowed time." Denton frowned. "At least that's the approach I'd take given the circumstances. Either Lazarus was killed by Molec's forces or by someone from the other dark side in retaliation for the theft."

"How can we verify that Lazarus has, in fact, been eliminated?"

"We'll stop by DC and have a little off-the-books chat with Speaker Collins. I'm sure Special Agent Knight can convince him to shed some light on this issue." Denton's tone was a cold and lethal.

Erik nodded. "The good padre gave us some names. Let's start shaking those trees and see what kind of fruit falls off the limbs."

"Tread lightly, gentlemen," O'Malley warned. "These men are involved in far higher stakes than just murder and corruption. They're dealing with powers and conflicts that transcend humankind—things no man should be involved with. Cross them and you risk confronting more dark horrors."

Erik nodded. "Duly noted. Our friends in Washington are playing with the worst kind of fire, Martin, and I believe we're about to get burned because of it. Molec has to be stopped. If his sphere of influence is such that he's able to orchestrate a ruse so vast it can confound both God and Satan, we need to tread lightly and carefully."

Bishop O'Malley studied the detective. "Are you prepared to take your rightful place as a Warrior of Light, Erik?"

The detective shook his head. "No. I'm ill equipped to fight the kind of war you want me to fight. I'll have my meeting with Speaker Collins and see what I can glean from him, but after that I'm stepping back. I have my family to consider, and I'm not going to put them in harm's way. I came here to help

Martin solve a murder and I've done that. I'm sure there are enough Lords of Light to handle this without me. If God is all powerful, and I believe that to be true, He'll clean up his own mess without me getting involved."

O'Malley shook his head. "Still you don't comprehend. God works through others, Detective, never getting directly involved. Lucifer is the same way. Molec is not. Molec will not play by the rules of ethereal engagement. Whether you wish to be or not, Erik, you are involved. Molec would not have sent a wraith against you if he didn't perceive you as a threat. If you think the Arch Demon will just stop because you've decided not to get involved further, I implore you to reconsider. Special Agent Knight, you're already hip deep in this conflict. You killed a powerful force of darkness and boldly challenged both the forces of Light and Dark during your combat. I assure you both sides heard your bold proclamation and consider you a powerful force. But your opponent isn't an agent of the devil. He wishes to replace the devil with his own brand of evil. If successful, the end of this world as we know it is imminent."

Erik shook his head. "Then maybe God should get involved and stop relying on other people to do His dirty work." The aggravated detective gestured toward Heaven. "He made the rules and He can break them, rewrite them or whatever He damn well pleases. He's God, Your Excellency, I'm not. I'm not all powerful and all knowing; I'm just a man that wants to get home to my family. Am I shaken and bothered by all this holy revelation? Hell yes! What sane man wouldn't be? Is my perspective of the world forever altered? Yes, you've succeeded in that as well. But that doesn't mean I'm going to get embroiled in some eons-old conflict fought by supernatural immortals that travel amongst the heavens like we walk through air and use entire planets to play a type of cosmic chess." The agitated detective closed his eyes momentarily, forcing down his anger. "I appreciate your situation, Bishop O'Malley, but I'm the father of a sweet little boy and the husband of a beautiful woman who likes me just the way I am and likes having me home at night, safe. The idea of getting involved in a huge conflict right now is not my choice."

O'Malley shook his head. "Sometimes, Detective, we don't

get what we want. I will confer with the cardinals and the Holy See and pass on all that we've learned. You and Mr. Denton will be escorted back to your suite."

Two Vatican guards gestured toward the door. Erik and Martin stood and began walking toward the ominous white barrier.

"A very determined lot." Martin mumbled as the two guards formed up behind them.

"Indeed. And I'm determined not to get involved in something way over my head."

O'Malley called out, causing both men to pause half in and half out of the ivory room, "Son of Adam and of the stars! You can deny your destiny, but you cannot change it. You can avoid this conflict but I fear it will seek you out and compel you. When that happens, please remember we tried to warn you."

Erik nodded and stepped out of the room. Martin followed behind him. The men walked back to their suite in silence knowing anything they said in conversation would be repeated to their hosts by their escorts. Erik nodded to the men as he closed the door to their suite. The detective flopped on the sofa. Martin went into his bedroom and came back out carrying a note pad and pen.

I'm betting we're bugged again.

Erik smiled and nodded, picking up the pen. *No doubt. Look at the table. The scramble box we left is gone, and the curtains have been changed.* He pointed towards a large picture. *That picture was hanging on the other wall when we left. I remember because I kept staring at it when we first settled in. I enjoy ocean scenes. Either our spies are incompetent or they're hoping we're observant enough to know we're being bugged.*

Denton produced another black box from his pocket, activated the unit and placed it on the coffee table. "You think we have an ally here in Vatican City?"

Erik shook his head. "I don't know." He pointed toward the picture. "That's a blatant mistake. Our friends are either sending us a message, or are just plain careless."

Denton's face flushed and Erik laughed. "That was a jibe, Counselor. Had I not spent fifteen minutes gazing at it a few days ago, I probably would have missed it too, considering all we've been through."

Denton laughed. "I must be getting rusty. I admit I'm not on my game right now."

"Martin, you've gone through hell, we both have at this point! My perception of the world is forever changed and..."

"And..."

Erik stood gazing out the large sliding glass door. "And I just need time to come to terms with all of this."

"Not to pick at it, Erik, but you're confusing me. I got the impression you were on board with all of this eternal war and good versus evil drama? I know I've seen enough to have me in a confessional once we get home. Hell, I may never sleep again."

The detective turned and nodded. "I get the threat and I understand the ramifications, Martin. I'm not running from a fight. I'm just not going to fight a battle on their terms as their patsy."

Denton nodded, gesturing back toward the couch as he adjusted to a more comfortable position. Erik sat staring at his friend.

"Do you trust them?"

Denton frowned. "Difficult question. I know what these men are supposed to represent and I understand they're serving a force of supposed light and decency, but I still see scandal and corruption. The very fact that Father Bashir and Timulty were bought and there are nun prostitute spies leads me to believe that the church, for all its supposed morality, is just as flawed and human as any other institution."

Erik sighed. "Or just as easily corrupted. O'Malley, the Archbishop, and the other men—they're all pure souls. The squeaky clean impression I get off them is undeniable. They have no real concept of malice which is probably why they seem so flatfooted dealing with the crap going on around them." Erik pointed. "So we're in agreement. You really don't trust them?"

Denton shook his head. "Trust has to be earned, Erik. Right now, the men here are reacting like ants that just had their ant hill kicked over. They don't know how to react to what's been happening under their very noses. If anything,

I'd say the amount of naivety among the church leadership is more a cause for alarm than any sense of mistrust. I believe the Archbishop and Bishop O'Malley are decent men caught up in a bigger game than either is comfortable with at this point." Denton sighed. "I trust them about as far as I can throw them … but not nearly as far as you could."

Erik snorted. "You know how annoying those long answers are, especially when you know I want a yes or no."

Denton shook his head. "I wish it was that simple."

"Me too." Erik stood again and began pacing, clearly agitated. "I know I have to do this, Counselor. I know I should be embracing this fight, but there's something out there, some missing piece I can't get my hands around, a part of the equation that's fucking up the math on my mental chalkboard. My gut tells me there's going to be a price to pay for wading into this battle full tilt." He looked over at his old friend. "And I know I'll be the one paying it."

"What price, Erik? You must have some idea?"

"None, just that annoying buzz in my head that keeps telling me I'm damned if I do and I'm damned if I don't."

"Okay, let's do the calculus together. The implications of not fighting are simple. Molec, in all probability, will take over the planet. From what our Vatican friends say, that won't be a good thing for anybody. If you do fight and are able to stop Molec along with the other forces of light, you'll save the planet including your wife and son."

Erik stiffened and a tear rolled down his cheek. "My son, Martin, the son that wasn't supposed to be born."

Denton tilted his head. "Okay you lost me."

Erik told his friend what he learned from Jakor and how the battle for good and evil took place on the Esper home world spilling over to Earth so many centuries ago. He also informed his friend that his son could not have been conceived without some sort of divine intervention.

Denton was silent for nearly ten seconds. "I don't know what to say, Erik. Is there any chance you were just experiencing some sort of drug-induced dream? They did have you on some pretty powerful painkillers."

"I don't think so, Martin. Jakor has been inside my head

ever since my change. A few years back he went silent and, to be honest, I was grateful to have my own mental real estate to myself again. I didn't try to call his essence up because I welcomed the solitude. What I experienced was real. I know it wasn't a dream. Shanda and I have been trying for nearly two years to have another child and nothing. That somewhat corroborates Jakor's tale."

Denton shook his head. "A whole city? He made a whole city in your mind?"

Erik nodded.

"Okay so Jakor is still inside your head, and knows what's going on. That's something you can use. But it still doesn't mean you and Shanda can't have a child. How could he know this? You said he was a bunch of programmed neural synapses wired into your brain, a set of active memory files. How could he know or even comprehend pregnancy or your state of fertility let alone have an intelligent conversation with you?"

Erik shrugged his shoulders. "Martin, I honestly don't know. I don't fully understand how Jakor's essence is able to exist in my head, but every time I've interacted with it, the advice I've been given has always been spot on. I have to believe that this time isn't any different. Why would he even bring up the topic if it wasn't of some significance? Jakor has no reason to lie to me … I don't think he's capable of lying."

Denton shook his head. "My God … add this to the list of unbelievable events. We're now referring to a bunch of neural cells in your head by name."

Erik nodded. "I know, but he is real, and he does exist inside my brain and he's made himself one hell of a home."

Martin placed a hand on Erik's shoulder. "Let me give you one piece of advice, my young friend, and take it as gospel. You have a son, love him always, and never let stupid things get in the way. Life is funny, Erik, and we never know how long we're going to have the people we love around us. I know you're heartbroken about not being able to have more children, but you have a wonderful son that loves you. Hold onto that and never let it go. You have a family. Take comfort in that as you wrestle with the issue of having more children. Some couples don't even have the one child you were blessed with."

Denton's voice broke and the old man turned away as a grief-wracked sob escaped him. "Hold on to your son, Erik. Don't make the mistake I made."

Erik felt the pain radiating from his friend as he succumbed to the grief. "I won't, Martin, I promise. But I want you to remember always, you're a part of our family, too. Our door is always open to you. EJ doesn't have a grandfather figure and he seems to really like you." Erik took a deep breath. "EJ will need your guidance and wisdom, just like I do. Family sticks together, Martin, and we're family. However odd and dysfunctional we may appear on the outside and despite all the weird shit we go through, we're family."

Denton looked up at his young friend and nodded. "Thank you."

Erik broached another delicate subject. "Were you able to see your son's body?"

Denton nodded. "Yes, they had all the pieces." The old man sighed. "He was torn apart like he'd been attacked by a bear."

Erik closed his eyes in dismay. "Are you bringing him home, Martin? Do you need any help with the arrangements?"

Denton looked over at his friend. "William will be buried here with his friends. While you were in the hospital, the Archbishop asked me if I would consent to having my son buried on holy ground. I know William would have wanted that and I was told it's a great honor. It's the least I could do for him and it's what he deserves."

Erik nodded. "That's good. Our Vatican friends are doing a noble thing. Your son deserves a holy resting place given his faith. I assume there's going to be a service or a Mass held for him and the others."

Denton nodded. "Yes, I was going to bring that up later. There will be a Mass and a special eulogy for the three of them next week. The other families are being flown in and I was invited to stay here in the suite until then."

Erik smiled. "That's good. They're doing right by him. I can call Shanda…"

Denton shook his head. "No, Erik. You've been away from your little one far too long and they both went through hell after that wraith attacked us. You go home and be with them and see if you can chase down a few leads. Your agent status is reactivated, so you'll have the resources of the firm behind you. I'll keep in contact periodically and let you know when I'm back stateside. There really isn't much more we can do here. The trail leads back to Washington and that's where we need to go.

Chapter 7. Hard to Kill

Vatican City: Palace of the Holy Office

Bishop O'Malley sat in the far corner of the cavernous room. He'd never been summoned to the Holy Office. This huge meeting place was a stark contrast to the mysterious 'White Room' used for strictly secret Church meetings. The décor of the room was beyond description, elegant life-sized statues of colored quartz and marble dominated each corner, and the artwork on the ceiling rivaled that of the Sistine Chapel. Three rows of well-padded chairs surrounded a forty-foot marble conference table. The rows were set back several feet from the table and filled with staffers who served the leadership seated at the table. O'Malley wondered if Michelangelo himself had been commissioned to paint the large ceiling here as well. O'Malley recognized several high-ranking cardinals of the Pope's personal staff but the presence of non-clergy was a mystery.

O'Malley recognized the US ambassador to the Vatican, and several high ranking clergy from the Greek Orthodox and Jewish faiths. The high-strung bishop also spotted two Muslim clerics conversing in the corner directly opposite him. Multiple clergy from the various denominations of the Protestant Church, were in attendance. O'Malley recognized representatives from the American Universalist Church, a powerful Baptist minister and several other distinguished representatives of faiths all around the globe. This was truly a meeting of historical importance and O'Malley wondered why he'd been summoned.

The large mahogany wood doors opened and the Holy Father was escorted in under heavy guard. Everyone rose from their seats. The Pope seated himself in the large ornate chair at the head of the table taking a few moments to personally welcome each representative speaking in Greek, Hebrew, French,

Spanish, Portuguese or English as required He turned toward the Islamic leaders and spoke to them in accented Arabic gesturing toward two empty seats at the table. The two men nodded, responding in Arabic and took their place among the other leaders of the world's religions.

The Pope spoke in that same soft tone use by the Archbishop. "Welcome, I thank you for dropping your plans on such short notice and making the trip to Rome. I wish we were coming together under more pleasant circumstances but I fear for the safety of all our faiths at this moment." The Pope paused as he studied each man and woman at the table. "The time for all people of faith to come together has arrived. It is imperative we put aside whatever squabbles we may have and move forward as one to avert a crisis of faith which impacts all of us."

The religious leaders nodded as the soft yet powerful words of the Holy See resonated throughout the room. "As my message to you all stated, our most holy relic has been stolen. Despite our differences in faith you all know the significance surrounding the Ruby Crucifix and the writings of the Apostle Paul regarding the fall of man and the second coming of Christ."

There was a small murmur and some tensed jaws from representatives of non-Christian faiths. The Pope continued. "Ladies and Gentlemen, let us put aside personal religious views for a moment and bear with me. While we debate and argue, over the true nature of God, Evil has flourished under our proverbial noses and is now threatening to take possession of this world. We have failed our God or Gods and we have all failed our faiths. Our squabbles have allowed Evil to hold sway over mankind for far too long. We are facing a crisis of unprecedented peril."

A Lutheran leader nodded in agreement. "Your words are wise. We need to put aside our animosity and personal bigotry. All of our faiths claim to teach peace and tolerance yet we've been shedding blood and tears in the name of religion and God. As we grow more concerned with our petty squabbles the forces of darkness grow emboldened enough to commit such a daring move. Do they not realize how they've escalated the Ethereal War?"

The US ambassador leaned forward, "Our sources say it wasn't Lucifer or his forces that committed this act." He looked toward the Pontiff. "Your Grace, perhaps you would be so gracious as to bring our friends up to speed so they may understand the degree of disparity this situation has wrought?"

The Pontiff nodded. "One of Lucifer's henchman broke away from Hell several thousand years ago. An Arch Demon of great power named Molec has been interfering in the Ethereal War not only here, but on other more advanced worlds. One of those races affected by that interference had their conflict spill over to Earth."

"The unpublished works of Apostle Paul," the Orthodox Patriarch injected excitedly. "It speaks of a great war in the stars ending here and that a prophet will come from a son of Earth, Adam, and of the stars."

The Pope nodded once. "Yes, the prophecy has come to fruition. We have met the son of Adam and the stars; he walks among us in form of a CIA cooler and private detective. In fact, he is investigating the theft of the artifact and the murder of three of our novices."

A few muffled gasps echoed at the Pontiff's revelation followed by dead silence. Each religious leader at such a high level had either read the secret writings of Paul or at least was familiar with the contents of the unpublished work.

"The End Days are upon us. Armageddon's Son walks the Earth." A Protestant leader visibly shuddered. "I confess I've read the writings of Paul but never paid them much heed. I assumed it was all metaphorical like most Biblical verse. If those writings are literal then this is the beginning of the end."

The Pope nodded. "According to the sacred writings, The Ruby Crucifix is the instrument to usher in the second age of man. Without that relic the coming Apocalypse will be eternal. There will be no Rapture, no souls will be saved and we will be living in a literal Hell on Earth. The Ruby Crucifix must be found and the growing evil stopped. I fear we are losing the war for humanity."

"The Rapture has been debated over several decades your eminence. My Orthodox brothers don't interpret the scriptures the way Vatican scholars do. But the theft of the artifact is troublesome and the spread of evil in our society is all too real."

"I've never heard of Molec or these writings. Our faith has been strictly scripture based on the New Testament." A Universalist minister sipped from her water glass. "I freely admit our religion isn't as old as many Christian faiths but I've studied the Bible and did my eight years of seminary study and nowhere have I ever heard of Molec or this ruby cross."

The Pope nodded. "That situation will be rectified shortly but I give you my word, Molec is real. The danger this demon poses is real and our world is in grave peril."

The Muslim imam narrowed his gaze. "You say you've met this Christian prophet slated to be the world's savior. Who is he or she for that matter?"

"Imam, the identity of this being is not important; it's what he represents that we must focus our immediate attention upon." The Pope's voice was calm and soothing, but there was a definite evasiveness in his tone.

"You are hiding something. You preach of honesty and trust yet refuse to answer a direct question." The imam stood, leaning against the table, "Who is this prophet that is supposed to save all of mankind and as your prayer goes, deliver us from evil?"

"Erik Knight."

The imam exploded. "The Silver Demon! The man responsible for Sarnia Fahaad's death and the death of countless Arab freedom fighters! You want us to align ourselves with the CIA's deadliest assassin?"

"We have sworn a death oath against this man; he is to be killed on sight!" The second cleric spat.

"Sarina Fahaad wasn't killed by Erik Knight. In fact she and Knight joined forces to root out the threat against the LaSalle family and expose the shadow government operating within the United States and now seemingly in other governments." The US ambassador handed out copies of a report to each attendee. "These are a few of the names we obtained through an interrogation of two spies Molec had here in Vatican City." The US ambassador leaned toward the imams. "Ask yourselves this question; who really controls your forces at this point. You're engaged in Libya, Egypt, Iraq, Afghanistan, Syria and you're still focusing on Israel. Is your objective to have a free state for your people as has been stated in the past, or simply be hell bent on war and destruction."

The senior Muslim cleric tried to speak but was silenced by a gesture from the Pope, "And what of your own government, Mr. Ambassador? Your nation's interference often does more harm than good."

"Truly," The representatives from the Jewish faith agreed, their cold gaze fell upon the ambassador. "America has not been the ally she has been in the past."

The ambassador looked over at the Pope, "I have no delusions your grace. The United States Government's hands aren't lily white. Man is corrupt and Molec is capitalizing upon that weakness. Our government is just as susceptible to the lure and influence of evil."

The Pontiff nodded, half smiling. "I didn't intend to come off like a hypocrite, William, considering our own current in-house situation."

The ambassador smiled. "Never Your Grace."

"A wraith!" A Protestant leader exclaimed leafing through the report.

"Yes. Agent Knight engaged it in combat, turning a one acre courtyard into a twenty foot crater leaving several of our buildings charred and windowless during the exchange of hostilities."

"Molec is unleashing the very creatures of the underworld. How is he able to summon such horrors to do his bidding? I thought the creatures of the Netherworlds were all locked away?"

"A breach between two dimensions," a Vatican official began. "Think of our universe as a large bubble in a sea of other bubbles. The Ethereal realm would be the ocean containing all the bubbles. A hundred or so years ago a tiny dimension, or sub universe, housing several of these terrors had a brief contact with our universe. Like two bubbles coming in contact each universe contracted slightly, their borders pressing against each other. Before the dimensions could separate again and continue to flow through ethereal space, Molec was able to punch a small hole in the fabric of both dimensions and bring through several of these trapped demons. In return for their escape from their universe they pledged eternal loyalty to Molec and also wanted vengeance against the forces of light that condemned them to their barren wasteland."

The senior Muslim cleric shook his head. "How has this Molec creature been allowed to run rampant for so long with neither the Light nor the Dark doing anything to put an end to his interference?"

"Another fair question Imam, sadly we have all been asleep at the helm, so to speak. Molec has worked discreetly behind the scenes very slowly until now. He's been manipulating events like a master puppeteer pulling the strings of those in political power, buying influence where he can and extorting it when his money isn't enough. This act of theft and murder was sloppy thinking on his part. Molec has been secretly and silently deploying his forces, buying influence and laying out the framework for his plan while we have been busy fighting amongst ourselves. The forces of light and dark became so focused on their own activities that Molec was free to act unnoticed and unchecked." The Pope picked up a copy of the report and tossed it back on the ornate conference table, "Until now. Now we must act. More importantly we must act together and share our knowledge and our resources if we are to avert this threat. The forces of darkness are also alarmed. Their minions were duped into stealing the relic and they in turn had it stolen from them by Molec. I'm sure the Lord of Dark is most put out right now. Being used by Molec will have Lucifer seething. Our Ethereal task masters are going to be focused solely on Molec right now and I fear that no good will come from the archdemon's schemes. He's been discovered, gentlemen, but he has the most powerful relic in the entire universe, maybe universes in his possession. None of us are aware how the forces of light and dark will react to this blatant and bold interference into their war of eternity." The Pope gestured toward Bishop O'Malley.

"I've asked Bishop O'Malley to bring us all up to speed on what we've learned and to give us his further impressions of Agent Knight, his colleague, Martin Denton and what we've learned regarding the henchmen who stole the relic from its place of concealment." The old man pointed toward the cowering bishop. "Come Bishop, tell us what isn't in the pages of this document."

O'Malley spent the better part of an hour providing a detailed narrative of the last few days. The nervous bishop provided detailed accounts of Knight's activities in the hidden chapel, his detection of all the surveillance equipment in the hotel suite and the unfettered power unleashed during his battle with the wraith. The bishop paused, taking a sip of water while his audience contemplated his report.

"You've given us excellent detail regarding Agent Knight and Denton's activities and capabilities, Bishop; I applaud your attention to detail. But what of the man himself?" An Orthodox leader challenged. "You've given us no idea as to what kind of man Erik Knight is or his partner. We aren't familiar with this man as you of the Catholic faith seem to be nor do we have an adversarial relationship with him as our Islamic friends have." The leader looked over at the two imams. "Much can be gathered about a man by his enemies also. Surely our Arab friends have some profile of Agent Knight they can share beyond their surface hatred of the man."

O'Malley frowned. "It's difficult to judge a man's personality after such a short time. Agent Knight is a cacophony of conflicting actions. Our officers told of his compassion and gentleness inside the chapel as he replaced statues and righted the holy tabernacle, I've also seen a darker, more brutish side to him. He seems rather quick and impulsive to act. He appears to be a man of action and deed rather than deep thought and contemplation." The bishop's forehead wrinkled, "Though his mind is sharp and capable considering the deep analytical reasoning he demonstrated when we met with him. The detective is able to piece together facts and has a powerful sense of deduction. I also sense within him a level of discomfort with himself. He is a man of great power yet he lacks the arrogance or confidence most men would possess having such capabilities." O'Malley looked over at the US ambassador, uncomfortable. "Forgive me Mr. Ambassador, for saying this, but most Americans in positions of power have a cocky swagger in their mannerism and their personality. Knight is devoid of these traits, he seems … possibly insecure or uncomfortable with himself to some degree."

"And Denton?" the Orthodox cleric pushed.

"He is a man grieving for his son, battling his own inner regrets over a relationship he feels he destroyed. His mind is razor sharp and he seems to have some kind of control over Knight, not in a sinister manner but more like a mentor would have for a pupil. The episode in the chapel revealed that both men have a deep affection for one another and a closeness that makes them both uncomfortable."

"Denton is the surrogate father Knight didn't have growing up." The Pope made a slight gesture and an aide poured a glass of water. "Denton fills that gap whether knowingly or unknowingly. Both men have found a way to fill a void. Denton found a surrogate son to replace the boy who abandoned him to come overseas, while Knight found a father figure he lost as a young boy."

O'Malley tilted his head as he considered the Pope's observation. "It could very well be, your grace."

"So, Erik Knight isn't a mindless wrecking machine. That's somewhat comforting. Is he someone we can direct and control during this crisis?"

O'Malley shrugged. "I don't think so, your grace. If he aids us, it will be because he chooses to, not because we compel him to do so. The Archbishop can attest, Mr. Knight is very headstrong and determined. We weren't able to fully convince him to take up our cause despite knowing the dangers. I believe he will fight in his own way on his own terms."

The Pope leaned forward, his hands shaking as he held his water glass. "Then we focus on Denton while he's here for his son's funeral. If Denton has sway over Agent Knight we can use that to our advantage. Erik Knight cannot be allowed to sit this out."

"Knight will be following up Lazarus and those connected to him, specifically the House Speaker in Washington. So he is, in a sense, working for us."

The Pope nodded placing his glass down on the table. "Lazarus isn't key right now, he's a minor annoyance we can deal with later. Lazarus was a pawn played by Molec against Lucifer and the Lords of Light. "

O'Malley's jaw dropped.

The Pontiff continued, ignoring the shocked looks around the table. "I understand your dismay, Bishop, and I'm not underplaying the vile acts committed by our turncoat vampire priest. Right now locating the Ruby Crucifix, thwarting Molec and trying to root out any of Molec's allies are of the utmost importance. I task you, Bishop O'Malley, to convince Martin Denton to rally Erik Knight to our cause. We need the unfettered power of the hybrid fighting on our side and following our direction. Having such a juggernaut running amok independently can only make things worse."

Bishop O'Malley frowned, "Your Grace, I'm confused. We agreed to send Agent Knight off to track Lazarus and the underground government back in America. Yet now you seem concerned about having this same man running amok out of our control?"

The ambassador smiled. "May I?"

The Pope nodded.

"Bishop O'Malley, sometimes it's better to let a fish run with your line awhile before reeling him in. Agent Knight needs to discover the severity of this situation on his own; nothing we do will convince him otherwise. Men like Knight are not directly led due to their force of will. Our dear detective will go to the capital, break a few eggs and turn over a few apple carts and discover through his own investigating that everything we've told him has been the truth. I'm confident if Lazarus is still alive, Erik Knight will find him and dispose of him. If, as Knight and Denton suspect, Lazarus is dead, Knight will dig into the mystery like a dog on a steak and find out the who, what, where, when and why to avenge the death of his mentor's son. In doing so he will force Molec's forces to adjust and adapt to his investigation, throwing them off balance and causing them to panic. They know how powerful the hybrid is and they don't want to be on the receiving end of what was done to the wraith here. Molec and his forces know one of his major players was dispatched and I'm confident no one else is eager to confront Agent Knight after the devastating display of power and aggression witnessed here. Knight serves our purposes doing what he's doing willingly or not. Sometimes the best course of action is to let a man think he's acting of his own purpose and volition. Our objectives, for now, are served. We can influence Denton while he's here and leverage that influence to get the hybrid further involved. If we can't, I'm confident Molec will tire of Knight's incessant interference and confront him. At that point Erik Knight will have no choice but to answer Molec's challenge and hopefully weaken or cripple the arch demon enough so the other forces of light can finally capture and dispose of him once and for all." The US ambassador grinned. "Knight will serve our cause whether willingly or unwillingly. By coming here he's already entwined himself in the ethereal conflict beyond his ability to become untangled."

O'Malley scratched his head. "With all respect, Ambassador, Molec is not one to confine his fight to just Agent Knight. The forces of darkness, whether they be of Lucifer or Molec will use any means to remove an impediment. We are protected here on consecrated ground; Erik Knight and those he holds dear are not. Not only will the detective be exposed, but his family will also be at risk should Knight, as you say, upset too many apple carts. Should we not inform Agent Knight of the possible danger he's facing?"

"No!" The Holy See countered. "There are forces watching over his family and the detective has taken precaution against human threats. If Agent Knight becomes too concerned for his family's safety our goals and objectives will be in jeopardy. We cannot have Knight diverted from this fight. His involvement is pivotal. He must draw Molec's forces out so we can deal with them."

"I confess to being slightly uncomfortable with the morality of placing innocent people at risk, your Grace. We are supposed to be 'The Good Guys' with scruples and morals. We seem to be plotting, scheming and manipulating innocents like those we oppose." The Orthodox leader shifted uncomfortably in his chair.

"We're in a war, gentlemen. A war we are in danger of losing. The price of our defeat is every soul on this planet. If we lose, the balance of power shifts and Molec will become a major player in the Eternal struggle. There will be two forces of darkness both grappling with each other and with us. Mankind will cease to exist. I am not eager to hold court in a Hell on Earth. If subterfuge and guile will aid us in the greater good then so be it. Molec and his forces should tread lightly around the detective since he turned one of their fiercest soldiers to dust. We will have entities watching the detective, as I'm sure Lucifer will. Molec will watch from a distance until the detective becomes a too big a thorn in his side. Once that happens, Molec will lash out in an attempt to extinguish the hybrid and bring forth eternal darkness and when he does we will be there."

The US ambassador frowned, "It's a desperate plan, your grace, but right now it's really all we have."

The Pontiff nodded. "It will have to do."

* * *

Vatican Guest Suites

Erik nervously paced back and forth, his motions that of a caged panther rather than a man. The detective kept staring at his wrist watch.

"You're going to wear a hole in the carpet my friend and it's now 6:35AM, five minutes later than the last time you checked."

Erik nodded. "Sorry, Martin. I'm just antsy today and I don't know why. That little voice in the back of my head is screaming and I can't seem to settle it down."

A knock on the door broke the tension. "Agent Knight, it's Neko. There's been a change of travel plans. We need to hurry!"

Erik looked over at his friend. "See! I knew it ... more problems."

Martin opened the door and Neko stepped inside along with a member of the Bishops' Council. Neko was panting and sweat ran down his forehead. "We cannot take you outside to the streets of Rome. Molec's soldiers are positioned throughout the area ready to engage in combat as soon as you leave the protection of our hallowed ground."

Erik swore as he cracked his knuckles. "I'm not running,

Neko. If Molec wants a fight I'm more than happy to oblige this time."

"No Mr. Knight, you can't. If you unleash your power in the crowded streets of Rome hundreds, maybe thousands, will die during the fight," the bishop who entered with Neko countered. "We have a helicopter waiting to take you to an airstrip outside the city that very few know exist. We have a plane ready to take you to London and you can catch a connection back to the United States from there. We had not counted on Molec deploying his forces so quickly after his last defeat."

"What about in here?" Martin looked out a window at the large crater that was the inner courtyard. "Do they possess more of that cosmic fiber that allows them to walk on consecrated ground?"

The bishop shrugged. "I don't know Mr. Denton, but several powerful warriors of Light are now patrolling God's city. There will be no more sacrilegious desecrations of our holy ground."

Neko gestured frantically. "Come, Agent Knight! My orders are to get you to the helicopter and get you out of here as soon as possible."

Denton chuckled. "I get the feeling you've worn out your welcome, Erik." The counselor turned and headed toward the door to see his friend off.

Erik sighed. His Esper senses were shrieking. He could detect the presence of powerful beings but not the hostility he felt during his encounter with the wraith. But there was still the sensation of danger. It was out there lurking just beyond the relative safety of Vatican City. He brushed his fingers across the silver belt and buckle around his waist. "We may see some more action my silver friend. Stay sharp."

The Sentient Staff growled a soft acknowledgment.

Erik and Martin were led to a seldom-used helipad. A small helicopter was already prepped for launch and the area was awash in rotor splash. Erik's long hair flew wildly in the wind as he studied the frail looking chopper.

"I see you're flying in style."

Erik dropped his duffel bag as he studied his ride. "Yeah, our friends really rolled out the red carpet."

The nervous bishop frantically gestured for Erik to board. As the detective entered the craft, the holy man handed him a small wrapped gift box. "For your wife, Mr. Knight. It is the finest gift we have in our shops."

The detective's jaw dropped. "You just saved my backside, Your Excellency. In all the ruckus I completely forgot."

"May God watch over you and your family."

Erik shook the man's hand. "Thank you." He turned toward his old friend.

"Looks like this is goodbye, Counselor," Erik placed a hand on his friend's shoulder. "I can stay, Martin. You don't have to go through this alone."

Denton smiled, his eyes heavy. "Thank you, but you need to get home to your family. I'll stop by as soon as I get back. I'll do what I can to keep digging here in the meantime. My gut tells me we don't have the whole story yet. There's more that our Vatican friends aren't telling us, that much my gut knows for sure."

Erik nodded in agreement. He glanced back at the bishop as the holy man walked away from the helicopter. "Yeah, I get that impression too. There's more going on here than we've been told." Erik shook his head. "As if this situation could be any more unbelievable."

Denton managed a smile. "If I find anything, I'll call you." He extended his hand and the two men exchanged a firm handshake.

"Just be careful and tread lightly, Martin. I don't need you getting killed by some 'creepie crawlie' that goes bump in the night."

Denton laughed. "That's the epitome of irony coming from you!"

Erik chuckled as he turned to board the helicopter.

As the detective settled in, he watched Neko escort Martin away from the helipad. There was a brief jerk and the helicopter ascended into the clear skies. Erik watched his friend continue to shrink as he was carried farther away. Whatever forces were outside of Vatican City waiting for him were probably quite put out. "God, please watch over my friend. I don't have many."

Barely fifteen minutes had passed as the small helicopter landed outside a small airstrip. The detective spotted a twin engine propeller aircraft at the beginning of the runway. The engines were running and the plane's flaps moved back and forth as the pilots performed pre-flight checks on the aircraft.

"A Douglas DC 3, Mr. Knight, it's not exactly a Learjet but she's rock solid where it counts." The helicopter pilot pointed toward the plane.

Erik smirked, his face must have telegraphed his surprise over the aircraft. "I'm sure it is."

He grabbed his bag, shook the pilot's hand, and headed toward the plane.

* * *

The chopper pilot watched as the DC 3's engines throttled up. The sound increased and a dusty wake formed a thin cloud behind the aircraft. The plane lurched forward, accelerating down the runway. The plane's rear wheel slowly left the ground as the speed increased. After another twenty yards the aircraft left the ground and ascended upward toward the clouds. The chopper pilot studied the plane, watching until it was out of sight. He pulled a cell phone from his flight suit. "You wanted to know when the American left. I just watched him take off. He's on his way to London."

The pilot listened briefly.

"I don't know what flight he's taking. There wasn't enough time to engage him in small talk. There are only a few flights to Boston from London. I'm sure your associates can cover each aircraft." He paused nodding to the voice on the other end of the phone.

"Yes, I'll let you know when the old man leaves too. Then my debts are clear, right?"

The pilot smiled and sighed with relief. "Excellent." The pilot throttled up the engine of his helicopter and headed back toward Vatican City. There was still time to make the floating poker game in Venice if he hurried.

* * *

Erik stared out the small window watching the sky overhead. The muffled sounds of the plane's piston engines took some getting used to. He stared at his cell phone and was shocked to see the phone registered a wifi signal. The detective needed information from a source he could trust. He hadn't reached out to his old friend for a few years and hoped the hacker he had in mind would be open to doing him a favor after so long. Erik walked toward the cockpit and leaned inside.

"I'm not much of an expert on flying and airplane electronics but I noticed I had a phone signal from a wireless source. Would I be screwing things up by making a phone call?"

The pilots laughed. "Not at all Agent Knight. This bird's old but she has the latest electronics and software. There's also a stocked refrigerator in the back, feel free to help yourself."

The detective nodded. "Thank you … I just may do that."

Erik went back to his seat and stared at his phone, it was 9:30 in the morning, which meant it was 3:30 in the morning in Boston. "Screw it! I know he's up." He dialed the phone number wondering how his old friend would react to hearing his voice.

"Hello, Charlie. It's been a long time."

"Erik Knight. Or should I say Special Agent Erik Knight, again. Did you find the life of a gym rat lacking in adventure and intrigue?" The voice on the phone responded in a friendly yet aloof tone.

Erik wasn't surprised Charlie Gallagher knew he'd been reinstated. Some computer somewhere registered his reinstatement and it was probably only a matter of seconds before the computer genius intercepted the data. Gallagher's aid was critical during Shanda's abduction. The ex-CIA computer analyst had a computer system that could literally hack and track any mainframe anywhere.

"You've been keeping tabs on me, Charlie. I'm touched. So, how's business? Hopefully the economic downturn isn't hurting you all that much."

Gallagher's laugh filled the tiny speaker. *"Come now, Special Agent Knight. You're fishing, my old friend. You know I always find a way to adapt and survive whatever the economic conditions. After all, knowledge is power and with my access to knowledge, I can pretty much rule the world."*

Erik knew his old contact wasn't simply blustering. Gallagher literally had access to every existing scrap of data and that made him more dangerous than any standing army or terrorist cell.

"Charlie, world domination wouldn't suit you ... dealing with petty politicians, political uprisings and a plethora of governments looking to terminate your rule would make you a nervous wreck. You strike me as a behind the scenes kind of guy."

"Ahh my old friend you know me too well. I'm happy taking my slice of the pie under the radar and invisible to the powers that be. But I'm already weary of this polite banter, I assume you have a reason for calling me at this ungodly hour..." the voice paused... *"And from over France in a slow-moving aircraft no less."*

The detective raised an eyebrow. Gallagher had managed to impress him again. "Charlie, I need to ask you a really far-fetched question. Please don't laugh."

"Fire away. I'll do my best."

"Have you heard of the Ethereal War, and have you ever heard of an entity called Molec?"

Erik's phone was silent for several seconds. There were several hisses and clicks but no response to his question. "Charlie? Are you there?"

"I'm here Erik. I just switched over to a secure burst mode. My friend, if you're involved with the Ethereals, I highly suggest you reverse course immediately. There are some pieces of information it's not healthy to have or even know. You're walking on that line. I strongly advise you step back."

Erik frowned. "So I take that as a yes."

"Yes."

"Can you do some research for me on a biblical topic?" Erik whispered, feeling foolish for doing so on an empty plane.

"As they say, Detective, what's in it for me?"

"My eternal gratitude and I'll owe you a favor."

"That's pretty thin but I'll take it. What do you need?"

"I need information on the Lost Scrolls of The Apostle Paul. Specifically sections that refer to the son of Adam and the stars. Is that something you can dig up for me?"

"I see you're going to ignore my warning."

"Sorry, I'm already past the line. Will you help me? It's pretty important."

The connection was silent for three solid seconds. *"Yeah, I'll do a search and see what I can find."*

"I'd appreciate that. I'll swing by when I get back. Do you still take your coffee black with three sugars?"

"I do, but right now you have bigger problems than buying me coffee. I'm tapping into a Russian spy satellite. You have five small blips closing in your location, Special Agent Knight. The returns don't read as metallic objects. They should be appearing on your aircraft's radar in about two minutes. I suggest you get that antiquated relic you're in on the ground or climb into a cloud bank."

Erik's danger sense triggered and his staff howled a low pitch hum. "Thanks for the heads up, Charlie. I'll let the pilots know." Erik closed the connection and moved to the cockpit.

The plane's radar had just registered the closing objects and the pilots were altering their course to avoid any chance of collision. As they adjusted the aircraft's heading the objects followed suit and continued to close.

"They're after us, no doubt." The copilot glared out the cockpit into the sky.

"But what are they?" Erik studied the five blips. "Can we go any faster?"

"Yes. These aren't exactly original equipment engines, but if push too fast we won't have enough fuel to make our destination. We'd have to land and refuel. Whatever connection you were hoping to make wouldn't happen."

Erik frowned. "These things aren't 'Friendlies.' My gut tells that much. I'd rather have to refuel and catch a later flight than dogfight in this prop-driven tin can, however tweaked it may be. Plus we're outgunned five to one."

The pilot nodded in agreement. He looked over at his co-pilot. "He who fights and runs away lives to fight another day. Let's get us some distance." The pilot pointed toward the unoccupied navigation seat. "I suggest you grab that empty chair and buckle down, Mr. Knight. The ride's about to get bumpy."

The engine roared louder and the plane lurched forward. The pilot banked the craft hard over, drastically altering their course in a desperate evasive maneuver. Erik felt his stomach churn as the plane creaked under the strain of the aerobatics.

"I'm gonna try for that cloud cover. It's another 8,000 feet up and off our flight plan but even at this increased speed, our friends out there are still closing."

Something was approaching the plane. Erik's enhanced vision saw it in the distance. "Bank to the left, hard!" he screamed.

The pilot looked at him puzzled.

"Do it or were dead!"

The pilot didn't argue. The plane pitched forty degrees off true, banking a hard left turn. As the plane lurched, a burning orb of fiery red passed the aircraft missing it by scant feet.

"What the Hell was that?" the copilot screamed as another searing orb sped to the right of their plane.

"We're under attack!" the pilot screamed as he studied his instruments. "Those blips are still closing."

Erik focused his Esper vision. His eyes burned fiery blue casting an eerie glow off the cockpit glass. He spotted one of their adversaries. Charlie was right. The thing wasn't metallic. It was a manlike creature with large beating wings–black bat-like wings. The creature looked like something from folklore. "A gargoyle."

"What?" the copilot stammered as he watched the detective's burning eyes study the horizon.

The plane shuddered as something slammed into the tail section. Alarms blared through the cockpit and the plane pitched forward, dropping altitude. Another fiery orb shot ahead of the falling plane just missing the wounded aircraft.

"We're losing hydraulics. I have to switch over to the back-up. She'll be a bear to handle now at this speed." The pilot desperately struggled to level the plane.

Erik could sense all five creatures. They had the same evil presence as the wraith. "We need to level the playing field somehow."

"We're unarmed, Mr. Knight. If you have any ideas, I'm open to suggestions. Right now we're a sitting duck, so to speak. I know you possess some unworldly abilities. Might I suggest now would be a good time to use them!"

"I'm working on it." Erik closed his eyes and gestured with

his hands. The sky around them darkened and black thunder-heads dominated the once clear skies. Heavy winds battered the stricken plane.

"If this is your idea of helping, I'd ask that you reconsider!"

The hybrid no longer heard the voices of the human pilots. His warrior senses were focused on the flying demons closing on the stricken craft. He manipulated wind currents producing a powerful vortex blowing two of the creatures miles away. He knew that wouldn't be enough to deter them. He focused on the static electricity building inside the black clouds. Telekinetic receptors and alien DNA projected inhuman commands. The elements, as if by magic, responded. Angry jagged arcs of energy shattered the darkness with a bright blue curtain of light.

"ANO' HAR OTAHL!!!!"

A lance of energy leapt from the massive ionized thunderhead striking a target. The creature exploded in a fiery plume, raining molten bits of armored flesh on the fleeing plane. A sea of hail and raindrops quickly extinguished the burning embers.

Another orb struck the DC3. The plane's left engine was enveloped in a sea of fire and smoke. Both pilots worked to shut the motor down and seal off the fuel supply to the burning engine. The plane bucked hard from the impact and plummeted toward the earth leaving a smoky contrail in the darkened sky. Three gargoyles followed the craft as it fell from the sky, continuing to fire more burning orbs.

Twin bolts of lightning vaporized two of the closing demons as the third managed to grab the aircraft with its dark claws. Armored flesh tore into the plane's thin metal skin and punctured the inner cabin.

"Mr. Knight! Mr. Knight! We're being boarded! One of those damn things is tearing through the cabin!"

Erik's senses slowly focused back on the cockpit as he heard the pilots scream. There was nothing more he could do. One of the creatures had made it to the plane, and they were still falling from the sky. The pilots had managed to level the stricken aircraft but Erik could hear the plane's one working engine sputtering and hesitating.

"What's happening?"

The copilot looked over, his face white with panic. "We're

losing our port side engine. Something's wrong with the fuel flow."

The wailing moan of air from the back of the plane caused all three men to glance back. A large eight-foot creature with burning red eyes stood at the tail section. Its mouth glowed with a burning hot fire."

"Staff!!! Shield, NOW!!"

Erik's brute force severed his safety harness as the Sentient Staff flowed like living liquid metal forming a silvery round disk on his left forearm. The creature launched a fireball from its mouth. The flaming orb slammed against the shield. Erik deflected the force of the impact but the flaming shards ignited the fabric seats and curtains covering the windows. "Fire!" he shouted to the pilots as he rushed the massive black creature. Erik slammed the rim of his makeshift shield into the large creature's throat. The metallic clang reverberated throughout the burning cabin. The gargoyle roared in rage and swung a massive club-like fist down upon him. Erik barely managed to raise his shield to absorb the blow. The physical strength of his opponent was staggering and the blow nearly drove him to his knees. Erik willed his body to grow stronger. The enhanced strength and power flowed through him. Before the creature could strike down again, he used his shield like a battering ram, pushing the beast backward. The creature fell onto its back and Erik slammed the rim of his shield into its throat again hoping to decapitate the monster. Even in his enhanced human mode he wasn't strong enough to cut through the beast's rocky hide. The creature swatted at him like an errant fly knocking him twenty feet backwards.

The gargoyle stood and tried to flex its massive wings in the cramped fuselage. Erik's senses briefly registered the sound of a fire extinguisher and he caught the odor of compressed CO_2. Erik tensed his forearm. Bioelectric plasma began to radiate as his body gathered more and more internal energy. If he couldn't out-muscle his opponent, he'd burn through it!

"No! You blast that thing in here, you'll do even more damage!" The copilot came up from behind the battered detective holding a second fire extinguisher.

Erik watched as the demon approached. He noticed the

floor buckling under its intense mass. He had to change completely. It was the only way to combat the gargoyle's power.

"You two seem to know a great deal about me and my
abilities."

"Vatican secrets are fleeting, Agent Knight. Right now I
can only hope you're as good as your press."

Erik nodded. "Let's find out. Take a step back. This is about
to get ugly." He willed his staff back to its cylindrical form.
"Okay you hellbeast ... you wanna dance ... let's dance! *I AM
THE WARRIOR!!!!* The detective rushed the gargoyle, his body
bursting out of his clothes. Chrome-armored flesh replaced
pale human skin in a matter of seconds.

The two powerhouses collided in the middle of the six-
ty-five foot aircraft. The impact sent a shock wave through the
DC3's metal skeleton. Even with the hybrid's expanded size,
he was still smaller than his lumbering opponent. The smaller silver warrior pushed his larger opponent back toward the
tail section of the aircraft, manhandling his stunned opponent.
The gargoyle slammed its fists into the hybrid's armored back
with its full, unfettered might. The powerful Esper warrior ignored the pain from those dreadful blows, attempting to keep
its larger foe pinned until the pilots could regain control of the
damaged aircraft. The silver warrior launched two uppercuts
into the creature's torso. Armored flesh slammed into armored
flesh. The weaker rock hide of the gargoyle fractured. The creature roared in pain and shock, flailing desperately to toss off its
opponent. Large stony wings thrashed angrily, damaging the
aircraft's frail inner structure.

*I have to end this. No matter what I do we're going to rip this
plane apart!* The silver warrior retreated, allowing its opponent
to advance. The gargoyle hissed angrily and its throat began to
glow a dull amber and red. The Esper Warrior didn't wait, but
leapt forward on powerful leg muscles. His right hand tensed
and fingers curled as razor-sharp silver claws tore through the
gargoyle's stone-covered throat. Green ichor and bile erupted
from the four deep slashes spraying the inside of the cabin.
The hybrid pressed his attack, launching a series of powerful
blows faster than the eye could follow. Each blow punctured
gaping holes in the stunned creature's body. More green blood

spilled as the creature struggled sensing its demise. It tried to attack again, but the hybrid caught its arm and with one quick twist, snapped the appendage. The sound of breaking bone and stony armor plate echoed through the cabin. The warrior dragged the heavy gargoyle toward the hole in the aircraft, and with a mighty heave tossed the creature into the air. The gargoyle was able to spread its wings and keep pace with the crippled plane. The dark creature cried out in agony as blood continued to hemorrhage from its mortal wounds.

This monstrosity isn't going to stop until its dead! It's like a programmed robot. The hybrid pointed his hand toward the creature and tensed his muscles. Again, plasma and jagged arcs of raw power enveloped the powerful forearm. With an almost casual gesture, he pointed toward the flying nemesis. A beam of pure blue energy launched toward the creature, vaporizing it instantly. The groan of tortured metal caught his attention. The tail section of the aircraft was badly damaged and a large chunk of the rudder and control flaps had been torn away and burned from the earlier attack. He could sense the overstressed and fatigued metal around the plane's frame and support joints. The DC3 was literally coming apart and nothing could keep the doomed plane from falling out of the sky.

"Agent Knight..."The pilot looked back seeing Erik's altered form for the first time. "Holy shit!" he screamed in panic.

Don't be afraid, it's just me! He projected into the terrified pilot.

The stunned pilot recovered. "We're losing altitude fast and I can't control the craft, our hydraulics are gone and the plane's control surfaces are shredded. We're going down and there's nothing I can do about it!"

He could hear the copilot's distress call.

Parachutes?

"No, we didn't have time to load any of the safety gear. This was an unscheduled flight and we were told we had to get airborne immediately. We barely had time to fuel the plane and run a pre-flight check before the call came in from Vatican City."

Wonderful. Are we near an airport or some kind of open area where we can drop this tub without endangering people on the ground and keep our heads attached at the same time?

The pilot was quiet for a few seconds. He looked at the hybrid's altered body then shook his head snapping out of his stupefied state. "Sorry, I'm not used to a voice inside my head like that. You are a most disturbing presence."

I'm sorry, but I can't speak in this altered form. This is how I communicate. He pointed toward the damaged fuselage. *What about this crate? Do we have any hope of landing it safely?* Erik felt another sense of danger, but it wasn't a threat to them. His wife and son were under attack!

* * *

Milford, MA

Shanda shot up from her bed. Immediately, she knew Erik was in some sort of danger. She tried to reach out to him but he wasn't answering. The fact that she could still sense his presence was a good sign. "Damn it. Why is this crap always happening to us?!"

A sense of dread raced through her body and the hair on the nape of her neck stood on end. She heard noise coming from outside the house in the side yard. She peeked out the window. The tree branches were rustling, but there wasn't enough wind to cause such a ruckus. She left her room and went to check on her son. EJ stared out the window, watching the trees. The boy trembled with fear.

"What is it baby?"

EJ pointed. "The ghost is trying to kill an angel."

"What are you talking about, hun?" Shanda closed the window and drew the shade closed. The noises outside grew louder and the shrieks sent shivers down her body. EJ's shaking grew worse.

"It'll be okay baby. It'll be okay. Just hold onto mommy."

A terrifying death shriek shattered the night, then the world fell silent. Shanda realized she'd been holding her breath. She exhaled loudly, still clutching her son. She reached over with one hand and moved the shade. There was no sound. Even the crickets had ceased their ever-present chirping.

"Is the ghost gone, mommy?"

Shanda brushed his thick hair. "Ghost?" she looked down at him confused. "I don't know, kiddo. The noise has stopped, but it's so quiet outside."

EJ shuddered. "It's coming, mommy! The ghost killed the angel. It's coming to get us." He buried his head against her. "I wish daddy was here. He scared the ghost away the last time."

"Huh? The last time? EJ, do you know what's going on?"

The window imploded and a deathly cold breeze tore through the tiny bedroom. The bedroom door slammed shut trapping the terrified mother and son. Several toys and garments launched around the room circling madly. A blood-curdling wail broke the night silence and the smell of sulfur tinted the air. EJ was forcefully ripped from Shanda's arms and tossed to the floor by his bed. A dark aura surrounded him, pinning him against the floor. He shrieked in fear, crying out to his mother.

An icy hand clamped around Shanda's throat, slowly squeezing the life from her. Chilling claws pawed at her nightgown, shredding the fabric and groping her exposed flesh. She screamed in utter terror as the unseen force attempted to violate her body.

"YOU WILL DIE SCREAMING IN AGONY, BEGGING FOR MERCY. ONCE I'VE VIOLATED YOU A DOZEN TIMES I'M GOING TO BREAK YOUR NECK, AND AS YOU LAY THERE, YOUR ESSENCE EBBING AWAY, I'LL MAKE SURE YOU HAVE JUST ENOUGH LIFE LEFT TO SEE ME BREAK YOUR ILLEGAL CHILD'S BODY LIKE A RAG DOLL"

Shanda brought her hand up and grasped the arm of the smoky figure choking her. To her horror, her hand passed through the body. She kicked with her leg and her foot passed through the smoky entity with no effect. She saw spots in front of her eyes and could hear her son crying out in terror. She focused her thoughts and projected a desperate plea for help.

ERIK! We're dying. It's killing us!

* * *

Somewhere Over France

The DC3 plummeted through the sky leaving a trail of debris

and smoke. In the cockpit, the pilots struggled to keep the aircraft stable while their passenger was inundated with a telepathic distress call.

Erik heard the plea for help. His wife and son were in mortal danger! What could he do? He was about to slam into the ground at over 300 miles per hour. His own mortality in question. The Sentient Staff buzzed angrily in his grip. He looked down at the weapon. There was a way! He couldn't get there, but his staff could. The Sentient Staff could navigate the ebbs and flows of Netherspace, the alternate space in between time the Seelak had used to their advantage during their war on Earth. The staff could literally travel through the dark netherworld, immune to the passage of time and open an exit portal in his home.

The Sentient Staff howled like an anxious dog. It sensed its master's wish and knew what had to be done. Erik willed the weapon to expand and with his very force of will he opened a black portal into the forbidden oblivion.

SAVE THEM. PROTECT MY WIFE AND SON! PLEASE!

The staff howled and vibrated burning white hot as it launched itself into the black void. Erik closed the portal behind him, praying his weapon would make it back in time to save his family. Erik looked up toward Heaven, *IF YOU'RE WATCHING, I COULD USE A FAVOR RIGHT NOW. TAKE ME IF YOU MUST, BUT SPARE MY FAMILY.*

The DC3 slammed into the ground exploding in a massive mauve fireball. A mushroom cloud of burning fuel and debris ignited the nearby forest.

* * *

Milford, MA

Shanda felt her body growing numb. The icy hand around her throat leeched her strength and blocked her windpipe. Her desperate gaze fell upon EJ. Some demonic force held her child immobile. She could hear his cries for help and his screams for his father. Erik wasn't coming to save the day this time. Her husband was in trouble half a world away, fighting God only knew what horrors.

Above the swirling satanic cyclone, she heard a familiar whine and drone. A dark tear in the very fabric of space opened in the bedroom. Shanda was convinced the very bowels of Hell had opened to claim them. A blinding silvery white orb bathed her helpless child, banishing the dark force keeping him captive. A searing beam of white struck the smoky figure. It roared in agony and lost its death grip on her neck. Shanda heard a savage hiss—the hiss of a battle-primed Esper warrior.

She looked over at her son. He held a burning silver staff in his hand. EJ had grown to nearly five feet in height and his eyes burned like two pale blue suns lighting up the darkness. His flesh was liquid chrome reflecting the radiant power from the weapon. Those burning eyes focused on the injured demon. She heard her baby's voice scream in her head.

YOU STAY AWAY FROM MY MOMMY!

EJ leveled the staff toward the demonic entity and blasted it again. The creature howled in rage and its body began to dissolve and vaporize. The child warrior showed no mercy as another searing blast of immense power burned a gaping hole through the smoky torso, vaporizing the back bedroom wall. The demonic entity was reduced to an amorphous blob of smoke which EJ incinerated with another searing blast of energy.

EJ studied the weapon in his hand. It purred and moaned, bathing the boy in a bioelectric haze. Slowly the child diminished. Silvery flesh gave way to human skin and burning eyes faded back to the innocent, terrified eyes of a child. EJ dropped the staff and ran to his mother crying out. Shanda wrapped her arms around him holding her son, unable to stop crying as both mother and child fell to the floor trembling.

"It's over baby. You're safe now."

EJ still shook, hiding his face against her chest. "Will they come back?"

"I don't know, baby." She stared up at the stars from the gaping hole in her roof. She also realized the entire back wall of EJ's bedroom was gone, as were the top halves of the pine trees in the side yard of their home. How the blasts didn't obliterate her was a mystery. "My God. What just happened?" She hugged her son tighter. A comforting sound broke the silence.

"Do you hear that, EJ?"

The child looked up. "What?"

Shanda started to cry. "The sound of crickets. The bad things are gone." She heard a faint buzzing. Erik's staff lay on the floor. "Daddy heard us after all."

Shanda grabbed a nearby towel and carefully picked up the weapon. She could feel the staff's incredible power. "If I didn't think I'd get zapped, I'd kiss you." She carried EJ and the weapon out of the destroyed bedroom, closing the door behind her even though the room was now blasted open to the outside. They'd sleep at her office tonight and hopefully she'd be able to reestablish contact with her husband in the morning. Erik sent help. That alone told her he was alive. "You're definitely your father's son, lil' man." The exhausted child was fast asleep.

* * *

20 miles west of Rouen, France

The flames continued to burn from the devastating impact. Trees burned and dry brush burst into flame from the oppressive heat. From the core of the hellish inferno, a lone silver figure walked unscathed. The massive figure looked up toward the sky, gesturing with powerful hands. Overhead, the skies darkened, thunder echoed, and heavy raindrops fell in a torrential downpour. The rain washed away filth and ash from the being's chrome, armored flesh. The powerful being continued to gesture, imploring the airborne elements to do his bidding. The rain fell harder around the silver sentinel. He stood unmoving for nearly half an hour, watching as the torrential downpour extinguished the fiery hell consuming the crippled aircraft and quenched the burning forest.

The hybrid watched in silence as the fractured skeleton of the DC3 was revealed beneath the dying flames and embers. He sensed the life force of his wife and son. They were alive. The psychic echo registered mild shock and exhaustion, but also a feeling of relief. He looked up at the sky, eyes burning like twin blue stars and commanded the rain to stop falling. Almost immediately, the rain ceased and the heavy cloud cover surrendered to the sun.

They're alive. Whatever happened they survived it! He looked up to Heaven. *I owe you one.*

The sound of rotor blades disturbed the tranquil yet sorrowful scene. Erik willed himself back to his human form and retreated behind a nearby half burnt tree. A large helicopter landed in the mud and ash-covered ground created by his rainfall. As soon as the craft landed, two men stepped out. Both wore black suits, expensive sunglasses, and black leather shoes. They carefully moved through the muck and examined the wreckage. Erik watched intently as the men gathered the plane's black box and examined the charred corpses. One of the men put his hands by his mouth and shouted.

"Erik Knight! Special Agent Erik Knight, can you hear me? I'm Andrew Foster with the CIA. We know you survived the crash and I know you're out here, watching. I know you can hear me. We're not here to harm you. We're here to take you home, sir."

Erik sighed in relief from his hiding place. "Would you happen to have a spare set of clothes?" He stepped out from behind the tree, doing his best to cover himself."

Both agents did their best to conceal their shock, then burst out laughing. "We have some flight suits on board, Agent Knight. Mr. Denton has been burning up the phone lines and bullying the French Embassy since your mayday was received. The French President, Pierre LaSalle and his daughter, Monique were most insistent when they learned you were in distress."

"It's nice to have friends." The detective blushed as he boarded the helicopter. The two pilots snickered but said nothing. One pilot tossed him a flight suit and undergarments from on overhead compartment.

"My clothes burned in the crash," Erik explained as he dressed.

Erik buckled himself in and the large helicopter launched. The nervous detective constantly glanced out a window scanning the sky for more of the flying demons.

"This bird is fully armed Agent Knight, anything comes within five miles of us without proper authorization will get blown out of the sky." The agent carefully studied him and Erik grew uncomfortable under the man's scrutiny.

"What's on your mind?"

Agent Foster leaned forward. "You certainly live up to your hype. There isn't a scratch on you from a plane crash that should have barbecued you just like those two pilots."

"They were good men."

"What happened, Agent Knight? What attacked the plane?"

"I don't honestly know. All I can say is they won't be attacking anything else, ever again." Erik's eyes were steel hard.

Foster nodded. He reached over and gave the detective a friendly pat on the shoulder. "You're a hard man to kill, Agent Knight. Thank God for that."

Erik nodded. "I already did."

Chapter 8. Revelations

E rik was tired, not in the physical sense, but emotionally and mentally drained. The detective had been away just a few days yet it seemed months had passed since he left for Vatican City. Every time he tried to come to terms with the revelations and the intrigue involving the Ethereals, the war of Light and Dark, and the involvement of a rogue creature called Molec, his mind cramped. Erik's brain function was enhanced far beyond human capacity but the cosmic implications of what he'd experienced the last few days threatened to overwhelm even his enhanced mental capacity. A voice broke into his brooding

"We're here Mr. Knight. Are you sure you don't want to go home?"

Erik stared at the Newberry Comics sign. Relief flooded through his weary mind and warmth saturated his heart. His pulse quickened knowing his wife and son were safely inside. He could sense their presence. "No thanks, this is fine." He stepped out, dropped his duffel bag while handing the driver a twenty dollar tip.

Loud music dominated the parking lot as he approached the glass door. He quietly stepped inside, blending into the busy crowd. EJ's distinct laugh spun his head. His friend, John, was on the floor in the far corner with his son playing Tonka trucks. His heart stopped as he heard Shanda's voice at the counter serving customers. He stepped into line, patiently waiting for her to notice him.

Her distinct telekinetic pulse washed over him like a warm blanket, soft and comforting. Shanda looked up, stunned, as she detected his presence. She ran from behind the counter rushing toward him, her face wet with tears. Erik caught her as she leapt into his arms.

He heard EJ yell 'Daddy' in the background as he lost himself in his wife's embrace.

Warm tears flooded his face. "Oh God, Angel, I'm never leaving you again!" He held Shanda tight, lifting her off the ground relishing the sensation of her skin pressed against him.

"Thank God you're back!"

Erik felt a tug on his leg. He glanced down to see his son. "Hey lil man! He bent down, scooping up his son. EJ wrapped his arm around his father's neck, kissing his cheek. "Daddy's home! Daddy's home!" the child screamed happily.

"I'm home, son. It's all gonna be fine now. Daddy's home." Erik looked over at his mountainous friend through his tear-filled eyes. "I owe you big," he mouthed silently.

"I'm not keeping score, my brother." The big man smiled as he headed out the door.

An exotic woman approached. "Well, you must be the famous Erik Knight."

Erik turned, adjusting his hold on a fidgety EJ. "I am." Before Erik could say anything more, Shanda stepped in.

"Erik, this is my dear friend and right hand, Carla."

Erik smiled. "Hello, Carla. I'd shake your hand but right now I don't have a spare one to offer."

The woman laughed. "I'm glad to see you're back in one piece." She looked over at her friend. "We've got this. You two need to go home and get reacquainted." She winked at them and Erik blushed a crimson red. Both Shanda and Carla laughed.

* * *

Erik awoke, his arms wrapped around Shanda. Birds chirped, greeting the morning sun. EJ stirred, hugged his stuffed bear tighter, and drifted back to sleep. He carefully untangled himself and silently crawled out of the sleeping bag. EJ was reluctant to be left alone in their bedroom, so Shanda suggested a living room campout complete with toasted marshmallows and roasted hot dogs on a stick. Erik glanced at the corner of the room. His staff lay tucked in its sheath. He reached out toward the weapon and it leapt into his open hand.

You saved my wife and son, he projected telepathically toward the weapon. *I don't know if you can understand gratitude, but I am grateful for how you saved my bacon with the wraith and you saved my family when I couldn't. I don't know if you understand what 'thank you' means, but thank you.*

The Sentient Staff purred and moaned in his hand. Erik could sense an emotional response emanating from the weapon. It knew! On some level, the weapon understood his meaning. "Keep eyes on them." He tucked the weapon back in its sheath and placed it next to his sleeping family. Erik tiptoed into the kitchen and prepared a pot of coffee. He studied the digital kitchen clock. "Ten in the morning. Cripes, it can't be that late." The mentally exhausted father couldn't remember the last time he'd slept so long or so soundly. He stared out the kitchen window watching several squirrels scamper down a large oak tree and hop across the lawn. The weary hybrid spent several minutes lost in thought, staring absently out the window.

"Good morning."

He turned, smiling. "Good morning, Angel." They shared a deep kiss.

The coffee maker sputtered as the last of the fluid dripped into the steaming pot.

"Yes!" She hugged him. "You made coffee!"

Shanda filled two mugs and gestured toward the deck. "We need to talk about what happened here."

Erik nodded, peeking into the living room at EJ. "He's still sound asleep. I don't want him to overhear anything."

"After what he's been through, he'll probably sleep for a few more hours at least. We'll keep the door ajar a bit. With your 'bionic' hearing you'll know when he gets up."

Erik laughed as they walked to the deck and sat under a shade canopy.

Shanda took a deep breath and described the terrifying events of the prior evening and how EJ transformed into a small silver-skinned Esper soldier. Erik got goosebumps as his wife painted a vivid picture of her assault and rescue. "Then he said, 'stay away from my mommy' and blasted the thing into oblivion along with most of the back bedroom wall." She shuddered. "I still don't understand how that blast could take out a wall, kill that black creepy thing, but not even scorch a single hair on my head. I've never been more frightened in all my life. After all we've been though, I never thought it could get worse. I was wrong. This was worse than the Seelak and the Observers put together."

Erik felt the tears run down his cheek as he squeezed her hand. "I'm so sorry, babe. I think our investigation into William Denton's murder had something to do with this." Erik described the events at Vatican City over the next hour.

By the end of the story, Shanda was pale and trembling. "I don't know what to say." She nervously braided her long hair. "I thought all that was fairy tales."

Erik nodded. "Martin is having what the church would call a 'Crisis of Faith.' The poor man has been a devout atheist all his life." Erik sighed. "You said the thing that attacked you said EJ was illegal. That ties into another tidbit I need to tell you. I'm sorry, hun, but you aren't going to like this." He placed both hands over hers and relayed his conversation with Jakor, emphasizing the conversation regarding his genetic incompatibility with human DNA. Erik struggled through tears as he told his wife he was incapable of fathering children and that divine intervention was required to conceive their son. "The one thing you want more than anything in the world, and I can't give it to you." Erik stood walking to the corner of the deck staring at the decapitated pine trees.

He felt Shanda's delicate touch on his shoulder. "Hey, you need to listen to me very carefully." She turned him around. "Yes, I wanted more children, but I love the life we have and the son we have, whatever the cosmic rationale for his existence. Right now, we have enough on our plates to keep us occupied. Our life is never boring, Erik, and I need you to believe that I am fulfilled. Please believe that I'm happy, extremely happy with our life together." She wrinkled her face. "I could do without some of the drama and cosmic revelations though."

Erik smiled as he held her tight. "I'm so sorry. I had no idea what we were walking into, and the revelations from the Bishops' Council were something I had absolutely no idea about. I really don't want to be some chosen champion of light. I just want to be a husband and father."

Shanda nodded. "I know, hun. But right now, let's deal with some smaller problems, ones we can solve." They walked to the side of their home studying the damage. The large tarps Erik placed over the gaping holes rustled in the errant morning breeze.

Erik studied the ground below the pine trees. His senses could detect the residue of a great struggle. He spotted an indentation on the ground and some burn marks roughly the shape of a body. "Something fell from the trees and landed here. I can only assume it was the 'Angel' EJ said was killed by the ghost or whatever attacked you guys." Erik shook his head, "Unbelievable! I can't believe that just came out of my mouth."

He looked over at Shanda. She was studying the damage to their home. Erik stopped his analysis as he felt her discomfort. He knew she was more scared than she let on. The realization dawned on him. She was the only real human in their family. Their son was a hybrid offspring willed into existence by a deity she never considered relevant to her existence and he was, as the church proclaimed, a son of Adam and of the stars. Erik wondered how any woman could cope with such bizarre revelations.

He walked up and wrapped his arms around her waist and she leaned back into his chest, her cheeks wet with tears. "My God, look at our home. How are we going to fix this? How do we explain this to the Petersons next door? You know Melissa will be asking a million questions about the house, and the trees." She shuddered. "How do we protect our son? That thing wanted to rape me and kill our son! It wanted to kill my little boy!"

Erik held her tight. "I know, but it failed. Right now, the most powerful weapon I know of is watching over him and protecting him. The staff knows to protect you both. It knows I value your lives more than my own." He gently kissed the nape of her neck. "Nothing will hurt either of you again, not while I draw breath."

He pointed up toward the tarp-covered holes. "I don't think supernatural attack is covered under our homeowner's insurance but that nice fat check with all those zeroes will more than cover this mess. I can make one quick phone call today to the firm and they'll have a crew out here by this afternoon to assess the damage and start repairs. As for the trees, I can drop the lower sections with a chainsaw and a winch. Tonight when everyone is asleep, I can change into my Esper form and carry off each section into the woods."

"What about work?"

"Martin's guys can handle it for one more day and Alissa already knows I'm back so I'm sure she'll be by to catch me up as I'm wrestling with this." He gestured toward the trees.

She turned and looked up at him. "Erik, I'm scared. I'm trying to be brave and understanding b...but this is more than I can handle ... my mind is spinning and I can't stop it. Why us? We've already had our share of 'fucked up' with the Seelak and then that crazy colonel wanting to dissect our son, not to mention an alien attack and now this! We have a demonic entity targeting us?" Shanda's body trembled. Her legs faltered. Erik held her up by his own strength as she recovered her footing. "And you're as calm as a rock."

Erik turned her to face her, eyes glistening with unshed tears and a deep, serious frown. "Babe, believe me, I'm scared too, when I fought that wraith I thought I was going to die. When I was plummeting from the sky and I heard you cry out for me I was scared, terrified for you and for EJ." His voice cracked and he took a deep breath before plunging ahead. "I didn't care if I died in a ball of fire or splattered like a pancake across some dirt field. All I cared about was the two of you surviving. I've faced alien battle craft that were over three stories tall and wasn't frightened as much as I was when you were in danger." Tears escaped. He sniffed and closed his eyes, finding inner balance. "Believe me, I'm as fed up with drama and intrigue as you are. We struggled these last few years but at least we had peace and I liked peace, a lot better than I like intrigue and drama. I liked being a normal married couple with normal married challenges. If you don't think this shit blows my mind you're dead wrong. I'm as disturbed and troubled as you are."

The early fall breeze picked up rustling the leaves, Shanda tensed. "I just want a normal life, like everyone else. Not just for my sake but for the sake of our son. For God's sake, why do they want our son?"

"I think I can answer that."

Shanda and Erik spun to face the voice. Erik's jaw dropped, "Charlie Gallagher, what brings you out of your computer fortress of solitude?"

"I came by as soon as I had confirmation of my data from my source as St. John's Seminary." The short, portly hacker pointed toward the tall, gangly man dressed in black. "This is Cardinal Rossi—retired—he's been a biblical scholar for nearly fifty years and has studied theology since he was a novitiate in his early twenties. He has over sixty years studying biblical passages and scrolls along with an IQ that's almost as high as mine." Charlie nervously scanned the yard. "'Where's your kid?"

"Inside, sleeping."

Gallagher shifted from one foot to the other, eyes scanning the surroundings. "Don't let him out of your sight, ever. There are forces active that don't want that child alive!"

Erik pointed toward the deck, "Okay Charlie, why don't you and your friend sit down and tell us what you found."

Erik guided Charlie and his elderly friend up to the large picnic table on the deck while Shanda went inside to check on EJ. She walked out a few minutes later with a fresh coffee pot and a boxed cake. "EJ's up. I put his favorite movie on and gave him some breakfast." She served their guests quickly, then sat down next to Erik placing her hand on his. She looked over at Erik's mysterious friends. "Okay, you said you know why this is going on, please, enlighten me."

Gallagher sipped the coffee and produced a folder from his briefcase. "I hacked into the Vatican mainframe as well as the Archdiocese database in Boston, I pulled all the relevant files pertaining to the Lost Scrolls of the Apostle Paul and I found more biblical prose that never made its way into the 'Good Book'. Each Apostle told of a great war in the heavens that carried over to Earth. They all wrote of the second coming, another prophet to usher in the second age of man."

"Yes," Erik nodded. "The Archbishop told me all about the prophecy and how they're convinced that I'm some sort of 'chosen one' to participate in the battle of Light and Dark."

The elderly cleric shook his head. "No, Erik. They're wrong. The script, the language in the Vatican mainframe was translated differently than the other file records from the other Apostles that made the same references. I've studied several of the lost scrolls while in Jerusalem and Cairo as well as the hidden libraries of Lebanon. All of the scrolls refer to the great battle that occurred on Earth and what we call the Ethereal War and they all speak of the second coming." The cleric reached a palsied hand and touched Erik's powerful forearm.

A slight tingle ran through his body like an electrical shock. He felt the cleric's mind studying him. Instinctively, he raised mental barriers and firmly but gently pulled his hand away. He now knew what it felt like to be probed. He'd be extra careful in the future about violating the thoughts of others. The cleric shuddered as he was abruptly forced out of Erik's mind.

"I'm sorry. I forget that my gift is sometimes beyond my control. Please forgive me, Mr. Knight. It was not my intent to violate your thoughts."

Erik flexed his arm. "No harm done."

"Mrs. Knight, may I read you?"

Shanda looked over at Erik. He nodded. "Your call babe."

Shanda held out her hand and the old man gently took it. She gasped momentarily and then the cleric released her.

"You have a powerful spirit, mother. Light chose wisely when they chose the two of you." He pointed toward Erik. "You, the most powerful man ever to walk the Earth and a woman of silk and iron to bear your child, the Bearer of Light." He gestured toward Shanda.

"You said the Vatican read the lost writings of Paul incorrectly." Erik pushed, growing uncomfortable with more biblical prophecy.

"My brothers read what they had correctly, but what they had was translated poorly. The Cherub script is very heavy in prepositional phrases. For you are indeed the son of Adam and the son of the stars. You are the warrior prophecy has described, but you aren't the chosen one. You have a pivotal role to play, Erik, as do you, Shanda, if I may be so informal. But the chosen one to wield the Ruby Crucifix and usher in the new age of man isn't you. The proper translation is 'The son of the son of Adam and the stars'."

Shanda dropped her coffee. The mug shattered on the wooden deck. "No, not my baby boy. Keep him out of this. He's just an innocent child, not a threat to anyone."

"I'm sorry, Shanda. Your son is a threat to every dark force involved in the Ethereal War. His birth signaled the upcoming second age of man and announced the arrival of Armageddon. Your child is destined to wield the Ruby Crucifix."

Shanda desperately looked at Erik. "Do something, Erik!"

"I'm sorry, Shanda, as powerful as he is, your husband cannot combat destiny or God's plan."

"Free will." Erik's voice cut as cold and hard as the edge of a sword. "We're responsible for the boy and for ourselves. We have free will. We can say no!"

Cardinal Rossi's head tilted as he contemplated Erik's challenge. "Yes, you have free will, as does your wife, and as does your son. When the time comes, the choice will be his; not mine and not yours."

"We're his parents and his guardians..."

"And Joseph and Mary were the parents of Jesus. Yet, he still chose to lay down his life for mankind's salvation. His parents didn't interfere with God's plan."

EJ walked onto the deck carrying his teddy bear. "Can I play outside?"

Shanda stood up and protectively shielded her son from the cardinal. "In a bit, lil man. Mommy and daddy's company is just about to leave." She cast a wary glance at Cardinal Rossi.

Charlie Gallagher studied his friend. "Erik, I'm sorry, but I figured you'd need to hear this in person. Look, I'm not really into any of this, but you wanted me to dig so I dug."

Erik shook his head in disbelief. "I'm not upset with you, Charlie. I appreciate the head's up and the in-person delivery. This, my friend, is the straw that broke the camel's back, but it does tie everything up in a nice little bow."

Charlie sighed. "Yeah ... dude, you're the new Joseph in this biblical yarn. Your pretty little bride is Mary ... and your son..."

Erik sighed. "Yeah, I got that."

Shanda came back outside, closing the door behind her. She leaned against the door, guarding it as if expecting the old man to attempt to abduct her son.

"Shanda, I won't harm a hair on your son's head, nor will I try to convince you of the importance of his destiny or your husband's or even yours." Cardinal Rossi folded his hands in front of him. "Your child is Armageddon's Son, the Light Bearer. Every dark force on Earth knows of his existence now and they will be coming for him in a desperate attempt to thwart destiny. I know the holy relic has been taken, but it cannot be shielded and hidden forever. Evil cannot hide and diminish such a power for long. It will make its presence known and no power in this world or any world can stop it. The war is upon us and forces are gathering. Exercise your free will and you herald in the end of mankind and every soul on Earth. The choices you now make threaten the cosmic balance of this universe."

About the Author

Greg Ballan is a graduate of Northeastern University holding bachelor's degrees in Marketing and Management. Greg enjoys several outdoor activities such as hiking, archery and shooting. Greg was an avid MMA fighter but realized after fifty, getting punched hurts ... a lot! He discovered the safer hobby, learning the acoustic guitar. When he's not working his full-time job as a financial analyst or exploring some unknown woodlands, he's crunched over his laptop putting his warped imagination into words or penning a column about the outdoors or his latest misadventure avoiding house and yard work.

Look for more action and intrigue as the adventures of the Hybrid and the Ethereal War continue in Battle Lines!